DIRGE

OF THE

WITCH

HAINTS

AN EZEKIEL CRANE NOVEL

J. KENT HOLLOWAY

CHARADE
MEDIA

Dirge of the Witch Haints

Copyright © 2023 by J. Kent Holloway

ISBN: 978-1-0882-9295-2

Charade Media, LLC
www.charadbooks.com

To Jen and Sherri, for putting up with all the wrong twists and turns before they became the right twists and turns.

To Kane, for having an amazing eye for those things that slip by and some great advice!

And finally, to the insatiable fans of Ezekiel Crane and his arcane and mystifying ways.

PROLOGUE

The Crawford Farm
Boone Creek, Kentucky
March 3
1:10 AM

L iz Crawford couldn't let herself fall asleep. She couldn't risk the dreams again. The images. The ghastly phantasms that had haunted her sleep ever since her husband, Tim, had been found dead in that ghastly Devil's Teeth, along with all the others. That had been five months ago.

And 'dead' might be putting things mildly. Perhaps slaughtered would be a bit more like it. Even though he'd only been missing for a few days, there'd not been much of her husband's remains that were close to identifiable. Not only had the ravages of rapid decomposition—brought on by that infernal mushroom suit he was found in—played its part in the body's mutilation, but the funeral director had told her that he thought the remains looked as if they had been hacked up by multiple hatchet wounds—the devastating consequences of an encounter with One-Eyed Jack.

Sheriff Tyler, of course, had denied it all. He'd said her husband, along with six others in the community, had been exposed to a fungus. An especially deadly fungus with spores that had multiplied inside his body, until they'd burst out of his chest with such explosive force that it simply appeared to have been hatcheted.

The very idea was nothing but tomfoolery. Ask anyone in town. No one believed him, which was why he'd been stripped of his title, and was soaking away his days inside a bottle. Not that it did her any good. Her husband was still dead.

So now she lay staring up at the ceiling, tears streaking the round contours of her plump face, as she struggled against the need to sleep.

It just wasn't fair. Her husband had been a good man...a good father. Hard-working. Dedicated. Sure, he liked to imbibe the occasional shot of whiskey from time to time, and could be rather irresponsible when it came to the chores and such, but she couldn't fault him for that. That's just the way his folks had reared him.

But now he was gone, and she was a widow. Her two children were fatherless. And it was all that scientist feller's fault. That Cian Brennan. Some fancy anthropologist from an Ivy League school, up north. He'd come down here to investigate the strange tales he'd heard about the Dark Hollows—more specifically, the Devil's Teeth—and his nosin' had stirred up a monster. One-Eyed Jack. An honest to goodness giant. A spirit guardian of the Cherokee injuns, who walked the mountains of Appalachia since well before her kin had ever set foot here.

Ol' Jack had attacked Brennan and his research team. The only one who managed to escape was that mean-as-a-snake Leroy Kingston. Her husband had found him on the side of the road, half-crazed and ranting, shortly after Jack had taken his first victim. Though Leroy managed to survive the ordeal, he hadn't exactly come out of it unscathed. A week after helping the good-fer-nothin' Leroy, Tim had disappeared...along with six other people from Boone Creek. They'd found their bodies a little later on when they discovered the body of a local waitress, Candace Staples, buried in a grave at the Teeth.

Even worse, all of them—except for Candace—had been covered head to toe in some weird suit designed to grow mushrooms. No one knows for sure who did it, though Liz would put a pretty penny on that devil, Ezekiel Crane, being behind it somehow.

She shuddered at the thought of Crane, then continued her musings.

Ever since her husband's death, she'd silently suffered from the night terrors that gripped her dreams, unwilling to share them with anyone, lest they decided she was too crazy to care for her kids.

But she couldn't help it, could she? She couldn't help dreaming about Tim...about him coming home in the wee hours of the morning, climbing the creaking staircase with short, jerky movements, and sliding up to snuggle beside her in bed. That was only natural, right? A wife misses her husband when he's gone. It shouldn't matter that the man in her dreams reeked of death or that his flesh was green and marbling. Shouldn't matter that his clothes were caked with the soil of his own grave, or that fat, squirming maggots crawled in and out of the jagged craters of the hatchet wounds that still marred his decaying face and chest. No, surely it was perfectly natural to dream such things when you were a grieving widow.

Of course, she shivered when she thought about just how real the dreams always felt. She would never tell another living soul that she could practically smell his rancid breath or feel how cool and wet the skin of his fingers felt, as they stroked the tears away from her face. She had had to remind herself on a number of occasions that it had been only a dream. A horrid and twisted nightmare that taunted her maliciously over the loss of her beloved husband.

It was for these reasons her mind refused to shut down and allow her the much needed sleep her body desperately craved. She just couldn't risk another nocturnal encounter with *him*. It would drive her near-mad with grief. And if nosey Margaret Evans were to ever find out about it, there'd be no end to the gossip spreading around...

Wait! What's that?

Liz sat up in bed, straining her ears to recapture the shrill phantom sound she'd just heard. But all remained still.

Was that a footstep? Is someone on the staircase?

Her heart thumped wildly inside her chest. Surely she'd just imagined it. Her overactive imagination playing harsh tricks on—

There it is again!

She was sure she'd heard it that time. A distinctive creak somewhere in the house...like a heavy-booted foot dragging itself up the stairs. Like every dream she'd had for the last few weeks.

Creeeeaaaaakkk!

The sound was louder this time, more deliberate. Someone had crept up the steps of their little two-story farmhouse, and was now standing stock still. Or at least, she thought they were. She couldn't be sure. All she heard now was the rush of her own blood, pounding through her head like Cherokee battle drums announcing a coming war. Each throb of her pulse echoed loudly at the base of her skull. She tried holding her breath, but the rush of adrenaline made it nearly impossible.

Who's in my house? she thought with wide-eyed panic. *What should I do?*

Her mind drifted back to Tim. The dreams. Surely it wasn't him. No. Of course, it wasn't. Tim was dead. Her nightly visitations had never been anything more than the cruel betrayal of her own mind. This was something else. There *was* someone in her house. Someone physical. Real.

Dangerous.

She heard a soft shuffling across the carpet, in the hallway just past her door, the gentle movement of feet trying desperately to avoid making any sound at all.

A lump swelled in her throat. Whoever it was, they had just walked past her door. Past her bedroom. They were slowly making their way to...

Oh dear lord! she thought, as she scrambled out of bed while being as quiet as possible. *He's heading toward the kids' room.*

Tiptoeing over to the closet, she crouched down, shoved a handful of wrinkled clothes and children's toys out of the way, and fought to recall the combination to the small safe.

10. 34. 12? No. No. That's not it, she thought as panic continued to build. She was running out of time. Whoever was in the house was surely in the kids' room now. *It's Isaac's birthday! That's it.*

With trembling hands, her fingers twisted the safe's knob right and left until she heard the satisfying click. She then pulled it open, reached in, and withdrew Tim's .357, still wrapped in lambskin from the last time he'd gone to the range.

Although she'd never much liked guns, she was now thankful her husband had seen fit to make sure she knew how to use one. And use it very efficiently. She checked the cylinder, and was satisfied it was loaded and ready to go. She flicked off the safety, and crept slowly over to the bedroom door. Her hand hovered over the door knob, indecision fogging her mind. Was she being foolish? Of course, it never hurts to check...

Her heart thrummed faster and faster, making her wonder if it might abruptly stop from sheer exhaustion. Or fright. But she had to look...she had to act. If there was the slightest chance her babies were in danger, she had to do whatever was necessary. She had to...

Taking a deep breath, she turned the knob with her free hand, and cracked open the door just enough to peek around the edge. The hall was empty. She moved further out, and tried peering into the children's room. The door was cracked open, but that was normal. Little Maggie, only six years old, still insisted on being able to see the warm, comfortable light from the hallway ceiling fixture. But try as she might, Liz could see nothing through the deep shadows of the room beyond.

She stepped out into the hall, and held her breath. She could hear the soft sounds of snoring coming from the room. Isaac. Already at age nine, the boy took after his dad when it came to snoring. But there was something strangely comforting in that nasal, growl-like breathing. At least the children seemed safe. Nothing had awakened them. Nothing had begun doing unspeakable things to them, as she'd imagined.

She exhaled, and that's when she heard it…

A gentle "shhhhhh" sound, followed immediately by a hoarse, raspy humming. The humming of a tune, though she couldn't place the song. There was something disjointed about the sound. Something not quite right.

Dear Lord Jesus, she prayed silently. *Someone's in my babies' room!*

The mention of Christ's name brought sudden recognition of the song being hummed. "Jesus Loves Me." But it was wrong somehow. Something that didn't sit right in the pit of her soul. Something dark. Deadly.

The thought brought a sudden wave of anger flooding through her veins. The song was special. Lovely. It should never sound like that. Besides…it had been Tim's favorite lullaby to sing the children to sleep, when he was alive. To hear it again, and in this way, after her husband's gruesome death, it was somehow perverse. Blasphemous, even. The sudden rage fueled her courage, and she stalked toward the room with the barrel of the gun trained at the darkness beyond the door.

The humming increased in volume as she approached. The voice sounded oddly familiar, yet so alien at the same time. Where had she heard it before?

She knew she couldn't think about that now. There was too much at stake. Her children were in dreadful danger, and she was the only one around now who could protect them. So before her newfound courage abated, she nudged the bedroom door open and stepped inside, with both hands firmly gripping the gun.

The light from the hall flooded past her trembling form, spilling into the room with warm, yellow radiance. Her eyes, adjusting quickly, flashed around the room, spying Isaac's Hot Wheels cars and Maggie's collection of stuffed toys, strewn willy-nilly along the floor. Finally, her eyes landed on the back of a rocking chair positioned just in front of Maggie's bed. A figure sat in the chair, rocking gently back and forth, as it hummed the eerie children's hymn with a gravelly voice. Liz looked past the figure and saw her little girl, still sleeping peacefully in bed, unmolested by the strange presence in her room.

Isaac lay in his race-car bed, his sheets kicked out onto the floor as he cradled a small pillow between his legs. His mouth hung open, oblivious to his irregular snoring. He appeared to be fine, too. They were both fine. Healthy. Unaware.

Steeling her nerves, Liz stepped further into the room and cleared her throat.

"Who are you?" she whispered harshly. "What're you doing in my house?"

In response, the figure merely continued humming its disturbingly inaccurate tune. 'Inaccurate' wasn't exactly the correct term. The figure was hitting the right notes, but occasionally, it would get stuck on a single note and hum it over and over again, until, like nudging a skipping record, the tune would suddenly continue again.

"I'm warnin' you. I'm armed," she said, her voice a little more forceful this time. "What're you doing in my house?"

And still, the humming continued, as if she had been as silent as a ghost in the room. A sudden rush of dread threatened to sap the remaining vestiges of her courage, but she willed herself forward. She took another step closer, trying desperately to look around the high back of the rocking chair, to see the face of the person sitting in it. But the shadows were too long. Too dark, despite the flood of hallway light.

To emphasize the danger the visitor was in, she pulled back on the hammer of the gun. "This is yer last warnin'," she said. "You either answer me or you get yerself shot."

Suddenly, the humming stopped. The figure, however, remained perfectly still. Unmoving. A dark statue resting menacingly in her grandmother's antique rocker. Then, after an ungodly amount of time, it spoke.

"Liz?" Its voice warbled uncontrollably with the single-syllable word, as if unused for a long period of time. It sounded hollow. Out of tune with the rest of the world. Like with the humming, there was just something…well, *wrong* about it. But her throat swelled three sizes larger in recognition of the strangely familiar baritone.

No. This can't be real. It can't be! This only happens in my dreams!

Unlike her dreams, however, there was no putrid stench of decay. No reek of the methane and ammonia that betrays all things dead. On the contrary, Elizabeth Margaret Crawford could almost smell the all-too-familiar scent of her husband's Old Spice wafting in the air.

"Tim?" The name all but caught in her throat, but she managed it in a hoarse whisper. "Is…is that you?"

The figure in the rocking chair didn't answer. He merely began humming that strange eerie tune once more, while he rocked back and forth. It was maddening. *Who was this? What is he doing in my children's room?* It couldn't possibly be Tim. People didn't come back from the dead. Those things just didn't happen.

Liz inched closer, the gun still fixed on the back of the figure's head. Closer and closer she crept, until she was just beside the rocker...until she could make out the rough, blood-stained hands clutching the arm of the chair. She looked closer, noticing the fingers and nails appeared torn or shredded, as if...oh she shuddered to even consider it. But she'd seen movies. She'd heard the stories. Men, buried alive, digging their way from their own casket into the world above. The world of the living.

No. No. It can't be.

She knew she had to be sure. She had to look at what the deepest recesses of her psyche were screaming against. She had to look into the face of the man that continued his infernal humming with unnervingly stark dispassion. She kept staring down...down at those horribly mutilated hands, unable to will up the courage to do what had to be done. She suddenly realized that she'd already lowered the gun. She had been completely unaware of it. She brought it up again with a quick jerk and moved further around the chair, her backside brushing up against Maggie's bed.

And after taking a series of deep breaths, she looked down into the face of her dead husband.

CHAPTER ONE

Boone Creek Municipal Park
April 27
12:24 PM

"Ladies and gentlemen, please give a warm hand for Jasper County Judge Executive, Joe Davis," said Mayor Mark Fowler to the crowded Town Square. The late April weather had been odd this year, to say the least, with the unseasonal drought that had been plaguing the region for the last few months. But with the clear skies and near-perfect mid-seventy-degree temperature, almost every person in town had put aside their concerns over crops and weather patterns to show up for what looked to be the event of the year. In fact, the barbecue/informal town hall meeting was becoming a serious contender for one of the most successful social events in decades. Of course, there was a good reason for all the hoopla. It wasn't every day seven well-respected and community-active citizens return from the dead, after all.

Kiera 'Kili' Brennan sat quietly at the picnic table under the oversized tent, just twenty yards from the pre-fab stage, which had been erected for the speakers. She'd already endured the town's high-school band performing a litany of Muzak's greatest hits, before having to endure another thirty-five minutes of poorly executed politician jokes from the town fathers.

To cap the day off nicely, she'd been unceremoniously stuck at a table between Ms. Delores McCrary, and her polite, but crotchety beau, Max Bertrum.

Though Kili would probably not admit it to anyone, spending time with the feisty elderly couple might have been the highlight of her day. She'd had a few encounters with Delores the last time she was in Boone Creek, but the two had never really spent a great deal of time together except for the period Kili had been recuperating from her encounter with 'One-Eyed Jack'.

Truth be known, after spending some time with Delores and Max today, she rather wished she'd gotten a chance to know her better the last time. She'd grown quite fond of them within the first five minutes of their acquaintance—although the doting older woman had begun to nag her incessantly when she noticed Kili had hardly touched the fried chicken Mr. Bertrum had heaped onto her plate at the buffet line. Still, she could live with all that as long as things would just move along. She'd come here for a reason—to learn as much as she could about the recent and undeniably strange events in the town. Although she'd found her table-mates to be warm and inviting, their constant needling repartee was beginning to grate on her nerves.

"Oh, swell," Max whispered over to Kili and Delores. "That blowhard judge will crow more than a rooster tryin' to take all the credit for the eggs. We ain't never gonna be able to git seconds now."

Delores glared at the old man before putting an index finger to her lips. "Shush now, Maximilian. Let 'im talk. This here's an important day. He's about to fill us all in on what them government scientists have learnt about the Kindred, and I for one want to hear every word." She stopped, then nodded over to Kili. "And so does she. So you act like a gentleman, you mean ol' coot."

Kili only smiled at the two, keeping her eyes fixed ahead, as the Judge Executive waddled up on a stage beside the town gazebo. It had been a little over four months since the injuries she'd sustained while investigating the legend of One-Eyed Jack had healed enough for Esther Crane to let her go home to resume her life as an FBI crime analyst at Quantico—the very life she'd practically abandoned to find her brother Cian, who'd disappeared in a dark patch of forest nearby, known as the Dark Hollows. Four months to wonder why it had all happened...to ponder the mysteries still left unanswered. Four long, haunting months wondering how a rare species of fungus could have mutated her brother into a crazed giant, who the townsfolk believed was the embodiment of an old Indian legend from pre-colonial days. Since that time, there hadn't been a day that went by that Kili hadn't mourned her brother's death at the hands of the enigmatic Ezekiel Crane—an act of mercy on his part, as well as self-defense—or questioned whether she had done everything she could to have saved him.

Warily, she scanned the crowd for Crane, but from what she could tell, he was nowhere around. This, of course, wasn't surprising. After all, he wasn't exactly well-liked around here. Besides the fact that he was supposedly a seventh son of a seventh son and imbued with all sorts of uncanny 'magical' powers, many of the Jasper County folk claimed he'd also made a pact with the devil himself as a youth, and Crane was cursed for his troubles. They said Death followed Crane around as close as his own shadow, and whoever got too close to him was doomed to die. Kili had witnessed first-hand just how terrified these people were of the strange man, and she suspected their fears might not be entirely unjustified. After all, she'd seen the things he could do first hand. He'd tried hard to make his amazing skills seem as if they were nothing more than down-home examples of scientific innovation, but down deep, she'd often wondered whether he tended to protest just a little too much. She began to develop a nagging suspicion that there might be a little more to Crane's amazing powers than hillbilly science. She'd begun to think the townspeople might not be as crazy as she'd first supposed.

No, it was no surprise that Ezekiel Crane wouldn't be here today. If he was, it was quite possible the town would stampede out of this tent, and run for their lives. This, of course, was ironic considering the nature of today's 'celebration'.

Two weeks earlier, Kili had come across an obscure article on the Internet about a strange phenomenon that had been occur-ring in a quiet little county in eastern Kentucky that had scien-tists baffled. It seemed that several of the local 'dead' were being resurrected. She didn't need to read the whole article to know exactly where the county was. It was precisely the kind of thing she'd expect from Jasper County.

She'd called Crane about it, and as was his customary fash-ion, he'd simply brushed her inquiries aside, told her there was nothing to the stories at all, and encouraged her to move on with her life. In fact, he'd been so cavalier about the strange events that she'd gotten the distinct impression he'd been trying to protect her from something. Something that had even the normally frosty Ezekiel Crane on edge. He'd sounded so nervous, in fact, that it had made her even more determined than ever to discover the truth about what was going on. The connections between the seven resurrected victims and One-Eyed Jack were just too numerous and too bizarre to be coin-cidence.

So, along with a virtual army of doctors, scientists, theolo-gians, and reporters from all across the eastern seaboard—as well as several from abroad—she had come to Boone Creek to investigate this strange phenomenon that had captured the imagination of the entire world. Of course, Kili wasn't interested in any of this for idle curiosity. She had another motive entirely. After all, if seven people, who had all died from exposure to the One-Eyed Jack spores—as Crane had begun calling the fungus—had risen from the dead, could it not be reasonable to suspect that her brother might still have a chance as well?

"Thank you, Mr. Mayor," Judge Executive Davis said, huffing for breath at the podium. His rotund frame glistened with sweat from the exertion of walking from his table and up onto the stage. Taking a handkerchief from his back pocket, he dabbed at his brow and cleared his throat in the microphone, eliciting a nerve-jarring squeal of feedback from the speakers. "Well, I reckon we've been keeping you'uns in suspense for a might longer than we'd planned on, but I figured it was high time to let everyone know what we've been able to discover about our resurrected friends." He nodded at several people in the crowd, and Kili assumed they were the people in question. "As you all know, we've had some of the best minds in the country—heck, in the world—taking a gander at our recently returned loved-ones. They've been subjected to a barrage of every sort of test on God's green Earth for the last few months, and only now have we gotten word that we could share with you. And none too soon, if you ask me! Heck, rumor has it that some of you have been a tad worried we might even be looking at the beginnings of some sort of zombie apocalypse or some such nonsense." He chuckled nervously at this comment, but he continued on when no one joined in with laughter at what he'd obviously hoped would be taken as a joke. "Well, I'm here to tell you'uns, there ain't nothing further from the truth. All the tests have come back, and everyone's perfectly fine. Alive as the day they took their first breath. Now, don't get me wrong... There still ain't no scientific explanation for it...but we're working on it. In the meantime, these people have been given a perfect bill of health and—"

Before the judge could finish, an older man sitting near the front stood up from his chair, and glared up at the stage. He was a thick-chested older man dressed in black with a white collar of a clergyman. Although his head was shaved, he sported a salt and pepper gray, bushy goatee and mustache. His sleeves were rolled up to reveal large, muscular forearms of a man who spent most of his life working hard in the outdoors. Kili imagined him chopping wood. Maybe even carrying entire trees down to the river on his broad shoulders.

"Uh-oh," Delores whispered over into her ear. "That's Reverend Jim Lorrie. We just call him the Preacher around here." She practically giggled with excitement. "Things are 'bout to get interestin' around here."

Kili had never heard of the man. She hadn't seen him the last time she was in town, and neither Crane or Granny had mentioned him either. But the reverence in which the crowd afforded him told her that he commanded a great deal of respect. And maybe, not a little fear.

"The only reverend I'm familiar with around here is Tom Thornton," Kili said.

Max turned his head, and spat at the name.

"Those two are about as different as a chicken and a goose," Delores said, giving her beau the evil eye for his rudeness. "The Preacher is about as godly a man as can be found 'round here. Ain't no one wiser neither. Even Granny goes to him for council every now and then. When he speaks, trust me…this town listens."

Kili turned her attention back to the old reverend with a new sense of awe. If Granny Crane respected this man, that was saying something. Apparently, the entire crowd felt the same way. The entire tent was silent as they waited for the Preacher to speak. But he simply stood, staring up at the Judge Executive, the mayor, and a severe looking woman seated behind the podium.

The air around them nearly crackled with energy. Then, Jim Lorrie opened his mouth, and spoke.

"Ya'll know how I feel about this."

Judge Davis wiped more sweat from his brow, then offered a nervous nod of his head.

"Nothin' good will come of this."

No one responded, though Kili noticed everyone's eyes shifting back and forth between the reverend, the stage, and various others sitting among the crowd.

Then, with a certain practiced grace, the man placed a wide-brimmed cowboy hat atop his head, stepped out into the aisle, and strode out of the tent without another word. The moment he was gone, a synchronized sigh rushed through the crowd, and the strange energy Kili had been feeling abruptly faded to nothing.

"What on earth was that about?" Kili asked, leaning over to Delores.

The older woman shrugged. "Don't rightly know. The Preacher hasn't exactly been quiet about his distrust for the *Kindred*." She said the last word—the name given to the seven people who had returned from the dead—in a hushed whisper as if uttering it was a taboo all itself. "Says they ain't the same people who died. Claims they're bodies with no souls. No minds. And especially no spirits."

"Is there a difference? I mean, between a soul and a spirit?"

"Oh, deary, of course there is. A soul is who a person is. It's their identity. Their nature. A spirit...well, a spirit is..."

"Sorry about that, folks," Judge Davis said, while wiping away a renewed stream of sweat. "That's the Preacher for ya."

A few in the crowd chuckled, but most shifted nervously in their seats.

"Now, where was I?" Davis shuffled through the notes sitting on the podium. "Ah, yes. Like I was sayin', each of the Kindred have been given clean bills of health and..."

"Your Honor..." A handsome blond man in his early thirties casually dressed in a blue Tommy Hilfiger polo shirt and khakis stood up from the crowd, waving apologetically. "Sorry to interrupt. Again. But the name's Alex Davenport. I'm a reporter working on the story, and although I'm not sure how that last guy felt about all this, I'm pretty sure we may be seeing eye to eye. I was wondering if you could clarify something for me."

"Well, son, now's really not the time," Davis said with an anxious, politician's smile. "This ain't exactly a press conference. It was supposed to be just for the town's folk and—"

"I know. I know," Davenport said, holding up his hands apologetically. "But I'm confused about something, and I have a sneaking suspicion many of your constituents are too. You see, since coming here two weeks ago, I've spoken with many of the families around here—some of the ones that have received their loved ones back and some who didn't. I've even talked to a couple of these...um, *Kindred*, as many of you have been calling them, and I have to tell you...something just seems weird about the whole thing."

An uncomfortable murmur erupted among the crowd, everyone's attention quickly turning immediately to the judge.

"I'm not sure I follow you, son," Davis said, wiping a rejuvenated stream of sweat from his forehead. "While, yes, on the surface, it's mighty unsettling for anyone when they consider the miracle that's occurred here. People don't come back from the dead every day, ya know. But medical tests have all been fine. CAT scans. MRIs. Blood work. They were all normal. Better than normal actually. A couple of them had diseases like diabetes and coronary artery disease before they died. Scars have disappeared. Heck, even Ned Campbell's ring finger grew back. They are perfectly healthy. Perfectly normal." He cleared his throat from the long winded diatribe. "Like I said...a miracle."

The reporter shifted nervously, looking down at his feet, as if trying to find the perfect response. Finally, after several uncomfortably long seconds of silence, he merely shrugged and pointed over at the closest of the Kindred.

"Come on, Judge, look at him!" Davenport implored.

All eyes turned to fix on the near-catatonic form of a man hunkered down in a motorized wheelchair. The man's eyes stared vacantly up at the sky, as a single line of drool slipped past the corner of his lips and down his chin.

"That's poor Tim Crawford," Delores McCrary whispered in Kili's ear. "It was him that was the first to return, they say."

Kili knew the name well. He'd been the one who had found her brother's guide, Leroy Kingston, in a crazed state on the side of the road. She'd never met Crawford during her investigation. He'd disappeared shortly after she came to town. Now, she scrutinized the man for several long seconds. Not only did he appear catatonic, but he also seemed dangerously emaciated...as if he'd not eaten anything in weeks. The skin of his gaunt face stretched tightly across a cadaverous skull. His jaw hung slack, absently moving up and down like a fish trying to take in water through its gills. But it was his eyes, she decided, that unnerved her more than anything. Though they were undoubtedly vacant, she imagined she caught the slightest trace of something intelligent in them. Something watchful. Patient. Unsettling. And she decided immediately that she didn't like staring into those blank eyes at all.

"Can you honestly tell me, Your Honor, that you can look this man in the face, and not see that something is wrong?" Davenport continued. "And it's true for all of them too. I've checked. Yes, they are *capable* of walking and talking, when the mood hits them. They are most definitely breathing. They eat food, but only rarely. But ask their families! Ask their friends... They're not even close to being the same people they were before their deaths. Something is decidedly wrong here, and you want everyone to believe that they've been given a clean bill of health from the medical community?"

"And how would you expect seven individuals who had been clinically—and I suppose quite literally—dead for varying amounts of time, to behave, Mr. Davenport?" asked the severe-looking woman sitting behind Davis on stage. The woman, wearing a striped pant suit and flats, with a coarse mane of copper hair pulled back in a tight bun, stood up, and strode over to the podium. Her face, which looked older than what Kili guessed to be her true age, appeared as skeletal as those of the Kindred, and her lips curled downward in an irritated scowl. "These people have each been through an unprecedented traumatic experience. They are unique in the annals of history. So you tell me, Mr. Davenport, in your *expert* medical opinion, just how should they look? How should they act?"

"Ah, Dr. Maher!" exclaimed Judge Davis, with an expression of orgasmic relief on his face. "I'm glad you're here!" He turned to the crowd and explained, "Ladies and gentleman, this is Dr. Ruth Maher. She's the lead investigator—sent by the Center for Disease Control itself—who headed up the medical panel that examined our friends. I'm sure she can explain the CDC's findings a bit better than me."

The doctor stared smugly at the local politician before she turned her burning eyes back to the reporter.

"I'd be happy to, Your Honor." She stepped down from the stage, and walked over to Tim Crawford's wheelchair. She gently laid a bony hand on his shoulder, and gave it a sympathetic politician's pat. "But I'd like an answer from our journalist friend here before I do." She paused a moment, then continued. "Mr. Davenport?"

The reporter looked at the doctor with unwavering, defiant eyes, then took a deep breath.

"Well, as you've pointed out," he said with an irritated smile, "No one knows for sure what to expect from people who've been dead for more than—what? A week or so? Every single one of these resurrected people have suffered from Lord-knows-what, and you've run a few simple tests, and declared them perfectly healthy? It just seems to me that prudence would suggest—"

"Prudence, Mr. Davenport?" Maher hissed. "Prudence? What on Earth do you know about that? Ever since coming to this town, you've been a busy little bee. You stood out from all the other reporters lurking about, so I thought it a good idea to research you a bit. I daresay that *prudence* is a word that is probably not in your vocabulary. Nor, might I venture, would be *credibility* or even *journalism* for that matter. After all, your last big story just happened to involve a pack of vicious gargoyles that came to life, and supposedly terrorized the good citizens of New York City a few months back, didn't it?" There was a deafening silence that blanketed the town square at this news, and the doctor was obviously savoring her imminent victory. The reporter's jaw fell open, unwilling—or unable—to form a rebuttal. "What newspaper did you say you worked for again? Oh, that's right. It's a supermarket tabloid called the...let me make sure I get this right...*The Fortean Inquisitor*?"

"Hey! I love that paper!" exclaimed an old lady in the crowd, which elicited a raucous surge of laughter.

The reporter's cheeks flushed, and Kili winced as the man's mouth opened and closed a half-dozen times in an attempt to defend against the attack. But apparently, he could come up with nothing to save face. Though she thought his occupation laughable, she couldn't help appreciating the man's desire to get to the real truth behind the Kindred. And he'd actually made a great deal of sense. Wasn't it a bit premature to stamp these people as perfectly healthy? Shouldn't there be more tests run? More observations made? Sleazy reporter or not, Davenport definitely had a good point.

She wasn't sure whether it was because of the logic of the reporter's argument or because she just couldn't tolerate bullies, but Kili stood at that precise moment and spoke out.

21

"Hold on a second. I'm kind of curious about this too," she shouted above the din of laughter still rumbling through the crowd. The moment she spoke, everyone once more fell silent. She doubted that there was a single person in the entire gathering—other than Maher, Davenport, and the handful of news crews that managed to sneak into the closed event—who didn't know who she was. There were probably several, as a matter of fact, who viewed her in as harsh a light as they did Ezekiel Crane. After all, she'd been in cahoots with the accursed one, hadn't she? Plus, her brother was blamed for riling up One-Eyed Jack, to begin with. Since Cian was dead, they'd readily turned their ire toward her. "Look, we all know that these people were killed by the fungal spores in the Dark Hollows. Every single one of them had some sort of connection to them anyway. And, as they did with everybody who came in contact with them, the spores entered the person, multiplied, and tried to change the victim's DNA. Those they couldn't change were simply used as incubators. Once the spores were mature, they exploded out of the body, and waited for the next victim to come along." She paused for effect, letting her words sink in. "I saw first-hand what the spores could do. I saw the 'hatchet wounds,' as many of you call them. The splitting and tearing of the skin from accelerated growth, and the spores ripping through the body. I'm looking at Tim Crawford now, and I'm asking myself, *What happened to the injuries? What happened to the wounds?* And then I'm asking, *If these deaths were caused by the spores, how do we know these resurrections weren't merely the result of the same DNA-alteration that affected my brother?*"

The crowd remained silent, soaking in her words with confused expressions on their faces. She had no doubt that more than half of them didn't believe one iota of it. Most still chalked the events in the Dark Hollows up to the spirit world. Magic, faeries, and Native American curses. They weren't ready to hear the truth, so they merely denied it.

"Ms. Brennan," Judge Davis said with a sneer. "I see you've decided to join us too."

"I've never given up on getting the answers to my brother's disappearance last year. Now that new evidence has arisen, I had to come see for myself."

"Ms. Brennan, I'm not sure what you *think* you know," Mayor Fowler said, standing up and walking over to the podium. "But there's never been a single shred of proof to Crane's cockamamie story about fungus spores that changed your brother into some sort of Boogieman monster. After all, he had our former Sheriff burn it all up before anyone of a scientific notion could take a look at it."

Former Sheriff? Kili wondered. *What happened to Tyler?*

"As it stands, we ain't found a single link between the Kindred deaths and One-Eyed Jack," Judge Davis continued.

Kili's veins began to boil with irritation. This ridiculous flim-flam team had another thing coming if they thought she was going to believe any of that. Taking a step away from the table, she glared at the two politicians on the podium.

"No link? Are you kidding me?" She was shouting now. "I was infected by the spores too! My body began to change just like my brother, and I would have ended up the same as him if it wasn't for the Cranes coming up with a cure.

"And I was still around when the Kindreds' bodies were recovered! I saw them with my own eyes during the autopsies. The injuries. The same ones I saw on Miles Marathe and Candace Staples. Are you saying now that *their* deaths weren't related to One-Eyed Jack?"

"What they're saying, madam, is that no one knows for sure what they died from," Dr. Maher said, her eyes burning a hole into Kili. "Your brother was cremated, under the direction of this Mr. Crane, before an autopsy could be performed. The autopsies you alluded to were performed by a quack deputy coroner, who everyone around in town seems to believe is some sort of witch-doctor. I find any diagnoses he established to be extremely suspect."

As the exchange grew even more heated, the buzz among the crowd rose. Tempers flared. Muttered rumblings echoed across the town square. The townspeople were becoming agitated. A clear line had been drawn in the sand, and they were taking sides. And through it all, someone started to sing.

It was the strangest song Kili had ever heard. Slow and melancholy, and darker than the darkest night. It sounded like a dirge...an old funeral song reminiscent of those sung at funerals in Ireland. Through the insanity that was boiling up in the mass of townspeople, someone had the audacity to sing such a song? She turned her head, trying to discern where it was coming from. *What a crass thing to do!* This was serious business, and some idiot chose that moment to sing a song of death. Carnage. But no... It wasn't just one person. The more she listened, the more she began to suspect the song was actually coming from a choir of some kind.

But as she looked around, no one else seemed to be noticing. They were still yelling at one another with beet red faces and spittle flying from their mouths, totally oblivious to the disturbing song that was now wafting all around them. What were the words? What were the singers singing? Something about death, she was sure...but whose?

"...know why we're even listening to her!" one man was yelling through the chorus. "She's as much of the devil as Crane is..."

If she heard the rest of what was being said, she couldn't remember. All that mattered to her in that moment was the sad, sad song that seemed to well up in the inner corners of her soul. Instantly, she was slammed with an overwhelming sense of loss. Torment. Anxiety. She wanted to drop to her knees and mourn for the loss of...

Her head whipped around again, scanning the crowd until

her eyes landed on the wheelchair-bound form of Tim Crawford. Once there, they slipped two feet to his left, to look at the prim, but portly middle-aged woman seated beside him. Crawford's wife. Something was about to happen to her. The song was for her. It was, Kili somehow knew, Mrs. Crawford's funeral dirge, and no one seemed to even be bothered by it. No one seemed to care. No one acted to save her.

Instantly, Kili dashed away from the picnic table, and moved toward the doomed woman, but it was too late. Just as the din roared to a crescendo, Liz Crawford cried out in an agonizing scream, silencing everyone. She stood from her chair, her face pale. Sweat trailed off her forehead, and she stared down at her feet in a subdued panic. No one moved. Even Kili skidded to an abrupt halt at the sight. All eyes fixed on Liz Crawford, as slowly, almost imperceptibly, her limbs began to shake. Gradually, the quaking became more intense, and a white froth began spewing from between her clenched teeth, just before she collapsed to the ground in a grand mal seizure.

In a rush, a group of paramedics, who'd been on standby at the barbecue, carefully moved Liz's two panicked children away, then knelt at her side to begin CPR efforts. Tim Crawford stayed glued to his wheelchair, staring blankly into the sky, unconcerned with his wife's plight.

The crowd's tension was palpable. No one spoke. No one moved. Which made it easy for Kili to catch something out of the corner of her eye. Someone was standing on a nearby hill in the park. Something. A human figure stood stoically looking down on the chaos. His dark robes flapped in the warm Spring breeze, which is what caught Kili's attention. Could he have been the source of the song she'd heard just before Crawford's collapse? For some reason, she didn't think so. It just didn't feel right for some reason. After all, the dirge had seemed to be voiced by a choir of children, not a full-grown man in dark robes and...what was he wearing exactly?

Slowly, she took in all the details of the figure, starting with the feet, covered with old-style riding boots, which were half-concealed by a thick wool cloak pulled tight around the figure's masculine shoulders. But it was the face that caused her to step back, and nearly collapse to the ground on weakened knees. The long, narrow beak of a crow stretched out from the face, with two perfectly round coal-black eyes nearly concealed by the shadow of a wide flat-brimmed hat. The initial sight of the thing had startled her, until she realized that she'd seen such a visage before. Something from a book, though she couldn't remember what it was.

She quickly glanced over at Delores and Max, to see if they'd caught sight of the strange figure, but their eyes were still fixed on the valiant rescue attempts of the paramedics. One of them, the chief EMT by the look of it, finally shook his head and looked up at the crowd.

"I'm sorry," he said, bowing his head low. "There weren't nothing we could do. She's dead."

At the proclamation, Kili turned her attention again to the hill, but the bird-like figure was gone.

CHAPTER
TWO

K ili watched as the funeral home's men loaded Liz
Crawford into the back of a mini-van, climbed in, and
drove away. When she asked where they were taking the body,
she had been met with cold, indifferent stares from the transport
crew. But one thing was clear; they had no intention of allowing
Ezekiel Crane, the county's deputy coroner, to examine the body.

From the moment the woman had collapsed, the crowd had
erupted into a panicked frenzy. Only the coolly detached Dr.
Maher and the new sheriff—though Kili didn't recognize the
man from her previous visit, she identified his position from the
brown uniform and the gold star on his left breast pocket—had
managed to keep the terrified masses from becoming a full-
blown mob. Something had certainly spooked them. Something
more than the strange and sudden death of a local.

Maybe they'd all heard the dirge too, she thought. *Maybe that's
what spooked them. It certainly spooked me.*

"Excuse me," Kili said, as she walked up to the new sheriff
and Dr. Maher. A pretty young blonde, wearing green nurse
scrubs stood next to the doctor. "Can you tell me where you're

taking the body? I'm friends with Ezekiel Crane. I'm sure he'll want to take a look at her before—"

"Ms. Brennan, I know exactly who you are," the sheriff, a gaunt little man of about five foot five, said with a scowl. "And I'm afraid that even though Crane's granny—who is the duly elected coroner in these parts, by the way—might have appointed him her official deputy, this here supersedes their authority." Pulling a few strands of hair back over the bald spot on his head, he glanced over at Dr. Maher.

"This is a CDC matter," she said tersely. Close up, her face wasn't as severe as Kili had first thought. Though her face was covered in frown lines that stretched down from thin lips and a few old pock-mark scars dotted her rigid cheek bones, there was the slightest trace of someone who could—with the help of a talented beautician—be somewhat attractive. Pleasant even. Instead, the haughty and upturned nose and angry demeanor helped to draw one's eyes away from anything resembling beauty. "And as such, confidential. We cannot discuss the incident at this time, though we will be sure to inform the public if there is a general health hazard with which they should be concerned."

"But I thought the CDC was here only to investigate the Kindred," Kili protested. "Are you saying that there is a connection between the resurrections and whatever killed Liz Crawford?"

"What I'm saying, ma'am, is that if you attempt to poke your nose any further in this matter, I'll instruct Sheriff Slate here to arrest you immediately," Maher said with a sour grin. "Now, leave it at that."

Kili could only stare at the woman in silence. She could feel the anger begin to boil, just at the base of her neck, over the doctor's haughty little threat, but could find nothing to say that would help her situation at all. If anything, she'd only make matters worse.

Despite this, she still had to try. "But I just wanted…"

"Good day to you," Maher said, brushing her off as the woman walked past with a sneer. The nurse, whose nametag simply read: HEATHER, gave her an apologetic look, and dashed off after her superior.

The sheriff remained in place, one eye fixed on Kili while his other, obviously a lazy eye, drifted off somewhere past her left shoulder. After a handful of uncomfortably silent seconds, he pulled a thick wad of chewing tobacco from a pouch and inserted it inside his cheek. "We ain't been formally introduced, Ms. Brennan, seeing as how I wasn't appointed until a month after you left town. Name's Slate. Gerald Slate." He spit a string of darkened saliva into the grass by his feet and smiled. "You should know one thing about me, right from the start. I ain't the pushover my predecessor was. I don't get swayed by the wiles of an attractive redhead. What's more, I ain't afraid of your friends, the Cranes, or their witchery. And I ain't the least afraid to tell you to leave all this well enough alone. As a matter of fact, knowin' yer reputation around here for stirring up trouble, I'm of a mind to tell you to flat out leave town." He tipped his hat slightly at her and smiled. "That'll be your only warnin', miss."

Without giving her a chance to respond, he stalked off after Maher, and disappeared into the crowd.

"Wow. Tough room," a male voice said from behind. Kili turned around to see the tabloid reporter leaning against a maple tree with his arms crossed, and a dazzling grin spread across his face. In one hand, he held an antique walking cane, which looked to Kili like fine ash. The cane was tipped with a silver handle, shaped like a dragon.

"Yes," she said. "Apparently it is." Not wanting to encourage him, Kili spun back around and started walking away toward Grand Avenue. Silently, she prayed that the man would get the hint and go away, but in the pit of her stomach, she knew that wasn't going to happen.

"I'm Alex, by the way," he said, hobbling with the cane to catch up to her. His blazing white smile hadn't even faltered at her rudeness, and Kili couldn't help wondering if the cane was a ruse to draw in women with the sympathy card. "Reporter. But I guess you already knew that, didn't you? I mean, from you being at the picnic and all."

She didn't answer. Instead, she kept marching; focusing her gaze two blocks down, where she would hang a left onto Main. She had no idea where Crane was, but she figured the best place to start looking for him would be at the used bookstore he ran downtown. Surely, he'd be able to fill her in on what was going on in this crazy little town. He might not like the fact that she hadn't listened to his advice to stay away, but he knew her well enough to expect she wouldn't actually do what she was told. When dead people who were connected with what happened to Cian started getting up out of their graves, and carrying on semi-normal lives, she couldn't just stand idly by and hope someone would eventually fill her in on what it was all about. No, Crane had to be expecting her.

"That was some craziness back there, wasn't it?" the reporter asked, oblivious to the cold shoulder she was fixing on him. "The wife of one of the Kindred—the very first one to reappear, no doubt—just drops dead for the whole town to see. There one second. Gone the next. I mean, what are the odds of that?"

Who is this guy, and why is he talking to me? Kili thought, as she turned onto Main Street, and headed toward Crane's bookstore. "Look, Mister…"

"Davenport," he repeated. "Alex Davenport."

"Mr. Davenport, I'm sorry. But I'm kind of in the middle of something now," she said, still avoiding eye contact. "I'm not sure what you want from me, but I'm not local. I can't give you any answers for your story. I'm just here to meet a friend, and then I'll be heading back to D.C."

The reporter kept stride with her, despite whatever disability that caused the pronounced limp in his right leg. "Heading back to D.C., eh?" he said with a laugh. "You're not a very good liar, are you?"

Kili didn't like being accused of lying...even if it was true. She stopped in her tracks and whirled around to face Davenport. "Look, buddy," she said, blowing a strand of bright red hair from her eyes. "I'm trying to be nice here. I'm not interested in anything you have to say, and I'm definitely not impressed by anyone who makes a living in a grocery store rag! So, drop the charm, turn around, and leave me alone."

Satisfied she'd given him the proper berating he needed, she resumed her progress toward the bookstore with a smile on her face. She wasn't a mean person. She didn't take pleasure in emasculating the guy. But the fact that she couldn't hear him following her filled her with a sense of pride over having dealt with the man.

"That crazy bird guy up on the hill sure was creepy, wasn't he?" Davenport called, bringing her to a halt.

"What did you just say?" she asked, turning around again to meet his gaze. He was now leaning forward, his full weight on the cane. Despite herself, she couldn't help being drawn to him. He really was a disgustingly good-looking man. Disgusting because he obviously knew it. The guy looked like he'd be better suited in front of a camera than behind a byline in some sleazy newspaper.

"You heard me," he said, a twinkle in his eye. "Guy in a weird bird mask standing up on the hill. He showed up right before Mrs. Crawford croaked. Disappeared right after. I know you saw him. I saw you looking at him. That's how I caught sight of him myself." He stepped closer to her and grinned. "So I wonder what *his* story is, and how he's connected to all this... don't you?"

Davenport had her, and he knew it, which was even more infuriating to Kili. There was just something about this guy that screamed trouble, and she was determined to make sure she kept the upper hand on him at all times during their acquaintance.

"Way I hear it, those guys have been popping up all over Boone Creek since the Kindred reappeared, actually," he added, before she could say anything. "Each time they show up, someone seems to die." He cocked his head. "If I'm not mistaken, the Crawford woman makes number three."

"Three? You mean two other people have been murdered since..."

Davenport shrugged. "No one said anything about murder. No one exactly knows how they died really. That Dr. Maher has kept a tight rein on things since she got here. And she's not saying anything about what caused these deaths...or what caused the Kindred to come back to life for that matter. Seven people come back to life—just like that—and she wants everyone to think everything is A-okay. Three people die mysteriously, and she expects everyone to buy the same load of crap? I don't think so." The man's smile had disappeared completely as he finished his diatribe. "Oh, and each of the victims has been related in some way to one of the..."

"...Kindred," Kili finished his sentence, before turning to walk toward Crane's store once more...only this time, the reporter had her attention. "Walk with me." The *tap-tap-tap* of his cane hitting the sidewalk told her she wouldn't have to tell the man twice, so she continued her train of thought. "And this 'bird man' is always around when someone dies?"

"Yep. But call them that to any one of these hillbillies, and see what kind of reaction you'll get."

Kili laughed at this. She was all too familiar with the superstitious fervor some in Boone Creek could demonstrate. "So what do they say this guy is?"

Davenport, now walking in stride with her, merely shrugged. "Not a darn thing. They're about as tight-lipped about him as they are about the zombie apocalypse they're having around here." He paused, his head leaning to one side as they approached bookstore. "Um, why are we going here? Is that friend you were going to meet, Ezekiel Crane?"

"Yes. Why? Do you know him?"

"Only by reputation," Davenport said. "I worked with a cousin of his in New York a little while back... He recommended I look Crane up when I got into town. But he's not been around since I got here. No one seems to have a clue where he's gone— though a few people in this town seem to think he couldn't have gone far enough, I might add. I think his grandmother knows where he is, but she's not letting on that she does. Matter of fact, she seems pretty worried about him at the moment."

"You've met Granny?"

His bright smile returned. "Oh yeah...best eating I've had in years. Like I said, Crane's cousin hooked me up. I've been staying with her while I've tried to sort this mess out."

Wow, Granny is a pretty good judge of character. If she's letting this guy stay with her, then maybe he'll be more useful than I first thought.

She jogged the last few feet up to the bookstore's door to see a CLOSED sign hanging from the window. Irritated, she let out a soft growl, twirled around, and leaned against the glass with her arms folded in thought. Davenport shrugged, turned around, and leaned against the glass next to her.

"So what now, boss?" he asked.

Boss? Wait a minute...

"What are you doing?" she asked, pulling away from him. "Why are you following me around? You don't even know who I am, for crying out loud. What's all this about?"

"Um, that's easy," he said, pulling out a reporter's notebook, and flipping through several pages. "You're Kiera Brennan—Kili to your friends and family. You work for the FBI. Your brother was Dr. Cian Brennan, an anthropologist who came here last year investigating some archaeological discovery in a place called the..." He flipped back two pages. "...Dark Hollows. Last October, he went missing. You came to town to find him... hooked up with Crane and his grandmother, and stirred up a hornet's nest in the process, if I'm not mistaken." He turned one more page and his face grew serious again. "And in the process, you apparently discovered some weird fungus that caused normal human beings to grow into giants. Your brother, for instance. I'm truly sorry, by the way."

Kili shrugged the apology away. "Everything you said is on the record. Doesn't take a super-journalist to know all that," she said. "What I'm curious about is...what do you expect me to do for your story?"

Davenport looked out toward the red-orange glow of the sun as it edged its way behind the emerald green hills in the horizon. She'd forgotten how depressing—how claustrophobic—this place could be around sundown.

"You want an honest answer, Ms. Brennan?" he finally asked after several seconds.

"That would be refreshing," she replied.

"Okay. Truth is...I'm not here for a story. I'm here for the truth." He motioned toward a nearby bench, then patted his leg. They walked over, and sat down as he continued. "I used to always be about the story. I'd step on anyone and everyone to get it. The crazier the better, I thought. Then, I got involved in that fiasco in New York..."

"Those gargoyles that Maher mentioned?"

He nodded. "Don't laugh. They were real. Absolutely real. And you wouldn't believe how scary. But that's not important. Point is, before that, the only thing I cared about was the story. A man I met while chasing those things down eventually convinced me there were some things more important than selling newspapers. Sometimes, the truth is the greatest reason there is."

"And this man? I'm assuming he's Ezekiel's cousin?"

"Second cousins, actually. But yeah. Why?"

Kili shook her head and smiled. "No reason. Just sounds like something special runs in that particular family line, that's all."

He chuckled but nodded. "Yep. I'd say you're right. Though if it wasn't for my friend, I would have never had my hip broken, and I wouldn't need to use this cane now."

She looked over at him. "Was it worth it?"

His pearly whites were brighter than ever. "You have no idea," he said, beaming. "Most definitely."

"Well, then," Kili said, standing up from the bench, and holding out a hand to help him up. "We need to get moving. The *Mystery of the Formerly Dead and the Bird Man of Boone Creek* isn't going to solve itself, ya know."

"What'd you have in mind?"

She started walking back in the direction of the park where she'd left her car. "Well, I happened to catch the name of the funeral home that took Mrs. Crawford's body away," she said, now allowing a subdued smile herself. "I thought we might pay *Overturf & Sons Mortuary*, in Morriston, a little visit later tonight."

"Ms. Brennan," Davenport said with a laugh. "I do believe I'm going to like you a great deal."

CHAPTER
THREE

The Dark Hollows
April 27
3:05 PM

There is a stretch of land amid the foothills of the Appalachians, in the county of Jasper, near the town of Boone Creek, Kentucky, which is comprised of a series of hollows. No one knows for sure just how many hollows, for no one who has ventured too deeply into the land has ever returned with his sanity fully intact. To most residents of Boone Creek, this region, known locally as the Dark Hollows, is a dead place. It's no secret that the vegetation becomes so thick within the 'hollars' that the roots of the very trees, in battle over prime real estate, strangle each other for any foothold they can muster. As a result, though rich with trees, shrubs, and bramble, nothing easily grows there...and fewer things ever blossom.

Even the animals, when they can help it, steer clear of the unholy place...which is well known to be haunted. Haunted by evil spirits. Haunted by the *Yunwi Tsunsdi*. And haunted by much older things that were forgotten even before the white man first set foot in the Appalachians.

So when a local explains that the woods that blanket the region are lifeless—dead—they are not exaggerating. They are not being quaint or using clever metaphors to describe the terrain. They most certainly believe that Death itself dwells in the land, and very few people have courage enough to venture there.

But there is one place—one small acre or so of land within the 'hollars'—that is a bit different than the rest. A marsh of near perfect circular symmetry lies near the southeastern most section of the Kentucky, Virginia, and Tennessee state lines. The tri-county border—commonly referred to as Briarsnare Marsh—marks a natural ley line, perfect for magical energies. A cross-roads of sorts, though no roads have been laid within ten miles of its boundaries. A place of power, some would say. A place where the green of the grass is the color of jade, and the rich lichen that coats the valley's boulders is as soft as down. And within that clearing, if one was either brave enough—or foolish enough—to journey into this pristine glade, they would find a grove of ancient weeping willows, basking in the sun's light, which is so foreign to most of the Dark Hollows. The sagging tendrils of each of the trees are said to dance on the currents of the breeze that dips fleetingly into the clearing. And in the center of this grove, weathered and worn, stands an old, ramshackle hovel, which leans precariously to one side, as if a sudden wind could topple it with the barest of effort.

Asherah Richardson knew that it would take much more than a mere gust of wind to ever knock down those walls, though. The shack's sole resident simply would not allow it, which was a testament to the power that resided inside its walls.

Asherah could not control the shudder that swept through her lithe, athletic frame as she stood there, looking at the place, by the silvery light of the full moon. With a chill, she reflected on the first time she'd ever laid eyes on it. She'd been just a young girl...around nine...already orphaned and taken in by Noah McGuffin, the area's resident drug kingpin. McGuffin, of course, hadn't brought her into his home out of the goodness of his heart. He'd had plans for her...dark plans. Both of the lascivious and the practical variety. The former, she pushed from her memories with a wave of nausea. It was the latter she wanted to recall today.

Noah had known of Asherah's heritage. A native of the Caribbean, her mother had learned magic from her grandmother, who had learned it from hers. It had been a cycle spanning back for generations, she supposed, all the way from Africa. But something had happened about three years before Asherah had been born. A tragedy she'd never quite understood sent her mother fleeing to the United States. She'd been running from something. That much, Asherah knew...but she'd never discovered from what.

When Asherah was around seven years old, her mother had brought her to Kentucky. The woman had fled into the protective arms of a young entrepreneur—Noah—who'd made a fortune cultivating marijuana when it was still the Blue Grass state's cash crop. Things had been good for Asherah and her mother for the next year and a half...until her mother died. Noah had stepped in, of course. Adopted her. And within days of the funeral, he'd taken her to this very spot. To the Willow Hag. To learn all about mountain magic and of the 'Old'uns'...they who can never be named.

She shivered as she stepped toward the shack's whitewashed door and raised her light brown fist to knock. The door creaked open before she could bring her hand down, and Asherah found herself staring into a thick, ethereal blackness that seemed to gorge on any light that became trapped inside.

"Come in," came a soft, soothing voice from inside. Asherah had never grown accustomed to that voice. It was the antithesis of the clichéd, crackly, nasal sound of a wicked old witch. Rather, it carried the sweet, soothing molasses of someone's dear old grandmother. It was a voice that should accompany the aroma of apple pie or warm cider on the stove. Though, as with everything else concerning the Hag, Asherah knew it was all an illusion. She had, after all, heard the crone's actual voice on more than one occasion, and it was anything but grandmotherly. "Come in, dear Asherah. I've been expecting you."

In the years that she had known the woman, the Willow Hag had always found new and inventive ways to surprise her. She'd certainly not expected so warm a reception. After all, the two hadn't spoken in more than fifteen years. Not since she had chosen Ezekiel Crane over her mentor. Her teacher. Her surrogate mother. For all intents and purposes, Asherah had been banished from the grove on the day she and Crane both had rejected the Hag's unthinkable offer.

"Are you certain, Mother?" Of course, the Hag was not Asherah's real mother. But for many years, she had indeed been a surrogate...her spiritual *Mater Matris*, and Asherah had been expected to address her as such.

She peered into the black miasma of the dwelling's interior, as she waited for a response. It was like looking into the eternal vacuum of a black hole...a living darkness of almost palpable vitriol, ready to pull her inside, to squeeze the life from her at the whim of the Hag.

"Of course, sweet child," the older woman cooed. "Bygones and all that." She paused a second, then chuckled to herself. "Here, let me give you some light to see by, shall I?" A second later, the warm glow of a candle flared to life, though Asherah had not heard the strike of a match or a lighter.

The single candle, resting on an old clay holder caked with generations of melted wax, sat on a wooden table in the center of the shack. The Hag leaned back in a creaking rocker just beyond the table, her form shrouded by shadows. Despite the candlelight, she would have been almost invisible, if not for the red-orange glow of a pipe that smoldered between her teeth, and the dried, leathery skin of her bare feet on the shack's earthen floor. Oddly enough, this was nothing new. In all the time Asherah had known the *Mater Matris*, she had never actually laid eyes on the old crone's features once. In fact, legend hinted that if one was to look upon her true form, they would die instantly. It was, of course, more likely that viewing the immortal creature—some type of nature spirit, similar to the Yunwi Tsunsdi according to the old stories—wasn't really the immediate cause of the unwary viewer's death. Rather, Asherah suspected it had more to do with the fact that the Hag would frequently feed on the life-force of the unsuspecting. The emotionally weak. The mentally unstable.

Tentatively, Asherah's own bare foot stepped onto the dirt floor, and she walked past the threshold, charged with the magical energies of the willows outside and the ley lines below. Energies designed to stop anyone unwelcome from entering the Hag's domain. Three steps into the hovel and she was standing next to the round table, looking anxiously across at the shadowy old crone.

"Now," the Willow Hag said, "let me have a look at you. Been too long. Been far too long."

There was a pause of a few seconds before Asherah had to suppress a shiver that ran down her spine. The old woman's invisible eyes were undoubtedly absorbing every pore, every hair, and every wrinkle on her body. Her light mocha skin had always been an object of contention with the Hag, who unabashedly hated any race other than white. It had been a surprise to even Noah when she'd eagerly agreed to teach Asherah back in the day. Asherah had never understood why, but she'd always been self-conscious of her skin color in the Hag's presence.

"Mmmmm...child," the Hag finally spoke up. "You are

every bit as bonnie as I remember. As pretty as a daisy in a graveyard, as my kin always liked to say. A daisy in a graveyard, indeed."

The pleasantness of the exchange set Asherah's nerves on edge. This wasn't going as she'd expected in the slightest. Forgetting the fact that she'd not been welcome in the grove in such a long time, the Willow Hag undoubtedly knew why she'd come...and she should be none too pleased by the questions now on Asherah's mind. Yet since her arrival, the *Mater Matris* had been nothing but kind...delightful even.

"Mother, I must speak with you," she said, absently pulling up the left shoulder strap of the sundress she was wearing. She wanted to berate herself for the obvious signs of trepidation she was displaying in front of the woman who had basically abandoned her. Fear was an emotion nearly foreign to Asherah. Men, women, and even children feared *her*, after all. There should be no mortal on Earth—save Ezekiel Crane himself—that troubled her. Yet the Willow Hag was a force of nature. If the stories were actually true, the woman was as old as the moss that carpeted the ground outside. She was beyond anything Asherah or Crane could possibly ever understand.

Asherah willed her nerves to settle as she took a deep breath and continued. "Why on Earth have you unleashed the Leechers after all these years? And if you're targeting Ezekiel again, why have they killed three people with the *Trial by Ordeals*? It doesn't make any sense to—"

The Hag's bony hand raised into the air, silencing Asherah. "Calm, child. Calm," she said with a hypnotically soothing voice. "It wasn't me what loosed the Leecher haints on the world. T'weren't me at all."

The Mother's response caught Asherah off guard. "W-what? But the bones...only you possess the bones of Smith and the other Witchhunters. Only you could possibly have summoned his judges to—"

"And when, pray dearie, was the last time you seen the undead lot of them, might I ask?"

The question was even more unexpected than the Hag's initial response. What was the woman getting at here? Of course, the last time Asherah had seen the hateful things, their murderous dead eyes had been locked on Ezekiel Crane. The Willow Hag herself had sent them to kill him, when he was still a teenager, as remuneration for his betrayal. But during the hunt, something had gone wrong. They'd targeted Crane's only surviving brother, Josiah, instead. Used their accursed Trials on the boy, which had put him in a coma that, as far as Asherah knew, he still suffered from to this day. Strangely enough, it was within the hour of that horrible incident that the Leechers had disappeared completely, until just recently. No one knew what happened to them, and Ash had believed, or rather hoped, that the Willow Hag had simply called them off the hunt because of the tragedy. Now, she was beginning to wonder.

"Y-you know when, Mother," she said nervously. "It was just after they witched Josiah Crane."

The old crone cackled before drawing another pull from her pipe. A second later, an exhaled plume of dense, gray smoke rolled out from the darkness toward Asherah.

"And you don't think, sweet child, that if'n I still possessed the Witchhunters' bones, I wouldn't have forced 'em to finish what they started?" she asked. "You don't think I would have made sure they kilt the elder Crane dead, if I could?"

"So...so you're saying?"

"That I ain't got the bones no more, dearie." Her voice was little more than a sad whisper. "Someone swiped them soon after the Crane boy was put through the *Trials*. 'Course I always suspected it was Esther Crane herself what took 'em. I've spent the better part of fifteen years tryin' to divine their location, but Granny's magic is strong. She's hid them good."

Asherah took a single step back at the news. To her knowledge, no one else—Witchhunters' bones or no—should have been powerful enough to summon the Leechers, much less commission them to perform the Trials. Esther Crane might be the only person she could think of who could match the Hag for might, but not for will. No, she couldn't see Granny doing anything of the sort.

But if it wasn't Granny Crane, then...

"*Mater Matris!* You're in danger!" she shouted.

The old woman let out a rasping chuckle that was part laugh, part cough. "I reckon I know where you're going with this line of thought, but don't you worry none 'bout me, child," said the Hag. "Everything is going according to as I've foreseen. Yes, indeed. Going exactly as I conjured, I'd say."

"But Mother, someone must obviously be looking for the one responsible for the raising of those dead people—the Kindred. Who has the power to do something like that, if not you? Which means, they must be trying to hunt you down."

The Hag's long-stemmed pipe blazed to life as she drew in several pulls of the sweet tobacco in silence. Then, disquietingly, she let out another low cackle. "But my dear...weren't *you* the one who discovered the strange properties of those toadstools near the Devil's Teeth? Weren't you the one who, among not a few witnesses mind you, openly experimented on the corpses of the very same people?" The old crone let her words sink in for several seconds before continuing. "And weren't you, sweet Asherah, the one who contacted that big city pharmaceutical company—the very one where Ezekiel's sister works, I might add?"

Asherah stiffened, as a dread thought whispered its way into her troubled mind. "But we failed," she protested. "We only managed marginal success. Though possibly suitable as a restorative agent, I was never able to do it. Never succeeded. I'm not sure if Jael Crane had any more luck after I gave up, but I can assure you... I had nothing to do with..." She allowed her words to trail off amidst the low, malicious cackles of the Hag.

"No, dearie, as you're only now startin' to understand, I'm afraid the Leechers won't have their infernal sights set on me. At least, not yet," she said, her voice no longer grandmotherly. Now it was dripping with venom and hate. "But don't fret none, *dearie*. You're perfectly right. Someone most definitely is controllin' them Leechers, and ultimately, they'll be lookin' fer me. Looking fer whoever's powerful 'nuff to raise the dead. And everyone knows the deal you and Crane tried to strike years ago...knows of your quest to bring the Dead back to life. So now, in everyone's mind, you will have succeeded. And whoever is controllin' the Leechers will eventually start wonderin' if you ain't been me all along, if ya catch my meaning. They'll come fer you. They'll come fer Crane. And though I no longer control the bones of Eli Smith—no longer control those malicious haints—I will finally be vindicated for the slight the two of you have done me. After that, I will deal with the insufferable fool that set the Leechers on my scent to begin with."

Panic was brewing deep inside Asherah's chest. She knew all too well the awesome terror the Leechers commanded. Crane had managed to fend them off once before—but only barely. She'd never known how he'd done it, but whatever trick he'd pulled from his sleeve to escape their dreaded axes, he'd been forced to leave town shortly thereafter. To sever all ties to her.

She couldn't let that happen again.

"I'll find proof!" she shouted, her voice laced with rage. "I'll discover how you did it. Show them it was you."

The Hag belted out an asthmatic fit of cackling laughter. "But dear Asherah, there is no proof to be had," she said, still chuckling. "'Cause I honestly had nothin' to do with it." She leaned forward in the rocker, but the shadows surrounding her seemed to come alive to protect her visage. "The deed was done by another. A new apprentice of mine actually, though she's not even aware of it yet. As foolish as she is, her slight indiscretion certainly has been a might fortuitous, wouldn't you say?"

Apprentice? To Asherah's knowledge, she herself had been destined solely for that role. When she and Crane had broken the covenant they'd made with the Hag, the title had been stripped from her. And what did the woman mean when she said the apprentice wasn't even aware of the apprenticeship? What kind of game was the *Mater Matris* playing?

Still, no matter what the woman meant, the news was grave indeed. If the magic employed to bring the Dead to life had come from some anonymous apprentice, it would be even more difficult to discover evidence to exonerate her or Crane.

Asherah felt the panic inside her begin to fester and boil, soon to be replaced with consuming rage. They were being framed. Set up. And as far as she knew, without access to the bones, there was no power on Earth able to waylay the Leechers, once their dark eyes were turned your way.

"You witch!" she screamed in a sudden burst of fury. Without another thought, she lunged across the table at the old woman, only to slam headlong into some invisible barrier. She crashed to the floor. Before she could get to her feet again, she felt a powerful force—like the weight of some great, invisible boot— shoving her deeper into the ground. Slowly, her face pressed firmly into the dirt, she felt the tendrils, legs, and claws of thousands of insects extricating themselves from the ground and swarming over her entire body. She tried to scream at the sensation, only to find a mound of caked soil wedged in her mouth.

"Be mindful, dearie, of how you address me," the Hag said, as if from a million miles away. "I don't cotton much to disrespect…especially from your kind. Next time we meet, you'd be wise to remember that."

Asherah's vision darkened as she struggled in vain to gasp for breath. Then, the invisible weight lifted from her shoulders, and she collapsed into oblivion.

CHAPTER
FOUR

Morriston, Kentucky
April 28
1:53 AM

K ili unbuckled her seatbelt as Davenport pulled his car
into a curbside parking space two blocks south of the
funeral home. She couldn't help cringing at the tabloid reporter's
posh ride. A brand new Audi R8 Spyder wasn't exactly incon-
spicuous in even the most upscale neighborhoods. Around here,
in rural Appalachia, if it didn't have four-wheel drive and a
rusted-out bed, it was downright suspicious. She chided herself
for letting the reporter talk her into taking it on their nocturnal
excursion into Morriston.

Reporter, Kili thought. *Yeah, right. What kind of reporter can
afford something like this anyway? It's a $200,000 automobile, for
crying out loud.*

For the moment, however, that was the least of her concerns.
The full-throated growl of the V10 engine idling in the parking
space was just one more blazing neon sign shouting to the
world: *Look at us!*

"Turn it off," she hissed, glancing around. But no one seemed to be paying them any mind. Of course, the fact that it was nearly two in the morning might have something to do to with that...which was the exact reason they'd chosen to wait so late.

Davenport shut the engine off and climbed out from the driver's side door. He then dashed over to her side as best he could on the cane and opened her door, before she'd even managed to find the interior lever.

"Allow me," he said, his smile nearly blinding by the light of the full moon.

Willing herself not to be drawn into an argument over chivalrous sexism, she stepped out of the vehicle, nodded her reluctant thanks, and motioned for him to follow. Slowly, they made their way down Johnson Boulevard until they came to the black, wrought-iron fence encircling the front lawn of *Overturf & Sons Mortuary*.

From Kili's vantage point, the place looked deserted. The façade of the establishment was as dark as her mood. Not a single light could be seen inside the classic Victorian-style structure, although the back portion of the building was concealed by a seven-foot privacy fence.

"See anything?" she asked Davenport, who shrugged in response.

"Not yet," he said. "Just a sec." The reporter reached into a backpack he'd had draped over one arm and pulled out a set of ATN Fusion Image night-vision goggles.

"Seriously, who are you *really*?" Kili asked, bewildered by the man's seemingly endless supply of expensive toys. Being a bit of a tech hound herself, she was well aware the asking price for the piece of digital optics was upward of $15,000. "That's quality gear. Like your choice of cars, it's not really in the salary range of your average tabloid reporter."

He smiled back at her, as he lifted the glasses to his eyes and peered into the darkness. "I'm a *really* good reporter," he said absently, then after a pause added, "but let's just say journalism is more a hobby than anything else." He pulled the goggles away from his face and shook his head. "I don't see anyone. Thermal doesn't even show any heat signatures for cameras or other surveillance equipment either. Looks like we're clear."

Taking one more look around, they made their way to the gate, lifted the handle, and stepped into the exceptionally mani-cured front yard of the funeral home. As they slowly crept up the concrete walkway to the front door, she took in the old build-ing. It had obviously been someone's home at one time. The two-story wooden structure, complete with intricately carved lattices sprawling up the four arching gables and two second-story balconies screamed of classic antebellum sensibilities. To Kili, who had grown up in the ever-evolving, fast-moving urban areas of the Northeast, the place just gave her the creeps.

"Are you just gonna knock on the door and see what happens?" the reporter asked.

"Huh?" His words had brought her out of the anxious stupor, and she found herself standing right at the two sprawling front doors. Nervously, she gave a quick glance over her shoulder, but from what she could tell, their clandestine outing still remained unobserved. "Oh, uh…no. Of course not. But I did want to get a better look at this." She pointed to a keypad fastened just left of the door. "Caught sight of it from the sidewalk. Looks new."

"Looks brand *spanking* new," the reporter agreed. "Like fresh out of the box."

"Yeah, that's what I thought too," she said. "From my last trip to this area, I can tell you…security isn't something these people pay much attention to. I seriously doubt a funeral home worries about too many break-ins. Plus, it just doesn't match the décor—the feel of this place. Grand old manor house gutted with twenty-first century cyber-security. These people are just too old-fashioned to have installed this on their own, which makes me think Dr. Maher and the CDC have had something to do with it."

Davenport bent down to look at the device, then shook his head. "It's unmarked. No manufacturer's logo, no serial numbers. Without knowing what kind of system it is, I'm not sure how we can beat it."

Kili gave the man a mischievous smile, reached into her purse, and pulled out a makeup compact. "Ever hear of something called a *scrying pool*?" she asked, flipping the compact open. Without waiting for him to respond, she held the mirror slightly up and to the right. She looked into it with wide eyes for several seconds, while her fingers hovered dramatically over the reflective surface. Then, as if under some sort of enchantment, she moved to the pad and punched a series of four digits into the device. Immediately, they were rewarded with the click of the door unlocking.

"How did you... I mean..." Davenport pointed to the compact. "A *scrying* pool?"

She giggled, folded the compact, and put it back inside her purse. "Witches use them for clairvoyance. Any reflective surface can work. One just needs to know how to open their eyes to divine the truth of things."

Davenport eyed her suspiciously. "And you just happened to divine the code to get inside, eh?"

She gave him a wink, then quietly pushed the front door open. "Nah," she whispered. "The theatrics are just something I picked up from Ezekiel. Truth is, I figure the hicks who work in this place aren't happy that Maher and company required these new security measures. They're not going to willingly memorize a really complex passcode, so the solution would be to use a number they're already familiar with. Something simple."

She nodded at the establishment's sign near the street. It read: OVERTURF & SONS MORTUARY. EST. 1923. 5434 Johnson Boulevard, Morriston, Kentucky 42038.

"Okay," he said. "I'm still not getting it."

"What passcode would you use for a place that has been in

the same location ninety years? The numerical in the address would be the most logical choice. To the employees, it would be easy enough to remember. I just used the compact to read the sign behind me, that's all."

Davenport grinned. "Nicely done. I am thoroughly impressed."

Absently, she pushed a strand of her crimson hair back behind her ears, as she blushed at the praise. She wasn't sure why she cared so much for the man's accolades, but inexplicably she did. Still, this was neither the time nor place for the flirting game. They were currently in the commission of a serious crime. Better to get in and out as fast as they could.

Putting on a more serious expression, she stepped into the funeral home's interior and waited for the reporter to follow. To his credit, Davenport had wrapped his cane's tip with a piece of wool to muffle his movements. She could hardly hear him moving behind her at all, though the grating creak of the door being shut behind her set her nerves on edge.

"Note to self," Davenport whispered near her ear. "Next time we break into a creepy old funeral home, bring oil for the hinges."

She gave him a sideways smirk, then put a finger to her lips to hush him. She crept forward down the long hallway leading away from the foyer. The only illumination came down from the silver-hued moonlight seeping in through the front stained-glass windows, which cast strange prismatic shadows all around her.

By the multi-colored light, the funeral home's interior was even more disturbing than the exterior. Not so much from the Victorian-era architecture, but rather from its anachronistic furnishings, straight from the 1970s. The décor, she supposed, was at one time designed to provide that faux serene environment that all funeral homes strive to attain. The dark wood paneling and the rose-colored shag carpet, along with an assortment of pleather-upholstered couches and chairs, would have worked beautifully back when the BeeGees were still in vogue, she supposed. Now however, the archaic style, along with the subtle blend of formalin and Pine Sol brought to mind images of Ed Gein and his furnishings of dried human skin. She half expected to see Leatherface—who'd been inspired by the real life serial killer—barreling out of one of the rooms with a chainsaw raised high above his head.

"Okay boss, where to now?" Davenport whispered, while turning on an LED flashlight that lit the hallway in a corona of white light.

"We need to make our way to the back," she said. "I haven't been in too many funeral homes, but I figure they store the bodies out of the way. Somewhere the public wouldn't accidentally stumble on them. I think we—"

There was a click of metal against metal from somewhere around the corner. The telltale sound of a door latch. But it was subtle. So subtle, in fact, she wasn't certain she'd actually heard it.

"What's wrong?" the reporter asked from behind.

"You didn't hear that?"

"What?"

She slowly shook her head. "I'm not certain, but I don't think we're alone in here."

The two stood transfixed for several excruciating seconds, their heads tilted to one side, listening. But nothing else happened. All remained still.

"It was probably nothing," Davenport said after a while. "It's an old house, after all. Probably just settling."

With a shrug of assent, Kili moved forward again while beckoning her companion to follow. When they came to the end of the hall, she pressed her back against the wall and peeked around the corner to see another hallway, much shorter than the first. At the end was a set of double doors. Silently, she motioned for the reporter to shine his light in their direction. In the illumination, the two could see the words stenciled in bold letters above the door frame: PREP ROOM.

"My guess is the refrigeration unit that houses the bodies should be in there," she said, taking a deep breath to calm her swiftly-unraveling nerves. "All right. Let's go."

She took a single step before Davenport grabbed her by the arm and pulled her back. "Wait," he whispered. "Look, I know why I'm here. To uncover the truth and get a great story while I'm at it. But why are you doing this? I mean, with your pull at the FBI, couldn't you just force your way into the CDC's investigation? Why risk your career with a burglary charge like this?"

Her throat constricted at the question. She'd avoided dealing with her suspension for so long now, it had become second nature. Her personal investigation into her brother's disappearance had been unauthorized. She'd even tried to pass herself off as a Special Agent to intimidate the locals into helping her. Her boss, who had never particularly cared for Kili to begin with, hadn't taken Sheriff Tyler's complaints lightly. As a matter of fact, she'd been thoroughly enthusiastic about demoting, then suspending Kili for two months. Sure, Kili was officially back to work, but she'd developed a stigma from the ordeal. She had been relegated to some of the most menial tasks within the crime analysis unit. She'd often joked that she was a reprimand shy of being sent down to the basement to join Fox Mulder. No, there'd be no support from Washington on this. As far as the CDC was concerned, she had no more authority than Davenport. Worse, if she made too many waves for the CDC doctor, Kili was sure her job would be forfeit.

"Let's just say I'm not exactly on the time clock here," she said. "We need to see Mrs. Crawford's body before they have a chance to autopsy her. Someone is covering up something around here, and I highly doubt Dr. Maher's going to just fill me in on everything if I ask nice."

Davenport nodded at this, as if considering her words. "All right. So I'm teamed up with a rogue G-Man." He broke into a huge grin. "Sweet."

Rolling her eyes, Kili stepped out into the hallway without another word, and moved toward the double doors. Like in the rest of the building, no light could be seen coming through the cracks underneath the doors. Gently, she pushed them open and looked inside. The room was large, about twenty feet long by nine feet wide, with ceramic tile lining both the floor and the walls, to make it easier to clean. To the far right, she could see three large workstations, complete with sinks, lining the wall. Three stainless-steel cadaver tables stood empty in front of the sinks. The smell of formalin was even stronger in here, and she winced from the acidic odor.

Davenport nudged her from behind. When she looked at him, he nodded across the room to four morgue drawers inserted in the opposite wall.

Understanding, she stepped into the room and made her way to the drawers. The reporter, close on her heels, shined his light at them, revealing two labels with hand-scrawled names: BLAZEMORE, HAROLD and CRAWFORD, ELIZABETH. The other two drawers, having no such labels, were presumably empty.

"We're in luck," Davenport hissed. "I think Blazemore was another 'Bird Man' related death."

"Did he have a connection with any of the Kindred too?"

"Yep. His wife…" He reached into his pack, pulled out his notebook, and thumbed through it. "Yeah, here it is. Jenny Blazemore. She was apparently a paramedic who disappeared soon after transporting some guy named—"

"Leroy Kingston?" she asked.

"Yeah. That's it. Anyway, she disappeared soon after, and

was later found in the mass grave with the others. She was one of the last of the Kindred to return, as a matter of fact."

Kili reached up to Blazemore's drawer, but couldn't quite get up the nerve to pull it open. "How did he die?" she asked instead.

Davenport scanned his notes again. "Apparently, he was working out in a field. Driving a tractor, when he just keeled over. Presumably a heart attack," he said. "But a neighbor I spoke with told me he'd seen the Bird Man—for some reason, they call this thing a *Leecher*—standing on a ridge just prior to Blazemore's death. The old man wouldn't tell me what this Leecher is, but I could tell he was scared to death of it."

"Doesn't surprise me at all," Kili said. "These people cling to their superstitions like they're super-glued to their psyches. I'm sure whatever the Leecher is, we won't find out from the average schmoe. We'll need to ask Granny about it."

Convincing herself that they had to get on with it, she grabbed the drawer's handle and yanked it open. A plume of fog fluffed from the open door as the cool air poured out into the Prep Room. Davenport moved to the other side of the drawer, reached in, and pulled on the tray inside. The nude body of an overweight, middle-aged man came into view. From the looks of the Y-incision in his chest, Blazemore had already been autopsied. Kili doubted much would be gleaned from the body, which had obviously been scrubbed down and cleaned after the postmortem had been concluded.

Still, need to get whatever evidence I can, she thought, while snapping a few photos with her phone. Something odd picked up by the flash caught her eye. "Alex, let me see your flashlight for a second," she said, leaning in for a closer look. She took the flashlight he offered without glancing at him and shined the light solidly on the deceased's right hand. The skin tone was discolored to a deep cherry red, and the flesh was caked with numerous nasty-looking blisters up to his wrist. A quick check revealed the same phenomenon on the other hand. "What do you make of that?"

The reporter leaned in and let out a low whistle. "If I had to guess, I'd say the man's hands have been severely scalded." He took a latex glove from a nearby box, slipped it on, and delicately lifted Blazemore's right arm. "Look at the wrist. There's a distinct line between the burned and unblemished skin. Almost as if—"

"Almost as if he'd held his hands down in a pot of boiling water," Kili said. "Yeah, that's exactly what I was thinking." She snapped a few more pictures, concentrating on the hands, then motioned for Davenport to slide the body back into the drawer. "Now, let's see if Mrs. Crawford has similar burns."

The reporter was just about to pull out the second drawer, when a soft thud sounded from the floor above them. They both paused, eyes wide.

"I *seriously* don't think we're alone here," Kili whispered. "You heard it that time, right?"

Davenport nodded slowly, looking up at the ceiling with a cocked head, as if listening. But no other sound followed. "Think some of the employees have rooms upstairs?" he asked. "Makes a certain kind of sense. Transport crews on-call 24/7 need a convenient place to sleep, right? Maybe one of them got up to use the bathroom or something."

She didn't respond. Her ears strained to catch the slightest of noises, but she couldn't pick up anything new.

"Okay," she said. "Let's look at Mrs. Crawford and get out of here quick. I definitely have a bad feeling about this."

With considerable more delicacy, Davenport slid open Crawford's drawer and eased her out to view. She remained, for the most part, exactly as she had appeared earlier that day. Her clothing was still intact, indicating that an autopsy had not yet been performed. The dead woman's eyes, cloudy and dry, stared blankly up at the ceiling; her mouth hung open in an unsettling grimace. Her skin was the deep mottled gray that only a corpse could be, and Kili could hardly contain the shudder that rippled down her spine at the sight.

Pushing the image from her thoughts, she took the flashlight and examined the dead woman's right hand. Nothing. It appeared perfectly normal. Not a blemish to be seen anywhere. The other hand was the same.

"Okay, so she doesn't have the same scalding burns as Blazemore," she said. "Must have nothing to do with—"

"Wait," Davenport said, his voice slightly louder than he intended. He paused several seconds to see if the noise had attracted any attention. When nothing happened, he pointed down her legs. "Look at her feet. There's something definitely wrong with them."

Kili moved the light down the woman's leg until it reached her feet, but she could see nothing unusual.

"The soles," Davenport hissed. "Look at the soles of her feet."

She moved down a bit more until she had a relatively good vantage point. Though the drawer didn't pull out far enough to get a full view of the bottoms of the woman's feet, Kili could distinctly see that they were blackened. They were charred, blistered, and lined with numerous red cracks where the skin had split in several places, as if the woman's feet had been held over a hot fire for a considerable amount of time.

"Dear Lord," she hissed. "What could have caused—"

Just then, the double doors flew open to reveal a huge silhouette moving wraith-like into the room. Instinctively, Kili brought the flashlight up, washing away the darkness with brilliant, LED illumination. But the sight it revealed turned her legs gelatinous, as her thudding heart leapt desperately into her throat.

The figure was well over six-feet tall—maybe over seven— with thick shoulders and arms draped in heavy, leather robes. It wore knee-high leather riding boots, and it's wide-brimmed, black hat was tilted slightly at an angle. The long, metal-tipped beak of a bird mask glimmered with the reflected light, while two tiny crimson orbs that acted as eye holes in the mask seemed to glare maliciously at the two of them.

"It's the Leecher!" were the only words that poured from Davenport's slack-jawed mouth, before chaos broke loose.

CHAPTER
FIVE

"**R**un!" Kili shouted, though she wasn't entirely sure where they could go. The Leecher lumbered in the doorway, blocking their path back into the main section of the funeral home. It muttered in hoarse, ghostly whispers that buzzed in her ear as if a choir of a thousand voices were murmuring all at once. The voices, if she could call them that, were unreal—ethereal—and seemed to be coming from somewhere inside her own mind, rather than through her ears. Even more bizarre, she couldn't be sure whether it was her imagination or not, but the temperature within the room seemed to be getting unbearably warm with the increasing beat of each indecipherable whispered syllable.

Before she could glance around to find another way out, the reporter grabbed her by the wrist. "Come on!" he shouted, pulling her to the opposite side of the room, where an ancient, green door opened up to a set of steps leading down into a cellar. There were no lights on below and no switch within sight.

"You want to go down there? Are you kidding?" she asked.

"It's either this or through him!" Davenport pointed at the bird-masked figure. The creature still hadn't moved, and Kili was uncertain whether that was something to rejoice about or dread. "But the way I'm sweating right now, something tells me we'd be much better off down here."

So Alex is feeling the temperature increase as well, which means it couldn't be my imagination.

Unable to think of a better alternative, Kili ran past the reporter and plodded down the rickety, wooden planks that acted as a staircase. Her companion pulled the door shut behind him and cursed when he could find nothing nearby with which to bar it. Giving up, he limped quickly behind her and nearly slipped twice as they descended.

Once safely down the stairs, they swiveled Davenport's flashlight beam around the room to catch their bearings. The cellar reminded Kili of every Hollywood dungeon scene she'd ever watched. The walls were made of rough-hewn rock held together by earth and crumbling cement. There was no flooring at all—only dirt with an occasional root or vine cropping up here and there to trip unwary trespassers. The chamber was large, easily taking up the entire space of the house's foundation. She'd half-expected to find piles of decomposing flesh—the discarded remains of the funeral home's former clients—rotting away in some macabre niche in the wall. But except for a large dehumidifier thrumming loudly in the center of the room, a single workbench with a hammer and other woodworking equipment, and an old water heater that had obviously seen better days, the room was unoccupied. What struck Kili as odd, however, was the inclusion of two worm-eaten wooden doors at the far end of the chamber, securely bolted shut from her side with wooden crossbeams.

The second oddity she discovered were a series of six posts placed sporadically, almost randomly, from floor to ceiling. Each post—obviously used to support the funeral home's foundation —was carved with an assortment of strange symbols over its entire surface. Forgetting their immediate danger, Kili stood transfixed at one of the beams, trying to decipher the arcane glyphs.

Strangely, she'd seen them once before in an ancient megalithic structure called the Devil's Teeth—the Stongehenge-like ruins that had so captivated her brother last year, and that had started the horror of One-Eyed Jack.

She had no idea what the symbols were doing here, who made them, or why. She couldn't fathom what a Victorian mansion and a Native American holy site had in common to elicit the glyphs' presence at both places.

Like those at the Devil's Teeth, there seemed no rhyme or reason to their placement among the old beams. On one side, she spotted a representation of what appeared to be an elongated spider hanging upside from a single strand. A rectangular object hovered mere inches from the arachnid's mandibles. A few inches down and over to the right, she saw an image that could only be a crow or a carrion bird of some kind, tangled in some sort of vine or serpent. She couldn't be sure which. And yet another symbol appeared to be the Greek letter *Psi*. Or maybe it was just a pitchfork. She wasn't sure, though Cian would have known if he was still alive.

She snapped a few photos of the strange carvings with her phone and moved over to the next post for a look.

"Kili!" Davenport shouted. "We don't have time for this!"

Before she could answer, the door at the top of the stairs flew open, immediately filling the entire cellar with the Leecher's otherworldly whispers. Looking up, they could see its hulking form filling the frame. A black leather riding boot stepped down onto the stairs as its jet black robes billowed out behind him.

"Time's up," Davenport said, while grabbing Kili by the arm and pulling her to the two ominous doors across from them.

A creak of wood from behind told Kili their pursuer was now slowly descending the staircase toward them. She had no idea where either door would lead, but she figured anywhere was better than here. The two doors stood only a foot apart from one another. Davenport chose the one on the far right, lifted the crossbeam from its supports, and shoved against it. But it was rotted from disuse, effectively blocking it from opening.

"Okay," he said. "Let's see what's behind Door Number Two." He leaned his shoulder into the second door and shoved.

Nothing.

"Crap! It's stuck too," he said, as he clambered down on his hands and knees to dig away at the assortment of roots jutting up from the earth. "Give me some help here!"

Kili risked a glance back and gasped. The Leecher had made its way to the bottom step and was now eyeing them with what could only be described as cold hatred—or at least, that's what she imagined when she pictured the eyes that hid behind the red orbs of the mask. There was no way she and Alex would break through the jumble of roots in time. They were trapped.

Suddenly, her cell phone began vibrating wildly inside her jean's pocket, making her jump. Despite their dire situation, she pulled it out and glanced at the caller ID.

Ezekiel!

She hit the green talk button, and Crane started talking as soon as the call connected.

"Listen to me," he said, his usually smooth, syrupy voice ragged with concern. "The Leechers...the Leechers are supernatural creatures. They can't abide running water—"

"Ezekiel..." Kili tried to interrupt him. She tried to tell him about their current danger. The Leecher was now only a scant twenty-five yards away. She had to force Crane to shut up so he could help her. "Ezekiel, please! We're in trouble!"

There was a pause on the other end, then a grunt of...*Was that pain?*

"I know," he finally said. "I'm trying to help you now. I know you're in the cellar. Know you've got at least one of them on your tail. Water is the trick. If you can find water, it should slow it down long enough for your reporter friend to dig the door free."

"How did you know we were down here? I mean—"

"Kili! You don't have time, and I can't go into specifics right now. They have a hive mind. If I say too much, they'll hear, and your pursuer will know what to expect. Just know… There is a good source of water inside the cellar. Find it and you'll know what to do with it when you do."

Water? What on Earth is he talking about? Where do I find water in a basement? What do I do with it when I do?

"Ezekiel, I need more," she said, keeping her eyes fixed on the agonizingly slow movements of the Leecher, as it took another step toward them. "I don't know—"

But the sudden silence on the other end of the line told her the call had been dropped.

She looked over at Davenport, still pawing away at the dirt like a ravenous hound looking for a bone. She then let her eyes roam around the musty old cellar for the miracle she needed.

The Leecher stepped past the work bench. The whispered maelstrom of words drifted in and out of Kili's mind while her heart raced. Then, her eyes landed on what she sought. Hope.

Risking drawing too close to the creature, she lunged over to the dehumidifier, threw open the back panel hatch, and pulled out the bucket inside, which was filled two-thirds with water the machine had pulled from the air. Just as the Leecher's claw-tipped hands reached out to grab her, she hurled the bucket into its face, eliciting an ear-splitting shriek from the thing. Though the creature seemed solid enough, the liquid flew right through and onto the floor behind it. Smoke or steam bellowed up from where the water had passed through, and the cloud seemed to get heavier the more intensely the thing wailed.

"Tell me you didn't just do a Wicked Witch of Oz thing," Davenport said, his neck craned around to see what had just happened.

Before she could respond, her phone buzzed again. She answered it on the first ring.

"The water won't stop it," Ezekiel Crane said the moment the two phones were connected. "But it'll have to spend some time drawing in energy from the air around it to reconstitute itself. Use your time wisely."

Kili looked over at the supernatural creature, its form slightly more shadow than anything else. Though its screams were now inaudible, it writhed in silent agony. After a split second, her eyes moved past the Leecher and back toward the steps.

"We can just go back upstairs and through the front door," she said.

"No, you can't. That way's blocked by at least three more," Crane breathed heavily into the phone, as if he was running. "Get the cellar door open. The one the reporter has been working on. Follow it around, and you should find a way out."

"H-how do you know what door he's working on?" she asked, her voice a mere whisper with anxiety.

"No time for that now. Help him pry it open. It'll only take the Leecher a few minutes to pull itself back together." And with that, the phone went silent again.

Kili slid over to where Davenport struggled to open the door. He'd managed to slip one arm inside, where he hacked away at the roots with the blade of his pocket knife. After a couple more minutes, he stood and gave her a nod. "I think I got it," he said with a nervous smile as he glanced back at the dark-robed apparition behind them. "Here. Help me push this thing open."

On the count of three, they simultaneously threw themselves against the door and shoved with all their might. Slowly, they felt it give beneath them, and the door swung free, causing them to spill to the floor on the other side. Leaping to their feet, they swung the door back into place, put their backs against it, and looked around for anything they could use to bar the door.

A quick search revealed an old weathered pick axe leaning

against the stone wall, a few feet ahead. Handing the flashlight back to Kili, the reporter grabbed the axe and shoved the handle against the door, while wedging the tip into the ground. Only after they felt it was reasonably secure did they relax enough to catch their breath.

"I've seen a lot of crazy stuff in my time, but this is freakin' nuts!" Alex said, sliding to the floor with his back up against the door.

"Welcome to freakin' Jasper County," Kili growled. She was breathing hard from their exertions and took a seat next to him, before shining the light forward to take in their surroundings for the first time.

They'd apparently stumbled into a long, black tunnel that twisted away from the house's foundation. From where they sat, she couldn't see how far the tunnel went or where they'd end up if they followed it straight through, as Crane had instructed.

"Okay," she finally said, breaking the momentary silence. "As much as I hate to say it, I don't know how long this door will hold that thing back." Absently, she wiped away at the sweat and grime that had accumulated on her brow. "We need to get moving."

The reporter didn't move. He just looked over at her with wide, blue eyes. "W-what the heck was that thing?" he asked. "Any idea?"

She shook her head. "No clue. Crane seemed to know though. He'll fill us in once we get out of here, I'm sure." Wearily, she climbed to her feet and dusted herself off. Glancing around at a pile of nearby debris in the tunnel, she found an old wooden plank and reinforced the door with it. "But I can tell you this...Whatever it is, it's not human. That water just passed right through—"

CRACK!

The door shuddered violently as something powerful slammed into it from the other side. A single crack splintered through the rotted wood, and the two could make out the long slender beak of the Leecher's mask through the crack.

"Looks like it's back!" Davenport shouted, leaping away from the door just as the silver gleam of an axe blade split through it.

Without another word, the two grabbed each other's hands and dashed down the dank stretch of tunnel for fifty yards, where it abruptly opened up into a new chamber, which was half the size of the original, with a low-hanging ceiling. This one, however, was pristine, with spotless white linoleum floors, plastered walls, and three rows of incandescent light fixtures mounted to the ceiling. It was furnished with state-of-the-art lab equipment and a computer that sat upon a stainless steel table on the northernmost wall. The unmistakable scent of formalin and antiseptic permeated the suddenly clean, oxygenated air.

"What the...?" Alex muttered as he rotated three-hundred-sixty degrees to take it all in.

"I have no idea," Kili replied, while examining a second table containing several rows of glass specimen jars. The labels on each of the jars read: AION PHARMACEUTICALS, then listed a number and a person's name underneath. "But I'd wager it has something to do with all the weirdness going on around here." Curious, she leaned forward for a better look at the jars. "After all, what does a run-down funeral home—one that seems to be working for that doctor from the CDC, mind you—have to do with a pharmaceutical company?" She swiped a hand across one of the containers, brushing a layer of condensation away, and shined the light into it. "Holy...!"

Instinctively, she jumped back with a start. From inside a two-gallon specimen jar, a pair of bulging, cloudy eyes stared back at her. After allowing a few seconds to calm her nerves, she took another look and discovered that the eyes were attached to a mass of misshapen organic tissue that looked like something akin to an oversized meatball. She leaned in closer, and nearly gagged when she noticed clumps of hair and teeth were jutting out from the mass as well. A quick inventory of the remaining jars revealed an assortment of other similar masses that seemed to be growing the same blend of eyes, teeth, and hair.

"What is this?"

She glanced at the name listed on the first jar. It read: "HENLEY, GORDON. XN: B232-23-4538". She'd never heard of the man, but the name on the second jar sent a chill down her spine. "CRAWFORD, TIMOTHY A. XN: B232-23-4539".

"Tim Crawford?"

The next jar was labeled with an equally disturbing name. "BLAZEMORE, JENNIFER L. XN: C232-23-2123". She quickly scanned the other jars. Each contained the same blob of tissue. Each was labeled with the name of one of the Kindred.

Kili noticed a larger container shoved toward the back of the table. The mass of tissue on this one was at least three times as large as the others—roughly the size of a soccer ball. Carefully, she shifted the jars aside, and shined Davenport's light on the label. Her knees nearly buckled at the name listed.

"BRENNAN, CIAN B. XN: A001-23-001."

The room began to spin as Kili continued to stare at the stenciled label. *Cian*? She glanced at the huge growth inside the jar. Three oddly shaped, cloudy eyeballs seemed to stare back at her from within the formalin. She tried to imagine the same eyes staring back at her from her brother's own face. Oddly enough, the image clicked. For all intents and purposes, they looked like Cian's eyes. But that made no sense. Ezekiel Crane had had Cian cremated as soon as his body was recovered from the cavern in which he'd died.

"What is going—"

The sound of the axe crashing against the door from down the hall brought Kili back to their current predicament. Though her mind reeled by this new piece of evidence—and the implications it presented to her investigation—the Leecher was still coming for them, and with that axe, it wouldn't take much longer to get through the door. In fact, it was an outright miracle it wasn't already on top of them even now and she had to believe the water she'd tossed at it was helping to slow it down. With that in mind, she turned her attention back to their escape.

"Okay. Time to go. As tricky as it was to get through that door, I'm betting there's got to be another way in and out of this room. We need to find it fast," she said, anxiously staring down the hallway from which they'd just come. Two heartbeats passed by without a response. Three. Then four. "Alex, did you hear—" She spun around to an empty room. The reporter had vanished.

CHAPTER
SIX

"A lex?" she shouted, her heart thudding even harder against her chest.

Where had he gone? Could this have been a set up? Could Davenport have been part of this whole conspiracy, all along? Had he led her here only to silence her? She didn't think so. He just seemed too sincere. Too determined to get the answers that she sought as well. If he'd been pretending this entire time, the man deserved an Academy Award. But it was more than that. If he'd led her down here to her doom, why had he given her the only flashlight? The tabloid journalist couldn't have gotten very far without it.

"Hello?" she said one more time.

Suddenly, there was a crash from the other end of the hall. The Leecher had breached the doorway. It would be on her soon. Kili spun around, the beam of her light cutting through the darkness of the clandestine lab. But there was no way out. The room was completely enclosed except for the narrow tunnel currently occupied by the bird-faced creature.

"But if that's true, then where did Alex go?" she mumbled to herself.

"Up here," she heard the reporter whisper from somewhere above her. She shined the light in the direction of his voice and saw a round hole cut into the ceiling. Davenport's feet clung to a ladder that stretched up into the blackness. She could just make out his smile beaming down at her. "Sorry about that. Found us a way out. I didn't want to get your hopes up before I checked it out first. There's a hatch up here that leads outside. Come on!"

Kili heard the scrape of a boot across the linoleum behind her. She turned around to see the Leecher lumbering into the chamber. Its shoulders hunched to avoid hitting its head on the low hanging ceiling. The whispers had returned to fill the room, and it was all she could do to keep from covering her ears from the wretched torment of those disembodied voices.

Catching sight of her beam of light, the creature lunged—its large, silver-headed felling-axe arcing through the air at her. Dodging the blow, she leapt up and caught hold of the first rung of the ladder, just as the Leecher's free hand took a bone-crushing hold of her ankle. Desperate, her foot slammed down on her assailant's arm. It didn't feel as though she'd struck anything solid at all, but the visceral shriek her kick elicited said otherwise.

As the Leecher's hand shrank away after the blow, Davenport reached down and pulled her up, until she was occupying the same tight space with him inside the shaft. His broad chest pressed against hers, while his free hand held tight around her waist.

"Th-thank you," she said, an uneasy wave of tingles trickling down her spine at his touch. What was going on with her? They were being chased by some sort of preternatural monster, and here she was feeling like a hormonally imbalanced pre-teen. The reminder of the Leecher below brought her back to her senses. "Okay, lead the way out of here."

"Ladies first, I insist," Davenport said with a fake southern drawl. "The gate is unlatched topside. I already checked."

Not arguing, she climbed past him and clambered up the ladder with practiced ease. She was within a foot of reaching the hatch when the Leecher's infernal murmuring resumed from below. This time, however, the words were different. The tempo was faster and more fluid. Kili found herself hit with a nauseating bout of vertigo, mixed with a case of claustrophobia. Even though the darkness of the shaft prevented her from seeing the tight confines around her, she clamped her eyes shut and clung desperately to the ladder's rung. She could feel the space pulling closer and closer around her as the world somersaulted topsy-turvy within her mind's eye. The brutal wave of disorientation hammered at her mind; chipping away the last vestiges of her courage. She was panicked. Weak. She felt her fingers, already moist with nervous sweat, begin to slip away from the rust-coated ladder rung.

From the moans down below, it sounded as though Davenport was fairing no better. If anyone had told her a year ago she would readily accept anything remotely resembling magic as a plausible explanation for any situation she might face, she would have laughed at them without the slightest trace of regret. But she'd simply seen too much since her investigation into Cian's disappearance. Learned too much. She'd have been a fool not to recognize what was happening to them now, and who was responsible.

"Alex!" she shouted, but she kept her eyes clinched as tightly as her death-hold on the ladder. "Hold on! It's a trick of the mind. Like a post-hypnotic suggestion. It will pass! Just hold on!"

"I'm t-trying," he replied, his voice shaking. "But not s-sure what's g-going on. W-what's happening?"

She tried to answer, but the words wouldn't come. Nausea entangled her mind as she hung only two rungs away from freedom. And still, the malicious whispers ruthlessly continued from below. They seemed louder now. More demanding. Every second she hung there, she found her perspiration-soaked hands weakening…slipping from their purchase, as if the debilitating enchantment had increased the effect of gravity.

Or I'm just getting tired, she thought. No magic required for that.

Without warning, the hatch above her swung open, and a tall silhouette, holding what looked like an old broom, peeked down the hole at them. With a flick of a wrist, the broom, along with a handful of long, iron nails were tossed down the shaft. She watched the curious objects fall to the floor near the Leecher, who instantly expelled a shrill, inhuman screech and leapt away. Kili's paralysis lifted almost immediately, and she looked up once more to see a hand reaching down to her.

"Take my hand, Ms. Kili," came the soft Kentucky twang of warm molasses. "Those talismans will keep it busy for a while, but not as long as we might like." He glanced furtively over his shoulder.

Without hesitating, she obeyed, and Ezekiel Crane pulled her up through the hatch. Without uttering another word, he got on his hands and knees and looked down at the reporter who was still struggling with whatever demons the Leecher's spell had conjured in the man's mind.

"Mr. Davenport, I presume," Crane said, glancing furtively over his shoulder. "I'd advise you to muster whatever strength you still have left and move. The Leechers are not to be trifled with. I managed to elude them earlier, but I'm afraid they've reacquired my scent. Even now, they are on the move. They'll be on us soon."

As if hearing the mountain man's voice for the first time, Davenport opened his eyes and looked up with a dumbstruck look on his face.

"Mr. Davenport, you're a guest in Granny's house," Crane continued, holding out his hand to the reporter. "She'd tan my hide if I allowed anything to happen to you. Now come on."

Kili had never heard Crane sound so weary. So...well, *uneasy* was the better word for it, she supposed. Even in the worst of times during their previous investigation, he'd always carried himself with an almost otherworldly calm...as though he was in complete control of anything that could be thrown at them. His voice was normally smooth like syrup. Melodious. The Kentucky accent very prominent, though articulate. Well-spoken.

Now, however, he sounded harsh. Anxious. His sandy-blond hair was disheveled, and his tanned face was more haggard than she'd ever seen it. His ice-cold blue eyes were even more haunted than she remembered.

Whatever is going on around here must really be bad for him to be this worked up.

"Alex," Kili shouted down into the shaft in a soft, under-standing voice. "It's okay. This is Ezekiel Crane. He's here to help."

Her voice seemed to pull the reporter from his malaise. He gripped the ladder rungs once more and began climbing—slowly at first, but gradually building momentum. A few seconds later, he pulled himself up through the hatch and dusted himself off.

It was only then that Kili was able to take in their surround-ings. They were outdoors in a well-maintained garden of shrubs, persimmon trees, and ceramic statuaries in the backyard of the funeral home. An artificial pond, no more than ten feet across, bubbled a few feet away from her. Motion within the water caught her eye, and she could just make out the form of what looked to be four giant goldfish zipping about. *Koi.* They were in some type of serenity garden. A place to soothe grieving family members after the loss of their loved ones.

At this time of the morning, with very little lighting and a supernatural killer hot on their tail, Kili could find nothing serene about it. It was every bit as unsettling as everything else she'd been through in the last twenty-four hours.

She turned her attention back to Crane and Davenport. The reporter was breathing heavily, dabbing a handkerchief across his damp forehead. Kili observed the curved, wooden handle of his walking cane poking out from his trousers around the waistband, and she realized that he must have tucked it into his pant legs when he first found the ladder. She tried to stifle a giggle at how ridiculous he looked, but was unable to do so completely.

The two men turned and looked harshly at her.

"Now is not the time for levity, Ms. Kili," Crane reprimanded, his face grim under his neatly trimmed mustache and goatee. "We are far from being safe. I wasn't lying when I said that more of them are undoubtedly on their way." He glanced at Davenport, then at the cane. "How is your mobility? Can you walk?"

The reporter gave a quick nod. "I can bloody well run a marathon if more of those creeps are after me. But I do need to catch my breath. Whatever was happening in that shaft was...was..."

"Magic of the darkest kind," Crane said. "Not to be trifled with at all."

"I don't get it," Kili said. "We were there to take a look Liz Crawford's body. I would have expected to be hunted by the funeral home guys or the CDC, but not that...that thing. Why did it attack us? Why was it there? Does it have anything to do with—"

"The Leecher, Ms. Kili, is no mere 'thing', as you put it. It's a *haint*, and its presence at the funeral home is indeed intriguing," Crane interrupted. "Up until about a week or so ago, they were acting predictably. Hunting the source magic behind these supposed resurrections."

"Supposed?" Davenport asked between wheezing breaths.

"*Haint?*" Kili asked a split second later.

"I'll explain both when we are relatively safe. Point is, a few days ago, the Leechers' behavior changed drastically. They began attacking people without cause—hexing their victims with the Trial by Ordeals, randomly trying to determine whether they were witches or not. Whatever else they are, the Witchhunter and his judges were never arbitrary in their judgment. Somehow, they always knew... They had an uncanny skill at ferreting out the real culprits without violence to the innocent."

Kili and Alex stared at the mountain man with open mouths, unable to speak. Unsure of what to say even if they could find their voices. Neither of them were absolutely sure Ezekiel Crane was making any kind of sense at the moment, so they both decided to just let him speak for now. To their dismay, the mountain man would make even less sense by the time he was finished.

"The only thing that made sense was that someone had gotten to the Witchhunter's bones," he said. "Since Granny had originally stolen them away from the Willow Hag a few years back—" Crane glanced over Kili, who stared back wide-eyed at him. "Long story. Point is, Granny last hid the bones somewhere we both thought safe. That's where I've been...took me a few days on foot, through the mountains, but I finally found the resting place for the bones. Not surprisingly, they were gone. They'd been dug up from the Witchhunter's final resting place.

"So obviously, whoever stole them are using the bones to control the Leechers. To send them on a crusade of the puppet master's choosing. So the big question now is..."

"What is the crusade they're on?" Kili asked with a confused shrug.

"Precisely! However, it looks like we'll have to ponder these things later. Mr. Davenport, I suggest you pull yourself together." Crane nodded toward the back door of the funeral home as it flew open as if by its own accord. "Because they're here."

As if on cue, a Leecher stepped out of the old manor house,

followed immediately by another. Then a third. Finally, there was a clang from behind them. Kili spun around to see that the hatch they'd just come through had been slung open again, and a fourth creature—the one that had chased them down in the basement—was scrambling from the ladder onto solid ground.

They were surrounded.

CHAPTER
SEVEN

The four robed figures spread out, encircling Crane, Kili, and Davenport. The metal tips of the bird-mask beaks caught the gleam of silver from the full moon overhead; all the while their burning crimson eyes glared malevolently after the intruders. Kili held her breath as the Leechers stalked slowly through the garden to block off every path of escape.

"You've no business here," Ezekiel Crane hissed, breaking the eerie silence of the bizarre stand-off. He glanced around the courtyard, as if searching for something before turning his gaze back to their assailants. His eyes narrowed on the Leecher nearest to him—the tallest of the bunch by at least a foot. Since the average height of each was nearly six and a half feet tall, this particular creature was the most intimidating of all, with a hooded cloak pulled over his head, as opposed to the wide-brimmed hat of his companions. "This is not a mission of ol' Eli Smith. You're not beholden to the one who holds his bones. Leave us be, and in return, I will not send you on to your final resting place." He paused to exhale a slow, methodical breath. "At least, not tonight."

"Uh, dude? You think it's a good idea to tick off the weirdos with the masks, right now?" Davenport asked. Despite his obvious trepidation, the reporter had pulled out his cell phone and was taking pictures of the ghastly quartet.

To help solidify the reporter's concerns, each of the Leechers reached into the folds of their cloaks and withdrew ominous felling axes—their sharp heads stained with something dark red, almost rust-colored.

"...'Til her head, the Leecher did hew," Crane muttered to himself.

"Excuse me?" Kili asked.

Crane shrugged, his eyes fixed dead ahead. "An old nursery rhyme. That's all. Though the Leechers have a variety of tools at their disposal for carryin' out their hellish mission, the axe is relegated to those they deem the worst offenders. Their belief being that nothing of the spirit world can tolerate the cold bite of iron." He actually chuckled at this. "Which is rather ironic given what they are."

"You're not making a bit of sense right now," Kili said, turning her head to keep track of the fourth assailant, as it slowly moved around to flank them. "You'd think I'd be used to it, but this is even more messed up than your usual nonsense."

He cast her a bright smile and then a wink. "Have no fear, Ms. Kili. All will become clear as the noon-day sun."

"Not if we don't figure out a way to deal with *them*," Davenport said, nodding to the deadly apparitions surrounding them. "Something tells me they weren't that impressed with your little threat a second ago."

Before Crane could respond, the Leechers moved two steps forward in unison, then stopped once more. A few seconds later, each of the creatures began emitting the strange whispers Kili had become so familiar with, though this time, something was different. The sound, disjointed as it was, could be heard audibly now. It was no longer something radiating through her mind.

She wondered why this seemingly insignificant difference unnerved her so much.

On the up side, she thought grimly, *they're no longer advancing.*

"Why aren't they just attacking us?" the reporter asked. "They've got us surrounded. Why not just kill us off and get it over with?"

"Because, they can't," Crane said. "Not outright anyway...no matter who's controlling them. They've got to judge us guilty first. They must perform the *Trials* and that takes time to set up."

"Trials?" asked Kili.

He looked over at her. "I already mentioned them. Part of that long story I owe you. But you've already felt the effects—at least, in part. Down in the cellar."

"You mean, that spell or whatever? That weird whispery thing it was doing?"

Crane's eyebrows raised. "You heard that?"

Davenport glanced between his two companions. "Of course, she can... They're whispering right now."

But the mountain man dismissed the comment with a wave. "I'm not talking about now." He eyed Kili warily, concern evident on his face. "I meant down there. In the cellar. You heard it then?"

"I don't think now is exactly the right time to discuss something like this, do you?" she said, pointing to their captors.

"No, now's the perfect time. Did you or did you not hear the whispers down in the cellar?"

Kili shrugged. "Yeah. Don't know why it's such a big—"

"Anything else?" Crane asked.

"Huh? What do you mean?"

"Have you heard anything else? Anything unusual the past couple of days?"

Her mind raced back to earlier, at the town picnic. The strange song she'd heard just before Mrs. Crawford's weird attack. The curious dirge that pressed down on her emotions so severely she'd wanted to buckle under the weight of it and cry. But for some reason, she felt telling Crane about it would be a mistake. Something about the look in his eyes—so dark, almost menacing even.

"No," she said curtly, her voice barely audible amid the swell of whispers filling the air. The way Crane looked at her sent a chill down her spine. He didn't believe her. But then, they had more important matters to worry about.

After several excruciatingly long seconds, Crane pulled his gaze away from her and withdrew something from around his neck. Handing the object to Kili, he said, "Take this. Wear it, and it should protect you." He glanced at Davenport. "Sorry, but that's the only one I have. Just try to stick close to her, while I work on something for all of us."

The mountain man crouched down to the ground and dug his forefinger into the dirt, effectively drawing a large circle—about four feet in diameter—around them, while mumbling incoherently as he did so. She looked down at the object in her hand. It was the over-sized rabbit's foot Crane religiously wore. The charm was not your typical gaudy-hued novelty item one might pick up from a local magic or costume shop. This was the real deal. The large hindquarter of a jackrabbit, bound by a leather strap. The thing still had claws, for crying out loud. No dyes. No 'Made in China' sticker taped to the mount. It was completely authentic.

Crane had once explained to her that the rabbit's foot superstition had never been about 'luck' per se, but rather, it was used to ward off hexes that might bring about bad luck. The way he told it, the foot had come from a jackrabbit he'd shot with a silver bullet, in a graveyard during a new moon. She'd never quite known whether he was telling the truth about the foot's origin. Nor had she exactly bought into the superstition herself, but after feeling the horrible effects the Leecher's spellcasting down in the cellar, she was willing to give the amputated foot a

try, no matter how superstitious—or disgusting for that matter—
it might be.

Muttering a silent prayer she only half-believed, she slipped
the charm around her neck with a sigh. As she did so, something
blurred across the corner of Kili's field of vision to her right. She
whipped her head around just in time to see something dark,
almost soot black, whipping into the garden foliage to their left.
The thing had moved so fast, she'd not been able to identify it,
but part of her would have sworn the speeding object had been
—well, spectral. Smoke-like. At the same time, she sensed more
than saw, that the apparition had been somewhat feline...
Whether it was the grace of its movements or something else,
she couldn't be sure. The problem though, in her mind, was that
whatever it had been, it was huge. Easily the size of a well-
grown Great Dane. Or maybe even a Saint Bernard. Something
much too big to suggest an average tomcat anyway. And that
worried her more than anything at the moment.

She turned back to look at Crane, who hadn't seemed to
notice. Instead, he was now hunkered down over a mound of
tobacco he'd placed dead center within the circle he'd traced
around them. Ripping open packs of sugar with his teeth, he
poured an even smaller circle around the tobacco.

He's making an offering to the Yunwi Tsunsdi, she thought with
an unbidden smile. When she'd first heard the term and learned
that it referred to the Appalachian equivalent of the 'Little
People'—the Fae Folk, as her own ancestors would have called
them—she'd scoffed at the very rustic notion of the thing. But
after her ordeal last year, when she began hearing their childlike
laughter and indecipherable chattiness, she no longer could
genuinely deny their existence.

"I'm not entirely convinced they'll help us this time," Crane
said, as if sensing her question. "The Little Folk aren't afraid of
much, but they do seem to have a rather healthy respect for
haints of any kind...and especially, the Witchhunter's ilk." He

added another dash of tobacco to the pile for good measure, then inserted a pinch between his lips and gums. "Still, it couldn't hurt to try." The mountain man continued to work on the protective circle while Davenport looked on in rapt fascination.

Or is that incredulity? Kili thought, remembering her own misgivings when she'd first encountered Ezekiel's so-called 'mountain magic.' But her attention quickly turned back to the Leechers, when she realized the whispers had taken on an actual pitch. The creatures' strange incantations were now fully vocalized. Even more disturbing, they seemed to be fully harmonized into an unsettling chant. And if things were bad enough, they were once more on the move, stalking toward the protective circle with deadly purpose.

"Uh, I don't think they care much for your little hopscotch circle, Crane," Davenport said, pointing at the hooded Leecher, who had lifted the axe high above its head as it took another step. "Any other tricks up those magical sleeves of yours?"

But if Ezekiel replied, Kili didn't hear it. Her gaze had been drawn to the shrubbery on the far end of the garden...to the silhouette of a very large, tailless cat. She stared at the thing, enthralled by the strange visage. She couldn't pull away from those haunting feline eyes that shined a ghostly green back at her. She tried to make out some details of the animal, but it had wrapped itself so deeply in the shadows of the garden, she could see nothing but its basic outline. Two very tall ears with tufts of fur sprouting from the tips, reminded her of pictures she'd seen of the caracal, cats common to parts of Africa and the Middle East she'd seen on the Discovery Channel.

As it sat quietly on its haunches, watching the scene unfold in front of it, she noticed the odd absence of a tail. If it hadn't been for the cat's foreboding size, she would have sworn she was indeed looking at the common bobcat. But to her limited knowledge, no bobcat alive would have ever stood chest-level with her while on all fours.

"...and I'm telling you, that isn't going to work on these things." Crane's words caught her attention, and she turned to look at her two companions.

Alex Davenport was standing slightly in front, still confined to the circle, and brandishing a sword he'd extracted from his walking cane. Briefly, she turned to check on the strange cat, realized it was gone, then immediately turned her attention back to the reporter and his sword in a surprised double take.

"What the heck do you think you're going to do with that?" she growled, already forgetting the weird feline visitor she'd just seen.

"Well, I thought I'd try something like this!" Just as the closest Leecher reached the edge of the circle, the reporter lunged forward, whipped the sword through the air and plunged it deep into the thing's gut. "Aha!" Davenport shouted, pulling the blade out and moving in for another swing.

But the Leecher, showing no concern over the injury, blocked the next strike with the wooden handle of its axe, jarring the sword loose from the reporter's grip. The creature then struck out with its pale, spindly fingers, grabbed Davenport by the wrist, and yanked him violently from the circle. In a single, fluid motion, it threw the reporter over its shoulder. He landed on the ground mere inches from the creature's still-chanting brethren.

"Alex!" Kili tried to run to his aid, but Crane grabbed her by the hem of her coat and pulled her back into the circle.

"No, don't move," he whispered, searching the shadows of the garden before turning his attention back to the Leechers, who were even now turning slowly in the reporter's direction. "Don't move a muscle. Something...interesting...is about to happen."

"Interesting?" Kili asked incredulously. "That man out there is in trouble. Those things are going to kill him if we don't do something, and you call that *interesting*?"

The mountain man gave her a reproving look. "That's not what I meant," he said sternly, before tapping the face of his watch with his finger. "But I need a bit more time...everything will be fine soon. Just a little more patience, and you'll understand. But be ready to run when I tell you, okay?"

The tempo of the chanting continued to escalate, reaching a feverish pitch. Davenport stayed huddled on the ground, looking up at the Leechers as they loomed over him, their axes raised above their heads.

"Problem is, we need to buy him some time as well," Crane whispered conspiratorially. "While he was in the circle, they couldn't perform their *Trial* on him. Now, he's fair game." Moving over to Kili, Crane bent forward briefly and examined her jacket with inscrutable eyes before letting out an enthusiastic cry. He then reached into the inner pocket of his coat, and pulled out a pair of tweezers. "Keep your eye on Mr. Davenport, if you please, Ms. Kili."

"I don't understand what you're doing... Why are you..."

Ignoring her protests, Crane brought the tweezers to the fabric of her coat and pulled back, revealing a light blonde hair. Taking a small twig he'd picked up off the ground nearby, he snapped it into four roughly equal parts and wrapped the hair around them tightly. He then pulled out a spool of bright red thread from his pocket and secured the hair and twigs together. Pausing, Crane gave a perplexed look before clawing at the dirt with his hands. After several seconds, he let out a frustrated growl.

"What? What's wrong?" Kili asked.

"Eyes, Ms. Kili! Keep your eyes on your friend." Without looking up, he pointed in the direction of the reporter. "He is in a great deal of trouble."

"Tell me something I don't know!" She edged to the thinly dug line in the dirt that formed the protective circle. Every muscle felt coiled, ready to spring if Ezekiel didn't do something soon.

"You misunderstand. The danger isn't as much from them as,

um, *something* else," Crane said, still searching the ground. "I'm working on a charm that will protect him from what's coming, but I'm missing something. Something of *his*. Your vigilance while I figure this out just might save his life."

"The hair," she said. "You found his hair on me." It had to have come from the reporter. Kili's own hair was a bright red hue. Crane's sandy blond hair was so dark, it was almost brown. No, the single blond hair that had been pulled from her jacket would have belonged to Davenport.

"Yes. Yes, of course," he said absently, as if not really paying attention to her. Abruptly, he stood to his feet and whirled around, searching the earth at his feet with an air of quiet desperation. "But unfortunately, Ms. Kili, it isn't enough. Typically, the protective charm would use a drop of his spilled blood or a fingernail clipping...something connected intimately with the individual who it is designed to protect."

"You mean, something the person never leaves home without? Something they keep with them at all times?"

"Precisely."

"You mean something like that?" She nodded down at the sword cane laying just outside the protective circle.

Slowly, a wry smile crept up the man's face. "Precisely like that, Ms. Kili. Well done."

A scream from Davenport interrupted their exchange, followed immediately by a series of strangled gurgles. It was then that Kili realized she'd failed miserably in the task Crane had assigned her. Instead of watching her new friend, she'd once again been drawn into the Ezekiel Crane enigma. She turned back to the reporter and watched in horror as he grasped desperately at his throat. His eyes bulged wide, while a stream of clear liquid bubbled from his nose and mouth like some macabre fountain spout. His face had already turned an unnatural shade of blue; his lips, purple. The man's air was being blocked. He was actually drowning on dry land!

"Dear Lord!" she shouted. She tried again to run to help him, but Crane restrained her. Furiously, she spun around on him. "He's dying! I've got to help him!"

"No, I'll do it. For now, you can't leave this circle, Ms. Kili," he said. "No matter what happens, don't leave this circle until I say it's safe. Agreed?"

Reluctantly, she gave a quick nod and Crane was off. He dashed out of the circle, scooped up the cane sword, and began tying the twigs and hair charm to its handle as he ran to assist Davenport. Kili watched helplessly as he raced past one of the axe-wielding Leechers and slid, feet first, next to the reporter. The mountain man whispered something inaudible to the reporter, and then he laid the cane into the man's lap. Instantly, the liquid seemed to dry up, and the reporter fell back onto the ground in a fit of hacking coughs. Crane turned him, tilting his head to one side to prevent any remaining fluid from rushing back down his throat. Kili tensed as the Leechers converged, their chanting now murderous.

But there was something else Kili heard within the garden, beside the strange melodious incantations. Something that had begun slinking its way into the outskirts of her consciousness as the horrifying scene unfolded before her eyes.

Purring.

Deep, resonating purring that seemed to vibrate from within her own core.

The cat! She thought, glancing around the darkness. It took a few seconds, but eventually she caught sight of it. Or rather, she thought she did. Something dark against the dim light, ducking behind the blossoming branch of a Rhododendron bush near the southeastern wall. Odd that even as far away as she was from it —amid the chanting and the chaos—she could hear the cat's purring.

"Ms. Kili!" Crane shouted, drawing her out of her reverie. "Get ready!"

While Davenport appeared to be doing much better, a trickle of dark red blood oozed down Crane's face from his nose and... *Oh God!* Blood was even coming from his eyes. Instinctively, she clutched at the furry object around her neck. Crane's rabbit foot. Whatever enchantment the Leechers were doing, without the charm, Crane was in just as much danger as the reporter had been. But this time, instead of water erupting from his lungs, it looked like the enigmatic man was hemorrhaging from every visible orifice.

She took a step forward, but one look from Crane's glaring, blood-stained eyes stopped her in her tracks. "Not yet," he mouthed with an almost imperceptible shake of his head.

Calmly, he wiped the crimson trail from his face with the sleeve of his flannel shirt, then climbed to unsteady feet and motioned for Davenport to do the same. "I want to remind you," he said, his melodious voice strong despite the pain he was obviously enduring. "I offered y'all a way out. It needn't have been like this." The unworldly chanting continued as he spoke. "You'd do well to remember that next time we meet."

"Crane, what are you doing?" Davenport asked between rasping coughs. "Don't agitate the monsters anymore, please."

"Ah, but my friend..." He reached into another pocket and pulled out something long and furry. The thing—it looked like some sort of animal's tail to Kili—was the color of night, and the Leechers appeared to sense some unseen danger at the sight of it in their enemy's hand. The chanting stopped abruptly as each of the creatures took a single step back. "Agitating these *monsters*, as you put it, is precisely what I intend to do."

And with a devilish smile half-hidden by trails of blood streaming down his face, Crane tossed the object to the nearest Leecher and shouted, "Now Ms. Kili! Run!"

Without waiting to be told twice, she dashed from the circle toward her friends, who had already made it to the garden's gate and were holding it open for her. The Leechers, in an inexplicable panic, seemed uncertain of what to do. They spread out, axes raised defensively as they moved erratically through the courtyard.

She was just within ten feet of the door when she heard the low, rumbling growl. She risked a quick glance over her shoulder and caught sight of a monstrous shadow bounding through the garden at one of the Leechers—the shadow of the tailless cat-shaped creature she'd been seeing from the moment Crane had erected the protective circle. But now, out in the open, as it pounced at their enemies with an insatiable hunger, Kili realized the creature was not an animal at all. It had no substance. It was as if the cat shadow itself was alive and stalking their enemies.

But that's crazy...

Her thought trailed off as her feet leapt over the object Crane had tossed at their attackers. Sure enough, it was the decomposing remains of some large cat's tail. It was much too thick and stubby to belong to any type of house cat. Kili guessed it belonged to something just a bit more wild, but couldn't place it.

Without realizing what she was doing, she stopped and turned to stare at the object more closely. The tail seemed to wiggle and writhe on the ground in front of her, and she couldn't help but stare horrified at it. Then, as if she were merely a marionette on a string, she felt herself involuntarily stooping down and reaching for it. Before she knew what she was doing, she'd scooped the object up and tucked it away in her jacket before running toward the gate once more.

She made it just as a great roar erupted behind her, followed by the sound of the most ungodly shrieks she'd ever heard. Crane slammed the gate shut the moment she passed through, grabbed her hand, and pulled her forward to the welcoming sight of Johnson Boulevard and freedom.

CHAPTER EIGHT

The Crane Homestead
April 28
4:28 AM

E sther Crane, 'Granny' to all who knew her, was getting worried. Her grandson still hadn't returned yet from his trip up the mountain pass—to the place where she'd hidden those accursed bones. He hadn't even called to let her know all was well, and to make matters worse, the Yunwi Tsunsdi had all but disappeared, ever since those nasty haints had returned. Or was it since the return of the Kindred? She couldn't be sure. All she knew was that the regular giggling and chattering she was so used to hearing had been replaced by nothing but the Dirge. The horrible song of mourning and death. The Little People were beside themselves with grief, and without their guidance, she knew she wouldn't be sure of anything through the dark days ahead. She might as well get used to it.

At any other time, she wouldn't have given Ezekiel's absence a second thought...but now? With the Witchhunter's Leechers on the prowl? She couldn't help but shudder at the thought.

Those vile creatures had had their sights on that boy since—well, for far too long anyway. Years ago, they'd been sent to kill Ezekiel by the Willow Hag herself...had irreparably injured her other grandson in the process. In her thirst for vengeance, as well as to protect Ezekiel, Granny had performed some of the darkest magic she'd ever done to steal the bones right out from under the Hag's control. She'd thought she'd put a stop to it once and for all. But now? It was just one more thing she was uncertain about. Though she was aimin' to find out.

But that would have to wait. Her grandson's current whereabouts was not her only concern at the moment. Her small, comfortable ancestral home on the apex of Ryder Bluff, overlooking their sleepy little hamlet, was getting a might crowded for her taste. *Heck, home isn't exactly the right word for it anymore,* she thought, while dipping a rag into a bucket of cool water and dabbing the moist cloth at Charlie Wrigley's sweat-drenched forehead. *It's more like a hospital around here than anythin' else.*

The illnesses had all started around the time the Leechers had returned. No one, not even those fancy doctors with the CDC, could make heads or tails of it. So, as was the custom in these parts, the townsfolk converged on the best doctor within a hundred-mile radius...Granny Crane.

The CDC, of course, was denying even the possibility of an outbreak. A mild flu going around, was all they would say, while their primary focus remained on the strange case of the resurrected Kindred. To the CDC, they were the only thing that mattered, and a few people catching the sniffles throughout the county were nothing to worry about.

But Granny knew better. Even without the normally ceaseless chatter of the Yunwi Tsunsdi, she knew these 'illnesses' were nothing of the sort. Not a single runny nose. Not a cough or a sneeze. Each victim was exhibiting specific symptoms not listed in any medical journal on Earth: spontaneous searing of skin tissue or water buildup in the throat and lungs. Her personal favorite—the most disturbing of all—was that a few people had suffered massive GI bleeds, which caused their abdomens to swell with so much blood they looked like an over-gorged tick. No, these weren't symptoms of some strange illness that had come across the land.

These were the telltale signs of Eli Smith's *Trials by Ordeals*.

Three people had already died from them. No, scratch that. With Liz Crawford, Granny supposed that made a total of four deaths. Their horribly maligned corpses had been taken to that funeral home in Morriston or carted off to Lord-knows-where by those CDC people. And Chuck Wrigley, blistered from the neck down with third degree burns, was about to join them. There just was nothing else she could do for him. *He is in the Good Lord's hands now*, she thought, stroking a strand of gray hair from the dying man's face.

A knock at the side door caught her attention. She knew her grandson wouldn't bother to knock, and her current houseguest, that nice reporter feller Obadiah had sent to her, had been given a key. And since she'd already given an ear-full to those other TV reporters and their *bull-in-a-china-shop* camera crews trouncing all over her property in hopes of learning more about the sick people she was currently caring for, that left only one other person.

"Jimmy, dear," she said, looking over at the eight-year-old boy who'd just walked into the living room carrying a fresh bucket of water for her. The poor boy had been through so much since the death of his mother the previous year. He'd been living with her ever since, and Granny couldn't have hoped for a better child to take care of in her advanced years. Jimmy's tender heart was outright infectious, and had been invaluable during this crisis. "Could you go let Ms. Delores in, please?"

The boy sat the bucket down beside her, smiled broadly at her with a nod, and dashed off to the front door. Delores McCrary, her current apprentice, had hit it off wonderfully with

Jimmy right from the start. A powerful bond had been formed instantly between the two, who had become almost inseparable when they were together. Granny supposed that Dee, as she affectionately called the woman, had become even more a surrogate mother to Jimmy than she had ever been able to, which was a blessing all on its own.

She leaned back in her chair next to Mr. Wrigley's deathbed, looked around at the twelve mesh sleeping cots that littered her living room, and sighed. Though few could look at her and guess how old she actually was, at that very moment, she was certainly feeling her true age.

Just so much to do. So much misery. Pain. Death. The majority of the hexed had come so suddenly. Just after the town picnic—after the death of Mrs. Crawford, starting with Edgar Winters. Before Liz, there'd only been a handful of the afflicted, some of whom she'd already cured. But within a span of nine hours, her entire living room had filled to near bursting. Though her 'medicine' seemed to be helping the majority, there were a handful she knew would never respond to her treatments. With her caseload being so heavy at the moment, she was thankful her old friend had decided to come to help.

She heard Jimmy open the door, and the kindly voice of Delores McCrary greeted the boy in her usual genial manner. But something was wrong. The woman's voice sounded strained. Tired. A few moments later, when she entered the living room with Jimmy in tow, Granny turned from her reflections to see Dee's pale, fevered face as she lugged in a box of supplies, cradled weakly in her arms.

"I came as soon as I could," she puttered, walking past the living room and into the kitchen. Granny immediately followed and watched, as the other woman set the box down on the table and turned around with a sigh. "But I should warn you.... Seems I got whatever's goin' 'round. First, my dear ol' Max— he's laid up in bed even as we speak—but soon, I found myself a bit under the weather too. I just dunno what we're gonna do."

Granny had been dumbstruck from the moment she'd caught sight of her old friend. Delores looked even more haggard than she'd sounded from the foyer. Worn out. Even worse, her entire face and arms were covered with rancid-looking, puss-oozing boils.

In recent years, Dee had become Esther Crane's unofficial apprentice in mountain magic. Though not a very powerful practitioner, what Dee lacked in strength, she more than made up for in compassion, and that was precisely why Granny had agreed to pass on the old secrets to her. After all, the Crane matriarch wouldn't live forever no matter what most in town might think. And although Dee looked at least fifteen years older, she was Granny's junior by more than twenty-five.

As with all water witches in these parts, Esther Crane would have to pass on her mantle to someone one day. Ezekiel was good. Powerful even. But he had his own destiny. Besides, the townspeople would never abide his appointment to the position. *The idjits still fear him too much to ever give him the chance.* So, one day, she planned for Delores to take her place instead. But since the Leechers' Trials were designed to identify witches or magic users of all kinds, their effect on her old friend was worse than on the regular folk. It was making its mark on her...making it easier for the Leechers to target her with their accursed axes.

Which begged the question... *What are those coonhounds up to?* They'd never unleashed their curses on the entire community like this. They'd always been focused. Precise in their judgments. That told her they had to be shooting from the hip...looking for someone specific, but with no real place to start.

When Delores started pulling the supplies from the box she'd carried in and preparing them for their patients, Granny's thoughts suddenly came back to the problem at hand. "Dee, what in Sam Hill's the matter with you, woman?" Granny gently rebuked while taking the woman by the hand and leading her to the living room. "Yer in no condition to even walk, much less tend to the others."

"Nonsense," Delores said, patting Granny's hand as it gripped her underneath her forearm for support. "I'm sure there's somethin' I could be doin' to help. You can't be helpin' all these here sick'uns on yer own after all."

Granny eased the younger woman down into her reading chair, straightened up, and smiled. Fortunately, being a student of mountain magic as she was, the Witchhunter's Trials wouldn't be lethal to Delores. That much she knew. They would definitely make her weak, though. And the pain her friend must be enduring would have been bad enough to knock down old Bear Boone, she was sure. But the inner strength and fortitude that shined from inside her protégé made her swell with pride. She'd certainly chosen her successor wisely.

"All right, Dee," she said, reaching into a pouch at her hip and pulling out an assortment of bizarre fetishes and arcane instruments, before getting down on her knees to look her friend in the eye. "But if'n yer gonna help me, I need to fix you up first. Then we can concentrate on the rest. Sound good to you?"

Delores, her eyes clinched in subdued misery, nodded once, then leaned back in the reading chair and allowed her mentor to do her magic.

CHAPTER
NINE

County Road 207
April 28
4:45 AM

K ili gently stroked the sweat-drenched hair away from Alex Davenport's eyes, as the mountain road raced past them. She and the reporter were in the backseat of Crane's crew-cab F-450 duel-wheeled pickup, while Crane himself managed the steering wheel as they sped up the winding road.

His frosty blue eyes, still caked at the corners with dried blood, looked back at her from the rearview mirror. "How's he doing?"

She shook her head and looked down at Davenport, whose head rested limply in her lap. "I don't know. He's breathing easier. Heart rate seems to be slowing down a bit." She paused, took the damp towel sitting next to her, and dabbed it at the corner of his mouth. "But he still seems to have fluid in his lungs. He keeps spitting the stuff up." She glanced back into the mirror to meet Crane's gaze. "What did they do to him? It's like he was drowning or something."

Crane negotiated a right-hand turn and accelerated down a roughly hewn dirt road. As the truck jostled over the uneven terrain, he glanced back at her once more.

"It's basically a supernatural form of the old Trial by Ordeals used in the witch-hunts of Eastern Europe and Colonial America," he said grimly. "The most famous of these involved dunking a suspected witch into a body of water, chained to stones. If she survived the ordeal, she was obviously a witch. Other, lesser known tests included the Trial by Boiling Oil, The Devil's Cake, and the Trial by Fire—placing a suspect's feet into a fire to see if they burned…"

"Just like Liz Crawford!" Kili said. "The soles of her feet were charred…like they'd been held over a fire or something. But that makes no sense. I was there at the park when she died. There wasn't a fire anywhere near her."

Crane's eyes gleamed in the dim glow of the dashboard lights. "Ah, but Ms. Kili, that's why I said they were supernatural. These tests—the ones vexing all of Jasper County at the moment—are special. They were perfected by a seventeenth century witchhunter, named Eli Smith."

"You mentioned him earlier," Kili said. "When the Leechers first surrounded us."

Crane's focus went back to driving up the long stretch of road. "He was a physician as a younger man…before becoming obsessed with witchcraft. No one knows exactly what prompted his crusade to hunt them down, but he quickly became the scourge of all practitioners of the Art. He came to see witchcraft as the Black Plague of the colonies, and he took to wearing an old medieval plague doctor's uniform as a means to frighten those he hunted."

"That's where I've seen those outfits before," Kili said. "I remember seeing something about them on the History Channel recently. They used spices stuffed into the beaks to drown out the smell of death and decay."

"Pretty much the same for Smith and his Leechers. Though for him, the masks were designed to blot out the stench of Satan and his evil, which was invading the New World," Crane said. "Then oddly enough, shortly after the Salem Trials, he just quit. His band of judges, who he called Leechers, which carried the double entendre of a medieval doctor and the notion of bleeding evil from the land, were disbanded.

"No one knows why for that, either. He simply left his home in Boston one day in 1698 and started making his way southwest. Eventually, he found a small settlement in what the Indians called Kan-tuckee, and he found it to his liking. He planted roots here. Started a family even, and he started practicing medicine again."

"Let me guess. That settlement? It eventually became Boone Creek, didn't it?"

Crane gave a short nod before making another left.

"So what happened? How are these Leechers still around after three centuries?"

"Simple. The Willow Hag...and her coven of three other witches."

"I remember hearing about her last time I was here. But only in passing. No one really explained what she was to me."

"That's because she's rather *difficult* to explain. She's a legend in these parts...as old as the Devil's Teeth. And yes, she resides out in the Dark Hollows, or rather in one lonely corner of it. Some say she's part of the spirit world—like the Yunwi Tsunsdi. She's an old crone who practices the darkest of magic, and she's a servant of the Dark Ones."

"The same gods that Tom Thornton and his church worship?" Kili asked. "The Nameless Ones, as Granny calls them?"

"The very same," Crane said. His eyes seemed to grow visibly darker for several moments before continuing. "Anyway, the Hag is said to be immortal. Supposedly finds young impressionable children to corrupt. She teaches them the dark arts, and then, when they're fully matured, she supposedly kills them, takes their skin, and wears it as a disguise to venture out into the world. Something akin to a Native American skinwalker, I suppose."

"You've got to be kidding!" Kili said, the very thought of it sending her mind whirling in a fit of revulsion.

"I don't believe it, mind you," Crane said, offering her a reassuring smile.

"The Hag?"

"Oh, no...she's real enough. And as old as the land itself, I'd say. I just don't think she actually steals the skins of her victims. I think she corrupts them—breaks their psyche—then simply transfers her own consciousness into them once she's done with them."

"I'm not sure that's any more comforting," Kili said. Suddenly remembering the ill reporter, she dabbed at his forehead once more with the washcloth. "So what happened to Smith? What does this Tree Hag have to do with him?"

"*Willow* Hag," Crane corrected. "And she stole Smith's only child...his eight-year-old son." Crane paused to let it sink in. "Not to train him up, mind you. No, the younger Smith was to be a sacrifice to the Dark Ones, on the summer solstice. When Smith figured out what was happening, he went to the town's fathers to drum up a hunting party. He tried desperately to get a posse together to go and save his boy. Unfortunately, when it came to the Hag, the town's elders were cowards. They wouldn't act. They simply barred their doors and windows, then waited the night out.

"When dawn came, the boy's body was found in the town square. He'd been eviscerated, and all his internal organs were missing. Grief stricken, Smith went into the Dark Hollows by himself to take vengeance on the Willow Hag. He was never seen again."

Crane let the truck slow just enough to turn into a short, gravel driveway. A small, unimposing ranch-style house sat under a stand of trees. The windows were dark, which wasn't exactly surprising, since they were still about three hours away from dawn, yet Kili got the distinct impression that the place was unoccupied.

"Whose house is this?" she asked. "Why are we here?"

Pulling under a covered carport, Crane put the truck in park, and turned to look at his two charges. "Somewhere safe," he said soberly. "Away from the Leechers' prying eyes and more importantly, away from whoever's stolen Smith's bones."

No one made a move to get out of the truck. Kili silently willed her friend to continue the story. When he didn't speak up, she decided to prod him on. "So what happened? I mean, if Smith was never seen again, how do the Leechers come into the story? What are they exactly, and what do they have to do with these bones you keep talking about?"

"Dr. Smith is the reason the Leechers exist at all. Legend says with his dying breath he cursed the town elders. Charged them with carrying on his crusade until the Willow Hag and all witchcraft were eradicated in the land. Problem is, the Willow Hag stripped Smith's flesh and used his bones from that point on, as a means to bind the Leechers to her will."

"You're seriously telling me that those...those things are some sort of zombie witchhunters from the early eighteenth century? Really?"

"The Leechers aren't zombies; they're *haints*, Ms. Kili. In other parts of the world, they might be called *liches*...beings who are neither living nor dead. Not exactly spirits, but not entirely flesh and blood either. Because they can manipulate the material world as easily as you or I, liches can create a sort of semi-corporal form at times, which makes them infinitely more dangerous than ghosts or other undead creatures."

Kili shook her head. "I think I've matured a bit since we first met, Crane. I've seen a lot of stuff I never imagined possible. I've become much more open-minded about these kinds of things. But this? This is just a little too unbelievable. I honestly can't believe you—as rational and scientific as you try to be—would even entertain such stories."

Without immediately responding to her rebuke, he reached into his pocket, pulled out a battered can of Copenhagen, and unceremoniously slid of pinch of snuff underneath his lower lip. "At the moment, whether you or I believe such tales or not is irrelevant. The cold hard truth of it is that the Leechers are here, and someone's using them to find someone else," he finally said, getting out of the truck and opening the door to the backseat. "My guess is, they're looking for a witch powerful enough to bring the dead back to life...and that's not going to be a very long list, I can tell you that."

"Do you think witchcraft is behind these resurrections?" she asked, sliding out of the truck before helping Davenport to climb out as well.

He gave her a sideways grin, as he pulled the reporter's arm over his shoulder and began half-carrying him toward the front porch, nearly knocking a potted fern off the rail as they climbed the two narrow steps. "Ms. Kili, you know me too well. The short answer is, I believe someone thinks witchcraft is behind it. But as you most eloquently put it, I'm not one to take up fanciful theories...especially ones without the slightest shred of evidence," he said with a chuckle. "And to be fair, I'm not entirely certain we're dealing with resurrections at all."

"What?" Kili asked. She watched as Crane fumbled for the correct key and opened the door. "But there's no doubt the Kindred were dead. You examined their corpses yourself, didn't you?"

He nodded an affirmative while guiding Davenport to an old, wool-covered couch in the front living room.

"And now they're alive," she continued. "So what else could

we be dealing with, if not a resurrection?"

Crane gestured her to take a nearby armchair, before crouching down to examine the reporter's eyes with a pen light. "I'm not sure," he said, silently coaxing Davenport to follow the light with his eyes. "But that's beside the point. Whatever is happening with the Kindred can wait for the moment. The Leechers and the one behind their obsessive hunt is our more immediate concern. If they're looking for who I think they are, it's possible that not a single resident in Boone Creek will be safe. That means, my priority is finding the person who stole the bones and stopping them."

"And I'll bet you ten grand easy, we know who it is, too," came a voice from behind Kili. She turned to see the haggard, emaciated form of former Sheriff John Tyler standing in a darkened doorway, leading down into the home's basement. His knuckles were whitened by the dead man's grip he held on the shotgun by his side. Besides the man's rumpled comb-over and sunken cheeks, there was something almost haunted about his eyes.

"Sheriff Tyler!" Kili said in surprise, rising from her seat to greet the man.

"Just John, ma'am," he said with a nod. "They stripped me of the title after the One-Eyed Jack ordeal."

"To be fair, John," Crane said, still examining his patient, "it was your association with Asherah and her doings that caused you to lose your job."

The ex-cop glared at Crane for half a second before letting out a curse and stepping up into the living room with an unsteady gait. "Don't kid yourself, Crane. It's your own particular association with that witch that's behind everything that's going on right now. You know as well as I do that she's responsible for all this." He turned his gaze back to Kili. "She has her eyes fixed on our boy there, and she ain't about to stop 'til he's her's."

CHAPTER
TEN

Crane Homestead
April 28
5:15 AM

E sther Crane recognizes the dream the moment she closes
her eyes. There is no question about it. She has been
having it every night since the Leechers first reappeared. And it
is precisely the same as the ones she'd endured twenty years
before, when Ezekiel and Josiah had both nearly been killed by
the creatures.

Gripping the broom, she busies herself with the chores of the
day. Sweeping the dirt, leaves, and detritus from the front porch.
It is unusually warm for an early December morning, but she
isn't about to complain. If the good Lord wanted to hold back
the approaching chill of winter, who was she to argue?

Enjoying her simple life, she begins humming the tune to
Amazing Grace, and as she works, the lyrics of the old spiritual
pours from her lips with such enthusiasm that by the time her
grandson Ezekiel's cries finally register, he's a mere thirty yards
away.

The boy—well, at the age of seventeen, she can hardly call him a boy anymore, she supposes—is desperately running through the recently cleared out tobacco field. His arms flail wildly, as he yells for her assistance. When he sees he finally has her attention, his gaze turns back over his shoulder. She follows his line of sight, and the world begins spinning out of control with the arrival of the thirteen black-clad figures in dogged pursuit.

The Leechers, their axes raised high, glide effortlessly over the rolling field, swiftly catching up to her grandson. But why? Why are they after him? What had he done to warrant their judgment?

She steps off the porch and toward Ezekiel before she even registers a blur of motion zoom past her. It's not until the soft, gentle arms of her granddaughter Jael are around her waist that she realizes what has happened. Ezekiel's two remaining siblings had been inside playing. They must have heard the commotion and looked outside to see what was happening. Impetuous nine-year-old Josiah, who worships his brother so, had seen the danger Ezekiel was in. Josiah was even now rushing out to protect him.

Esther Crane closes her eyes at the realization of what was to come. She always did. She couldn't bring herself to watch it all over again. She hears Ezekiel and Jael crying pitifully over their fallen brother. Hears Ezekiel lament the sound of the horrible dirge that only he could hear, and his confusion over where it was coming from. The song of anguish and grief—sung by the Yunwi Tsunsdi when mortals are about to die—would haunt him for the rest of his life. He couldn't possibly understand at that moment that it was a curse placed on him for a promise reneged upon. Not yet. But soon, she knew, he would understand. The curse, which could potentially drive the young man mad with anguish and grief, would be a part of his life forever, and there was nothing he could do about it.

And then her mind, just like in all the other dreams before, opened once more. She knew before even looking where she'd be. She knew without doubt she would be...

...in the hospital room. How many years had passed? How many times had she visited this same room? The passage of time could be marked only by the progressive change in technology: the heart rate monitor, the style of bed, even the perennially unused television screen mounted high on the wall. They were the only things that ever changed about the scene. And of course, the face of little Josiah. As she watches in horror at the unmoving form of her youngest grandson, his face begins to age. Just a young boy at first. So innocent. So full of life. Then, suddenly, he is man. Stubble grows on his chin as his sweet, devoted nurse scrapes the hair away with a straight razor. The nurse—for some reason, she struggles to recall the poor girl's name—smiles warmly at the Crane matriarch. Assures her that her grandson is getting better...that one day, he'll be up and walking again. But one look at Josiah's atrophied arms and legs tells her otherwise. He's just too deep in the coma. He'll never recover.

And it was all that witch's fault. The Willow Hag. The immortal demoness of the Dark Hollows, who feeds upon the lives of the insane, the emotionally disturbed, and children of all kinds.

Instantly, Esther Crane finds herself removed from her grandson's hospital room and once more in the strange, unearthly glade of the Willow Grove. But something is different this time. The place, usually crisp, green, and alive, now appears dead. Where lush grass and neatly trimmed shrubs had once been, there are now only weeds and bramble. The ring of ancient willow trees that circles the glade is withered. Diseased. The branches hang down in gnarled knots upon the ground.

Oddly, Esther doesn't care. She has only one thing on her mind at the moment. She must put a stop to the Hag's control of the Leechers, and the only way to do that is to find Eli Smith's bones yet again. But before she can begin her search, she turns to see a curious sight.

A Leecher. The chief Leecher, Eli Smith himself, with his hood pulled up over his mask, instead of the wide-brimmed hat the rest of his judges wore. He just stands there, yards away, looking at her through those beet-red eyes. In turn, her own eyes are pulled down…to the felling axe hanging near his hip and the old chopping block to his right. She blinks, and there is someone—a woman—resting face forward, on the block. Esther cocks her head, trying to see who it is, as Smith slowly raises his axe into the air.

Panic wells up inside her as she strains to see the face of the woman on the block. But no matter what she does or where she moves, she can't get a good vantage point. Something is blocking her view. She turns her attention to the object keeping her from getting a good look at the execution and realizes another person is standing in front of her. She doesn't understand. In all the years of having this dream, this has never happened before. This is all new. She's not sure what to expect.

And yet she is compelled to reach out and ask the person in front of her to move. She simply must see the execution. Must know whose head is on the block. Nervously, her index finger taps on the offender's shoulder. The person turns around, and she's immediately greeted with the leathery, mummy-like face of the Willow Hag. The old crone looks over at Esther and casts a snaggle-toothed malevolent smile, just as the axe begins to fall. The Hag's face suddenly shifts and folds in on itself, and it quickly transforms into the kindly visage of Delores, then the arrogant smirk of Asherah. It changes again to Josiah's nurse, then strangely enough, to the cadaverous face of Candace Staples, little Jimmy's mother, who was killed by One-Eyed Jack the previous year. Finally, and perhaps most surprising of all, the face shifts to that of Kili Brennan, whose kind emerald eyes smile sadly at her.

Esther Crane pleads with the pretty, young redhead, though no words form on her trembling lips. *'Move! I must see the execution!'* she starts to say, but the air is ripped from her lungs just as Kili steps aside, revealing the chopping block once more, the falling axe now only inches away from its target's head.

Without warning, everything stops. The axe hovers. The Leecher is frozen in mid-swing. And a voice calls out from the surrounding countryside. The voice is barely audible at first, but it gradually begins to build, until she hears it as clear as day. The old nursery rhyme. Only bits and pieces are actually audible. Fragments really, except for one complete verse that drifts through the air on a familiar voice. The voice is her own grandmother, singing it to her, as the woman had done with Esther when she was only a little girl.

Oh sweet little deary, never tire or weary
Of choosing the right thing to do.
For the Leechers are comin', to the beat of the drummin'
And it might be your head they'll hew.

Tears well in the corners of Esther's eyes. It's exactly as she feared. The omen is now certain, and there is nothing she can do about what will happen soon. She knows instantly with those strange, familiar words, exactly why she's been given this vision, and she shudders at what it truly means—for Ezekiel. For the people of Boone Creek.

There's no need for her to look at the victim on the chopping block now, but as movement begins to flow again, and as the axe's descent is renewed, she looks over at the huddled form of the intended victim, and the tears begin to pour down her cheeks.

"I'm so sorry," she says, looking into those doomed eyes across from her. "I failed y—"

THE KNOCK at the door roused Granny from the brief catnap she'd allowed herself not ten minutes earlier. With the implications of her bizarre dream still in the forefront of her weary mind, she scrambled out of her reading chair, then looked around the room at her patients to make sure they were all still sleeping soundly. At this stage of their therapy, rest was the most essential and she was doing everything in her power to make sure they got as much uninterrupted sleep as possible. The intrusion at her front door—her *front* door, of all places. Everyone who would be welcome there would have known to go to the side kitchen door—was an annoyance she wouldn't take lightly.

Whoever was outside knocked again.

"I'm comin'. I'm comin'," she whispered while tip-toeing past the cot on which ol' Selma Blakely slept. Once she'd negotiated the maze of cots and sleeping bags, she made her way to the front door, unbolted the lock, and opened it to find a bent stick-figure of a man, dressed in the blackest of black suits on God's earth, leaning on a hickory cane with one hand, and holding a wooden bowl, a fork, and a spoon with the other. The man's head was covered in a burlap sack with holes for both eyes and his mouth cut into it.

The man stood there without saying a word. Instead, he held out the bowl to her in the humble gesture of a beggar pleading for some food.

Granny's eyes narrowed. "We didn't call fer you, Sin-Eater. You know I don't cotton to yer ilk."

But the man held his ground, nodding off into her lifting

room. Granny followed his gaze, which came to rest on the still form of Charlie Wrigley. She glanced back at the Sin-Eater, then back to Charlie.

"Oh, dear Lord." Though she'd expected the elderly man to pass sometime soon, she'd prayed he make it to the light of day —or at least that she could be with him the moment he breathed his last breath. Quickly, she moved around her sleeping patients, and knelt down at Charlie's cot to check his pulse. Sure enough, he was dead, though not yet cool to the touch. She looked back over at the door, but the Sin-Eater had followed her into her house without so much as an invitation. He now stood next to her; his bowl and eating utensils held down to her in silent supplication.

"You know I can't abide by this pagan practice," she said to him with a scowl.

He didn't budge. Instead, he nodded at Charlie Wrigley and wriggled the bowl in his hand. The meaning was obvious. Though Esther Crane didn't agree with the age old custom of the Sin-Eater—a custom dating back to Roman times—Charlie Wrigley's family had a long tradition of honoring the ritual. It would have been disrespectful for her not to allow it, no matter how much she reviled the practice.

With a grunt and a nod, she took the bowl from the cadaverous Sin-Eater, motioned to her reading chair for him to take a seat, then marched into her kitchen to prepare the ritual meal that would be used to supposedly absolve poor Wrigley of his sins.

THIRTY MINUTES LATER, Granny watched as the Sin-Eater knelt down at Charlie Wrigley's cot, and placed the bowl of stew she'd hastily prepared on the corpse's distended belly, before bowing his burlap-covered head.

"I give easement and rest now to thee, dear man," the Sin-Eater hissed. "Come not down the lanes or in our meadows. And for thy peace I pawn my own soul. Amen."

He took his spoon—made of the same wood as his bowl—dipped it into the stew, and took a bite. He then muttered another, similar pronouncement before taking another bite.

Of course, Granny had seen this all before. Many times, in fact. Thankfully, it was a custom that had all but died out in Appalachia in recent years, but there were still vestiges of the tradition still clinging to life here and there. It shouldn't have surprised her that Boone Creek would be one of the places it was still employed religiously.

The Sin-Eater tradition had been brought over to the New World with the Irish and Welsh. When these descendants of the Celts traveled west, settling in the mountains, the Sin-Eater's role seemed to grow even stronger in the fertile fields of death caused by the hardships of pioneer life and Indian raids.

The tradition itself involved employing a lone man in the community—usually passed down from father and son—who would travel to the places where people were dead or dying. They would then barter for food that would be placed on or near the corpse's body, and the Sin-Eater would then take the person's personal sins into themselves by ingesting the consecrated feast. Though the dead person would be supposedly absolved of all their sins through the ritual, the Sin-Eater's soul was irreparably damned, according to tradition, making them the pariah's of the community. Outcasts. Feared and reviled until a loved one's soul was at stake.

The whole thing was simply blasphemous to Esther Crane, who held firmly to the belief in the atonement of sins through the blood of Jesus Christ alone. Still, despite her own reservations, she couldn't, in good conscience, deny Charlie Wrigley his own customs, so she sat there and watched the ritual unfold with strained patience.

Ten more minutes passed, and the Sin-Eater set his spoon down in the empty bowl, bowed once more, and stood to his feet. Picking the bowl up off the body, he turned to Granny, and held out an empty hand, palm up. Granny reached into the pocket of her jeans, withdrew two dollars, and placed the money in the man's hand. With a nod of thanks, he stuffed the money into the pocket of his black coat pocket, picked up his cane, and started heading toward the door. Before leaving, however, he turned and looked at Granny through the roughly cut eye holes.

"More's a comin', Granny." His voice was like the sound of a brood of snakes in a garden. "Beware, 'cause that means only one thing."

She stared back at him, unwilling to respond.

"The Ghostfeast will be upon us soon if'n you and that boy of yer'uns don't put a stop to it. Ain't nothin' I can do neither." The Sin-Eater looked down at his mud-encrusted black boots. "Soon, the Sin-Eater will be no more, and the Ghost-Eater will take his place in Boone Creek. And there ain't nothin' I can do to stop it."

With that, he gave Granny a courteous bow and slipped out the door, closing it behind him.

CHAPTER
ELEVEN

John Tyler's Residence
April 28
5:00 AM

"And I'm telling you, you've been obsessed with Asherah ever since you concocted the irrational notion that she witched you for betraying her, John," Ezekiel Crane yelled at Tyler, his voice unusually frigid. Standing up from Davenport's side, Crane moved over to the front door and flipped the deadbolt locked. Once satisfied it was secure, he grabbed a broom leaning against the wall and laid it down in front of the door. "You've been hiding down in your cellar for the better part of three months—convinced that her curse is coming for you. You're not exactly thinking rationally here."

"Is that why you're broomin' the door, Zeke?" Tyler said with a mocking smile. "Because *I'm* being irrational?"

"The broom," Kili said, nodding to the innocuous object on the floor. "You threw one down into the cellar earlier tonight, and now you're laying it across the door. What exactly is that about?"

He gave a quick shrug. "Legend says that witches—or any supernatural creature for that matter—can't pass a broom without counting all the fronds. They're compulsive that way," he said. "It doesn't exactly banish them, but it slows them down long enough to escape."

"And since Asherah is this town's resident dark witch, there ain't much reason to do that unless she's a threat," Tyler said. "You know as well as I do...she's dangerous."

"There are darker things out there than Ash, John," Crane said, moving from one window to the next, laying garlands of some strange plant along the locks. "I'm warding the house against them, not—"

"Wait a minute...hold on," Kili said, interrupting him. "Granny is a witch. Are you telling me she couldn't resist the urge to Rain Man any broom someone threw at her?"

Her friend cocked his head at her curiously, then chuckled when he grasped the movie reference's meaning. "Granny's not *that* type of witch," he said. "She's a water witch. A diviner. A finder of lost things, if you will. And she's a healer. Though most wouldn't classify it as such, she uses a deep understanding of nature—physics, botany, chemistry—to help those in need. The witches I'm talking about are a bit more..." He paused as if trying to come up with the perfect word. "...*unnatural* than that. These are the witches of old fairy tales, Ms. Kili. The kind that ride brooms and throw young children into stews. Witches like the Willow Hag and her sisters."

"Sisters like Asherah," Tyler said with a sneer. "The Hag, after all, trained her, and you know it."

"And you, my friend, speak without having the full story." Crane's eyes now burned with a rage Kili had never seen from him before. "Take care about such things. As I said before, I think when it comes to her, you are slightly biased."

Kili leaned forward in her chair and turned to look at the former sheriff. "I don't mean to change the subject—lots of info to absorb after all—but what exactly happened between you and Asherah? Last time I was here, I thought you were tight with her and her boss, the drug lord. Thought they'd keep you in office 'til Doomsday, as long as you stayed away from their business. How *did* you get fired?"

Tyler scowled at her, obviously annoyed with her accusations. But knowing she was speaking the gospel truth, he knew better than to argue her point. "I got fired on account that I helped that witch out with some mighty dark things. Experiments she was conductin' during the One-Eyed Jack incident." He pointed a finger at Crane. "Experiments, I might add, on the same corpses what are walkin' 'round town this very day."

"As you know, Ms. Kili," Crane interjected, "several people associated with the treatment of young Leroy Kingston disappeared around the same time as your brother. Our friend here, however, had found their corpses in the Dark Hollows during the exhaustive search for Cian.

"But instead of going public with the discovery, Asherah convinced him she had use for the bodies. We've no idea what exactly she did to them, but…then, you saw the strange mushroom suits the bodies had been buried in at the Devil's Teeth yourself. I suspect Asherah knew of the One-Eyed Jack fungi's unique properties and was working at different ways of harvesting them for Noah McGuffin. Of course, John here knew nothing specific about the operation at the time. He merely succumbed to Ash's rather substantial charms, and aided her with experimental subjects. He eventually came clean, which almost landed McGuffin with an indictment if not for certain unscrupulous members of the state senate."

The room was silent for several awkward seconds as everyone tried to sort out their thoughts. Slowly, Kili became aware of a strange scratching sound from somewhere in the room. She turned toward the couch to see Davenport sitting up and scribbling away at a narrow reporter's notebook.

"...unscrupulous...members...senate," he mumbled to himself before looking up at them with a big grin. "This is amazing stuff. Keep going."

"Mr. Davenport," Crane said, a sincerely warm smile spreading across his face. "It's good to see you feeling better."

"Thanks," Davenport said, returning the smile. "Glad to be alive. But seriously, don't stop. What happened to the bodies after they were buried? How did they come to life again? And what role did this Asherah person's experiments play in these resurrections?"

"See?" Tyler growled, gesturing toward Davenport. "Even *he* doesn't think the witch's involvement is coincidence." He turned to look at Kili. "What about you, FBI? Do you think it's coincidence?"

"I never said it was," Crane growled before Kili could answer. His cold gaze returned to fix on the former sheriff once more. "I believe she's most definitely involved in some way, and I plan on meeting with her soon to find out exactly what she knows.

"However, as formidable as Ash is, I don't think she has the strength necessary to raise people from the dead, either. I'm not sure even the Willow Hag could pull something like that off. No magic is powerful enough to raise the dead. Only God has the power to overcome death. More than likely, we're dealing with something else entirely, but I need more information before I'm comfortable enough to speculate further.

"In the meantime, as I already mentioned to Ms. Kili, the Leechers present the most immediate danger. I believe it's high time we formulate a strategy to deal with *them* before we can move on to the Kindred."

"And how do we do that?" Davenport asked, while scribbling frantically in his notebook. "If those things aren't real, then how can we stop them?"

"Don't confuse supernatural with not being real. They're

real enough." Crane moved over to the living room and sat down in an armchair next to the couch. He then grabbed another pinch of snuff from the can in his pocket, added to what he already had in his mouth, and nodded at Tyler politely when he was given a paper cup. After discreetly spitting into it, he continued. "But the simplest way to deal with them is to find the Witchhunter's bones. Find the bones, stop the haints. Simple as that."

"Once again, I bet if we take a gander at Asherah, we'll find them bones of yours," Tyler growled. "She's the most likely suspect as I can imagine anyway."

"Look," Crane said, pointing at the former law man. "I'm getting rather tired of—"

"What about the Lil' People?" Kili asked abruptly. It was an awkward attempt to break the growing tension between the two, but if it worked, she wasn't going to complain.

"Wait. Stop. Did you just say the *Lil' People*?" Davenport didn't bother trying to hide the smile. "Please tell me we're talking about a group of midget acrobats or something, and not something like...well, like elves or faeries or something like that."

Kili laughed. "This coming from a guy who swears a flock of blood-thirsty gargoyles went on a rampage in New York City last year."

"The Yunwi Tsunsdi are Granny's thing, not mine," Crane interjected. "And she seems to think they've disappeared since the reappearance of the Leechers. Though I wouldn't know, since I've never personally spoken to them. Even if they were around, I'm not entirely sure whether I could make contact with them or not." He paused, fixing her with an unnerving stare. "Unless..."

"What?" she asked. The lump forming in her throat began to constrict her breathing. She felt his suffocating gaze bare down on her—almost accusatory.

"Granny's not the only one that seems to have an affinity for the Little People." Crane nodded at her. "They've spoken to Ms. Kili here."

"But that was just the once." It was a lie. In fact, throughout her entire investigation last year, she'd been haunted by their constant chattering. Even worse, they'd never really stopped. Had actually seemed to follow her back to D.C. when she returned, but she'd told no one this...including Crane. Something about the entire thing bothered her and she fought against the notion that their intrusion into her life was real. If she'd told Crane about it, she'd simply be admitting to herself that it was, and she wasn't quite ready for that. "And I was under the influence of the spores at the time, too."

"Were you under the spores' influence tonight when you heard the Leechers' whispered incantations?"

"No, but..."

"And were you under their influence tonight when you actually laid eyes on the Tailypo?" Crane gave her a knowing grin.

"The what?" Davenport asked. "What the heck's a T-tail, um, poe?"

"Tailypo," Crane repeated. "A creature of the spirit world. A tailless cat-like animal. The stories always reminded me of the Cheshire Cat from Lewis Carroll's tale of *Alice's Adventures in Wonderland*, but of course, I've never seen it, so I could never be sure. The legend says that years ago, a starving hunter shot at the Tailypo one night and took off its tail. The Tailypo has been searching for it ever since."

Unconsciously, Kili slowly reached into her pocket and felt for the fur-covered object inside. Assured that the strange tail-like thing was still there, she felt her heart thud against her chest as she absorbed the story. She hadn't been certain she'd seen anything at all, in the garden. Up until now, she'd pretty much chalked the whole thing up to a panic-induced hallucination. Now, Crane seemed to be implying that what she had observed was one hundred percent real—right alongside the strange song she'd heard at the picnic the day before and the Leecher's strange whispers earlier that night.

"I saw you throw some sort of furry object at the Leechers earlier," Kili felt the unmistakable compulsion to protest, no matter how weak it might sound. "It looked like some kind of cat tail or something to me, but I'm not sure I saw anything..."

"Don't deny it, Ms. Kili," Crane said. "I saw the expression on your face when you first caught sight of it in the circle. Then, later as you ran toward the garden's gate. You saw it. I'd carried the Tailypo talisman with me for just such an emergency... hoping to summon the creature if it became necessary. But I've certainly never seen it with my own eyes. You, however, did. Which, I might add, is not surprising to me in the least. Ever since the encounter with One-Eyed Jack, I'd suspected it...but you have the gift of Sight. You can see—and sometimes hear— the creatures of the spirit realm. The Yunwi Tsunsdi. The Tailypo. Even a certain raven." He gave her a knowing nod. She had indeed seen all these things, including the strange raven that seemed to follow Ezekiel Crane around like an insubstantial shadow. She'd first seen it her initial visit to the Dark Hollows while searching for her brother. Then, later at the hospital when they'd gone to visit Leroy Kingston. But, like the Little People, she'd never confessed these things to Crane. "You can see these things, Ms. Kili, just like Granny. A remarkable gift really."

The expression on his face as he spoke the words, however, was anything but encouraging.

Kili shook her head. "Even if you're right, I'm not sure how that's going to help us right now. I haven't had an encounter with the Yunwi Tsunsdi in over a month. Granny's right. They've disappeared."

Crane's eyes widened at this. He stared at her in silence for several moments, probing the chew in his mouth with his tongue, as if in deep thought. "So you've had encounters with them even after leaving the Hollows? Since returning back to Quantico?"

She chastised herself for the slip, but forced to confront it head on, there was no way she could honestly avoid it now. The Little People had been making unwanted, frequent visits with her, ever since her ordeal in the cavern. The things they'd confided in her were enough to send even the most rational of individuals spiraling mentally out of control. And yet, they persisted in speaking with her...even during those times she'd undeniably asked them to leave her alone.

Slowly, she nodded at Crane in the affirmative.

His grin widened at this. "Excellent! Then we have the next phase of our investigation."

"And that is?" Tyler asked.

"Simple. Ms. Kili and Mr. Davenport will head out to the Dark Hollows." Crane gave a sympathetic shrug to her. "I'm sorry, Ms. Kili. I wouldn't ask it of you, if it was not absolutely necessary. But you need to head to the Devil's Teeth and try to establish a connection with the Yunwi Tsunsdi. It's a place of power. A place where they'd be less fearful of the Leechers. I need you to go there, establish contact with them, and find out what you can."

"But I..." Kili tried to protest, but Crane held up a hand.

"Don't worry if contact can't be made," he said. "Just see what happens. And have no fear...you two aren't going alone. I'll send Bear Boone up there to meet with you. He'll be your guide, and he should be a pretty formidable bodyguard as well."

"What about you?" Tyler asked. "What're you gonna do?"

He gave the question some thought for several seconds. "Exactly what I said I'd do," he finally said. "I'm going to pay Asherah a little visit and find out what she knows."

CHAPTER
TWELVE

Crane Homestead
April 28
6:30 AM

"Esther?" Delores McCrary said, concern evident in her voice. "Esther, you okay?"

Delores had gone home to check on Max a few hours earlier, after the more debilitating effects of the Leechers' Trial had been alleviated. Her sudden intrusion on Esther Crane's private thoughts startled her.

Granny stepped away from the front door, where she'd been absently contemplating both the Sin-Eater's ominous warning and her own fearful premonition, and turned to look back at her old friend. The poor dear. Delores looked like a nervous wreck. But then, she could only imagine how she, herself, must look after the night she'd just had.

"I'm fine, dear. I'm fine. Just thinkin', is all."

"Have you gotten any sleep?" Dee asked. The concern still reflected in her eyes.

Granny shrugged. "Just a little."

"Bad dreams?"

Granny gave a weak smile, then nodded. "Just the usual. Nothin' new about that, I suppose."

"You need to pace yerself, deary," Delores said, putting an arm around the older woman, and leading her over to her reading chair. "Even you have yer limits."

Little Jimmy came in from the kitchen, carrying a glass of ice water and a handful of crackers on a silver tray. He dutifully handed the items to Delores before stepping back to allow the two old women to continue their discussion.

"I'll be okay," Granny said, wiping the sweat from her wrinkled brow. "Any news?"

Delores handed her the water and nodded. "Y-your grandson called." Dee was a dear, but she was just as unnerved by the dark rumors surrounding Ezekiel Crane as everyone else in town. Just as distrustful. "He's fine. He said you weren't answering your phone, so he decided to call me. Told me to tell you...hold on a sec. I wrote it down. I want to get it exactly right." She rifled through the pockets of her apron until she came to a crumpled yellow sticky note with a shout of triumph. "Ah-ha! Here it is. He told me to tell you that it is exactly as you two feared. The *relics*—he didn't elaborate on what those were—have disappeared, but he didn't want you to worry none. Him and his friends were gonna look into some leads they—"

"Friends?" Granny asked, suddenly stiffening. A rush of adrenaline shot through her veins as the dream returned to her mind's eye with crystal clarity. "What friends?"

"Why, I reckon ol' Bear Boone and Sheriff Tyler to start," Delores said with a comforting pat on her hand to reassure her. "He was at Tyler's house when he called, as a matter of—"

"Who else?" She was getting frantic, but she already knew the answer.

"Well, I think he mentioned that reporter feller too," Delores said, oblivious to the rising panic growing in her friend. "Oh yeah, and that sweet Ms. Brennan. She and the reporter were headin' out to the Devil's Teeth from what I gathered. By the way, did I tell you I saw her at the picnic yesterday before all this chaos broke loose, and before I got myself sick with the..."

But as Dee rambled on about her first real meeting with the Brennan girl, Granny's mind had already wandered off to another place. A darker place where the willows were gnarled and decayed, and a great axe hovered in the air waiting to crash down on its unsuspecting victim.

I'm so, so sorry, she thought silently before turning further inward to pray for the days to come.

CHAPTER
THIRTEEN

The Dark Hollows
April 28
8:45 AM

The Devil's Teeth had changed quite a bit since the last time Kili had laid eyes on it, though it was every bit as foreboding and sinister as she remembered. Nestled in a small clearing in the middle of a dank, primordial series of valleys the locals called the Dark Hollows, the monolithic structure was comprised of thirteen giant slabs of marble jutting up from the earth in a circle.

When she'd been there last year, the place had rested on a blanket of emerald green moss covering a small knoll; surrounded by a thick wall of vegetation on three sides and one of the largest crops of pot she'd ever seen—cultivated by the town's infamous Noah McGuffin—on the fourth. Now, the rough tracks of bulldozer treads dotted the terrain, which had churned up the moss-topped soil around the monument. Numerous miniature orange flags stuck up here and there near the stones, as evidence of recent archaeological excavations to investigate the giant skeletons interred centuries before within the megalith. And perhaps most notably, the acres of marijuana plants that had once canvassed the eastern slope of the valley were completely gone—a charred patch of earth where the crop had been torched by authorities, was all that remained.

Despite the dramatic change, the oppressive, perhaps arcane, force that had clung to the Teeth for centuries was still all too present, and Kili found herself shivering involuntarily at the sight before her as she, Davenport, and the burly forest ranger known as Bear Boone, walked up the slope to the monolith.

"Holy wow," Davenport murmured, his eyes wide with disbelief, while taking in every facet of the structure. After a few awe-struck moments, he quietly brought his camera up and snapped a handful of shots. "This is absolutely unbelievable. It's like…like looking at…"

"Like looking at a set of fangs pushing up from the ground," Kili said with a nod. "Yeah, I know. Hence, the name of the place."

"Are you'uns sure you need to actually go inside, Ms. Brennan?" Bear asked. His normally deep, baritone voice warbled as he spoke, elevating a few octaves like a prepubescent boy. "I know what Zeke says 'bout the place. That it was never haunted by One-Eyed Jack or his brothers…but there's still odd goin's on around here, I tell ya. The spores may all be gone, but I ain't entirely sure the spirits have followed suit, if you take my meanin'."

Kili smiled up at the large bearded man. Of all the citizens of Boone Creek she'd met on her first visit here, Bear had been the most kind. Understanding. Almost childlike in many ways. Standing almost seven feet tall, with a sturdy, muscular frame to match, he was extremely formidable to look at. But within the giant forest ranger beat a heart of pure, mushy gold. His only fault, if Kili had to say, was that what he gained in sheer size and strength, he lost in a strict adherence to the folklore and superstitions he'd grown up with—which in turn, affected his courage.

The first time he'd guided her and Crane up to the Teeth, he'd basically abandoned them to their fate. Sure, he'd remained on the edge of the forest watching over them, but he wouldn't step foot within the circle of stones. It looked to Kili as if he was having the same hesitations now, as well.

"It's okay, Bear," she said still smiling. "If you want to wait by the truck and keep watch, that'll be fine. I don't even know what I'm doing here myself. Ezekiel seemed to think it would help, so I agreed to come and check the place out. We'll just be a few minutes, okay?"

The big man gave her a sheepish nod and backed slowly away from the monument. "No need to go back to the truck," he said after backpedaling about fifty yards away. "I'll just stand guard right here. How's that?"

"Perfect!" She threw him an encouraging thumbs up and turned back to the Teeth with a nervous sigh. If she was honest, she'd rather hang back with him than take a single step past the twenty-foot stone directly in front of her. Despite her own trepidation, it looked like she had no other choice. Crane had told her that if there was any hope of communicating with the Yunwi Tsunsdi, it would require coming here. Though, truth be told, she'd spent quite a long time getting the little buggers to quiet down once they'd attached themselves to her. She wasn't exactly chomping at the bit to bring their constant chattering back into her life. But, she supposed, she had no choice.

Taking a deep breath and pulling her backpack up over her shoulder, she nodded to Davenport and stepped inside the circle. Upon entering, she felt an immediate increase in the gravity around her; as if giant invisible hands had begun pressing down on her shoulders.

This is new, she thought, moving to the center of the circle, where a great stone altar rested.

"What now?" Davenport said in a hushed whisper. One glance at his wide eyes told her he was feeling just as uncomfortable.

"Now, we do what Crane told us to do before we left this morning," she said while reaching into her pack and pulling out a one-pound bag of sugar, a bag of gummy bears, three shot glasses, and an unopened bottle of Jim Beam bourbon. She placed the items on the altar, then reached once more into the bag and pulled out a strange looking set of wind chimes made up of glass shards painted pitch black.

"What are those for?" Davenport asked, nodding to the chimes as she drove a shaft into the soil and attached them to it.

"Long story, but basically, Crane says the chimes will signal us if any spirits are nearby." Kili paused for a second, looking at the darkened glass. "Oops, sorry. The black glass means that they'll detect any dark or dangerous spirits lurking nearby. They're sort of an alarm system for what we're about to do."

The reporter gave her a sidelong glance, as if expecting her to fill him in on some unspoken joke. When it finally sunk in that she was being serious, he scratched at his head with a few conceding nods. "Okay," he said. "I'll take your word for it. So what's the whiskey and sugar for? You trying to take advantage of me in an Indian graveyard? Kinky."

Rolling her eyes, she ripped open the bag of sugar and poured the contents into a circle on top of the altar. "Crane always uses tobacco for this little ceremony," she explained, trying to ignore Davenport's flirtations. "But he says it has to be something the individual actually uses, for it to work. Apparently, the Little People are huge fans of tobacco, candy, and booze. So I figured if I offered them at least two of the three things on their Christmas list, they might be more likely to show up."

Once the sugar circle was complete, she laid out a pile of

gummy bears in the center, then filled each of the three glasses with whiskey.

"And what? They're going to drink all that?" Davenport asked.

"Nope. You and I are. Well, we're going to leave one glass for them. But our drinking will symbolize our intentions of friendship with them. It's a gesture of good will to have a drink with a friend, after all, right?"

"Um, sure," he said, not entirely convinced. "But I'm curious. Was Mr. Crane right about you? You've actually seen these... these...um, what exactly are these things anyway?"

Rubbing her forehead with the palm of her hand, she let out another sigh. They'd already gone through this at least three or four times. Granted, if she was honest with herself, she had to admit she'd had just as difficult a time with the concept of the Little People when she'd first been told about them. As a matter of fact, she'd been far more skeptical. The reporter had apparently experienced some pretty strange things in his time, so it was a little easier for him to accept...bizarre phenomenon and crazy ideas.

"The Yunwi Tsunsdi is the name given to a race of spiritual beings, by the Cherokee tribes that used to live in the region, before the white man arrived," she said while still placing all the objects of the ritual in the places and ways described to her by Crane. "Best I can figure it, they are the Native American equivalent to the European myth of the Little People, or more specifically, faeries."

"And these faeries...these Little People," he said, snapping a photo of the ritually adorned stone altar. "They're real? They actually exist? You've seen them?"

Kili shrugged. "Honestly, I don't know. I mean, I've heard them. Sure. All the freakin' time." She let out a frustrated sigh. "And something certainly helped Ezekiel and me escape from the cavern my brother brought me to last year. Something unseen. And while under the influence of the One-Eyed Jack spores, I hallucinated an entire conversation—in Gaelic, I might add—with the creatures." She turned to look the reporter in the eyes. "And when I returned to Quantico, in the middle of the night, while deep in sleep, I dreamt about them. Such strange dreams. So real. But I don't think I've ever actually *seen* them... I mean, while alert anyway."

A gentle breeze swept between the stones of the Teeth, whipping Kili's hair in front of her face, but she paid no attention. Her mind was on other things. Dreams. Visions. The dark silhouette of the tailless Tailypo she'd seen the previous night. The strange, sad dirge she'd heard at the picnic the day before.

Why was Crane so convinced she could communicate with the Yunwi Tsunsdi? That she could summon them? Even more unbelievable, that she could compel them to give her the information they needed, to discover the truth about what was going on around here? She wasn't like Granny. She'd never held conversations with them—well, at least not while she was conscious, that is. So what made her enigmatic friend believe this would be any different?

"Kili?" Davenport's voice sounded nervous. Shaking. But she didn't have time to answer any more of his inane questions. The sooner she got this over with, the sooner they could get out of here.

"Not now, Alex." She didn't look at him as she took a shot glass from within the circle and nodded to the second glass, indicating that the reporter should take it. If only the wind would ease up. The speed had picked up considerably now, and she could hardly see in front of her with her scarlet red hair whipping about her face, as it was.

"But Kili, I really think..."

"Alex! We need to do this now," she said, her tone a little more biting than she'd intended. "Take a drink."

"But the chimes..."

The moment the words eeked from his lips, she suddenly understood. The wind that had been building. Why had she not paid attention to it? The glass and metal shards of the chimes were clashing against each other, drumming up a cacophony of chaotic sound.

Oh, crap. This can't be good.

Crane had given her the device almost as an afterthought, just before they pulled out of Tyler's driveway that morning. He'd used a similar set of chimes the last time they'd been here, though that time he'd claimed it was only to determine the direction the wind was blowing. However, he'd also shared the more superstitious, Appalachian use of the contraption. Though she'd never fully bought into his tale, he'd told her chimes such as these were used to detect the presence of ghosts. The hill people had a deep-seated belief in such things. They felt that ghosts lurked in almost every shadow, waiting to do mischief the moment a mortal's back was turned. The chimes would help the living to know when *not* to turn their proverbial backs.

But when her old friend had given her these chimes—the one with the glass shards of obsidian black—he'd explained that these were slightly different. Because her mission was to attempt to conjure up the Yunwi Tsunsdi in the darkest, most mysterious section of the southeast United States, he'd felt a more specific warning system would be necessary. Something designed to detect the darker, less friendly spirits in the area. Spirits that would possibly want nothing more than to make her suffer for trespassing on their domain.

Slowly, her eyes lifted from the altar and turned toward the suddenly quiet Davenport, only to find him being held by two brutish men wearing dark, hooded robes. A quick glance over their shoulder revealed that Bear was equally as indisposed, with another robed figure holding him at bay with a sawed-off shotgun.

"Well, well, well," came a familiar, gravelly voice behind her.

"If I recollect, I warned you about coming to this here place last time you were in town."

Kili turned to see the hooded figure of the 'Reverend' Tom Thornton, owner and operator of the Tegalta Mining Company, as well as Boone Creek's very own cult leader. Normally rather small in stature, except for an obvious beer paunch, he seemed much larger now with his robes cascading down from his shoulders and an AK-47 gripped tightly in his hands.

Last she'd heard, Thornton and several of his 'church' were wanted by federal authorities in connection with the death of her brother's research assistant, Miles Marathe. Ezekiel Crane had proven they'd shot Miles with a shotgun after he was already technically dead, but the feds still wanted to have a little chat with the prune-faced man nonetheless.

Thornton pulled back his hood to reveal the white minister's collar around his neck, a mockery, if not outright blasphemy, to the office it represented. "This here's our sacred land," he said while stroking his thick, salt and pepper beard. "And you ain't got that devil Crane 'round to witch us this time."

Irresistibly, Kili burst out with a laugh. "Seriously?" she asked. "You guys openly worship some weirdo gods called *Those Who Cannot Be Named* or some crazy name like that, and you say Ezekiel is of the Devil? Really?"

The instant the words left her mouth, her heart vaulted into her throat. Why on Earth would she try to goad these guys? One look into Thornton's deep, black eyes told her he was in no mood for games, and here she was taunting him on mere impulse.

The hardening of the man's face told her he'd not appreciated the jab in the slightest. In response, he nodded casually to the muscle-bound goons holding Davenport. Understanding the silent command, the largest figure balled up his fists and struck the reporter across the chin, dropping him to the ground. Another one of Thornton's men raised Davenport's cane high above his head and brought it down on the man's legs in three powerful blows.

"Stop it!" Kili cried. "Just stop!" Immediately, they complied with her plea, and she turned to face Thornton. "What do you want?"

Smiling lasciviously at her, a rancid line of decaying, yellow teeth spread from under his bushy mustache. "I want you to come with me, darlin'," he said with a chuckle. "Someone mighty important wants to have a bit of a pow-wow with ya. Someone mighty important indeed."

"Who?"

"Don't matter none who it is, I reckon. You're comin' with us, if you don't want yer pretty little beau here and that good fer nothin' ranger to come to harm."

Kili's resolve was made up. It might cost them their lives, but she wasn't going anywhere until she knew who wanted to see her. At the very least, she hoped Davenport or Bear could let Cranc know where she'd been taken.

To demonstrate her determination, she squared her shoulders and glared at the cultist with unabashed defiance. "Who?"

Thornton's black eyes locked onto hers for several, excruciating seconds. She watched as the man's jaw moved back and forth, as if he was grinding his teeth with irritation. Finally, he revealed that same Death's Head grin she'd come to know so well, and nodded.

"Sure. No harm in tellin' ya now," he said with a hoarse chuckle. "But you're gettin' quite the honor fer an outsider. You've been summoned for tea and biscuits by the Willow Hag herself."

CHAPTER
FOURTEEN

The McGuffin Estate
April 28
9:55 AM

The McGuffin Estate was nestled in a heavily forested region of Jasper County, just a few miles south of the Dark Hollows—the perfect locale to run an international drug empire amidst a predominantly superstitious culture. The manor house, an old Victorian mansion built soon after the Civil War, was well maintained, with large, Corinthian columns along its front porch, painted in off-white and contrasting perfectly with the rich burgundy of the outside façade. Two good-sized balconies protruded from the second floor on both wings, overlooking the gorgeously manicured lawn of emerald green grass. Shrubbery, perfectly aligned, ran in rows along a blacktopped driveway, stretching for a quarter of a mile.

Ezekiel Crane sat in his pickup truck at the front gate, waiting for someone to answer the call-box button he'd just pressed. His eyes swept past the fifteen-foot wrought iron gate in front of him and scanned his surroundings. From what he could see out there, Noah McGuffin employed patrols of well-armed security guards with dogs, walking the perimeter in irregular, seemingly random intervals. From where his truck idled, he'd been able to spy at least nine different infrared security cameras, along with a handful of motion detectors along the path, as well. And he was fairly certain the place would have an extra, very *special* layer of defenses set up by Asherah herself.

He shuddered to imagine what those might be.

A bird cawed outside his truck, breaking his attention. His head swiveled outside the driver's side window until he caught sight of the familiar raven that had haunted him since the day of his infernal curse. The bird glared at him with unsavory black eyes.

"Don't suppose you'd be inclined to help me with this little investigation, would you?"

But the raven continued to stare silently back at him, quite comfortably perched on the highest point of the fence.

"Didn't think so."

"Can I help you?" crackled an elderly female voice with a stilted Mexican accent, from the call-box, interrupting his one-way conversation with the enigmatic bird.

"Yes, ma'am. Ezekiel Crane. Here to see Ms. Richardson."

There was a long pause. Though he knew it was utterly ridiculous, Crane had the sense that it was a particularly nervous pause. He could just imagine the maid or whoever was manning the call box, developing a state of frightful indecision at that very moment. She would have no doubt heard of him... more than likely would be just as frightened of him as most others in Boone Creek, but she was probably even more terrified of her mistress (and rightly so). A meeting of two such as they could not be a good thing in the maid's eye. Oddly enough, he suspected there would be little concern over how Noah McGuffin would respond to such a meeting. In recent months, Noah had become less and less visible among the community, and speculation abounded about the cause. Some, of course, believed him to be just one more victim of the malevolent One-Eyed Jack. Others believed he'd been witched long ago by the 'Harlot of the Manor' and was now probably on death's door. And still, there were other rumors even more ludicrous than these.

Crane, on the other hand, believed the reason for McGuffin's withdrawal was probably much more mundane, though he wasn't naïve enough to discount anything nefarious behind it all. No, he had become unequivocally convinced that Asherah was actually the one running the illustrious drug empire now. The notorious drug lord, if Crane was not mistaken, had long since become little more than a puppet for Ash's own machinations. As a matter of fact, if he had to guess, he would say that the lecherous old man no longer even resided within the manor house itself, but more than likely had been relegated to one of the more run-down staff houses that dotted the estate.

"Um, what is thees about?" the woman asked, her accent becoming even more pronounced than before.

"She'll know," he said in his best soothing tone. "Trust me, my dear. She *will* want to speak with me."

Nearly sixty seconds passed before the motor at the gate began to whir and the doors swung open. Taking that as an invitation, Crane drove up the winding driveway until he came to a roundabout at the front of the house. A man dressed in a very expensive black suit, obviously packing a concealed weapon underneath the well-tailored jacket, was standing there to open the door of Crane's truck, once it was in park.

After Crane climbed out, the man motioned for him to turn around and face the windshield of his vehicle. Crane complied without protest while the man gave him a quick pat down, only confiscating a folding case knife that had been attached to Crane's belt. Satisfied there were no other weapons, the security guard ushered him into the house, led him down a long hallway, and directed him to sit on an antique divan in the downstairs' parlor.

"Ms. Richardson will be here shortly," the man said sternly. Unlike the old woman on the call-box, there wasn't the faintest trace of an accent in the man's speech. His size, close-cropped hair, and disposition easily identified him as ex-military. Probably special forces of some kind. Obviously not local, no-nonsense, and deadly. "I'll be right outside the doors if you need anything."

It was a warning. Or a threat. Crane figured it really didn't matter which. If push came to shove, he was more than capable of handling the man. He'd just need to keep his eyes, as well as his options, open. He didn't believe Asherah truly wanted to harm him—she'd had plenty of opportunity for that since his return to Boone Creek the previous year—but she was not opposed to playing games. Sometimes very cruel, dangerous games. Despite the inexplicable connection he had with the woman, he could never trust her...never truly let his guard down, where she was concerned.

Crane sat back on the divan and took in the room, while waiting for his hostess. The parlor was as lush and extravagant as the rest of the place, sporting darkened, cherry-wood floors, an exquisitely rare Persian rug, and claw-footed furniture straight from the Edwardian era. Bookshelves, from floor to ceiling, were built into two entire walls and were filled with ancient leather-bound tomes running the gamut from Chaucer and Spenser to rare arcane texts exploring everything from witchcraft to demonology. One section of the bookcase in particular caught Crane's eye. Standing up, he walked over to it and shook his head in quiet amusement. The entire section of interest comprised a veritable treasure trove of old, dog-eared, paper-back romance novels with yellowing paper and ridiculously silly covers featuring muscle-bound pirates ravishing women.

"See any you haven't read yet, Ezekiel?" cooed Asherah

Richardson's silky feline voice from behind him, as he rifled through the titles.

Crane slowly turned to see Asherah's lovely mocha-colored face smiling brightly at him. Her teeth were as white as porcelain, and they seemed to gleam in the soft light of the Tiffany's chandelier above. She'd always thought it amusing that he, who had a handful of advanced degrees in a variety of disciplines— including a Master of Arts in the Humanities—could be so enthralled by the ridiculous 'drivel', as she put it, of trashy romance novels. Though he'd hardly admit the vice to anyone, he had found them immensely cathartic over the years—an escape from the insanity that had ruled over most of his life. She'd never understood his own disdain for the preternatural world, in which they both lived. Never fathomed his need to delve into the mundane, albeit melodramatic, of which the romance novels allowed a glimpse.

"A couple, actually," he said with a polite nod. "But at the moment, I have more pressing matters to discuss with you than literary criticism."

"Oh, sounds ominous." With puckered lips and fluttering eyelashes, she gave him a mocking look of wide-eyed innocence, gestured for him to take a seat, then glided across the room in his direction. As she moved, Crane soaked in everything about her. From her flawless light brown skin underneath her form-fitting, low-cut sundress, to her long shapely legs and bare feet with painted toenails, the color of blood. Her kinky, black hair fell past her shoulders, forcing her unconscious habit of brushing it back behind her ear. Slowly, seductively, she moved over to the same settee he occupied and melted into it beside him. After waiting a few moments in a silent, but similar appraisal to his, she nodded. "All right, Ezekiel Crane, what would you like to discuss?"

He stared at her with a single raised eyebrow. "Just like that?" he asked, amusement flavoring his words.

"Whatever do you mean?"

A cockeyed grin spread up one side of his face. "No games? No flirtations? Straight to business, just like that?"

"What can I say? I'm a business woman now, Ezekiel," she said playfully. "No time for such adolescent trivialities like in the old days. You have a problem, you came to me. I'm touched. Honored. I'll do whatever I can to help you." She paused, mirroring his own lopsided smile. "Besides, plenty of time for fun and games after."

"Ash, you and I need to talk about the—"

"How's Tyler doing?" she blurted.

Crane sighed, shaking his head. "I thought we weren't going to do this."

"Do what?"

"The games, Asherah. The games. You know exactly why I'm here, and so, as usual, you want to stall...want to avoid the serious discussion."

"Maybe I don't want to give away anything for free?" she said smoothly. "Maybe this is a game of tit for tat. You scratch my back and...mmmm...I'll scratch yours." Her smile broadened. "So, I'll repeat myself—something I don't do for too many men... How's my old friend, John Tyler? He doesn't call. Doesn't write. Makes a girl feel completely unwanted."

"All right, Ash. I'll play it your way," he said, his voice stern and without a trace of humor in it. "If you've hexed him, call it off. The man's about to die from the anxiety of it all."

She giggled quietly at this, then tilted her head back for a full throated fit of laughter. Crane's own fierce façade cracked, and he soon found himself laughing right alongside her.

"A hex, eh?" she asked, after they'd both caught their breath. She wiped an errant tear from her eye as she grinned at him. "Really?"

"Yes." He continued to smile as he said it, though he reined in his own amusement. "Poor man's wasting away in his canning cellar. Hasn't taken a shower in weeks, and he's about as paranoid as you can get. He's been absolutely insufferable to work with, I can assure you."

She laughed some more, but veered away from the subject. "And I take it you've performed all the necessary rituals to break such a curse, if one *had* been cast at him?"

Crane nodded.

"Had him carry a glass of water across a creek?"

"Yes."

"Carved his name, as well as my own, in a stick..."

"Buried it for seven days, then stomped on it with my boot. Yes," he said with a frown. "All of them I knew. A few I didn't and Granny had to do. But the man will not allow himself a moment's peace. He continues to torture himself with the belief that you will get him for his perceived betrayal." He paused, then leaned toward her and whispered soberly in her hear, "So I'm going to need you to leave him alone."

"But you just said you performed all the hex breakers yourself. Surely you don't think..."

"I know you, Ash. I won't ask you again. Call off the curse."

"Can I get you something to drink?" Another deflection, Crane knew. "Some Apple Pie moonshine perhaps? I also have the straight stuff if you'd rather have that." She paused, eyeing him for a bit. "Nah, I know. You'll just have some sweet tea."

Without waiting for a response, she picked up a small bell on the coffee table in front of them and rang it. "Vincent?" she mewled. "I need you." Immediately, the armed thug poked his head in, his Sig Sauer 9 millimeter firmly in hand and ready for action. A distinct look of disappointment flashed across his face, when she instructed him to bring in some refreshments for the two of them, but he complied without complaint.

"Ash," Crane's face was suddenly somber. "This isn't a social call, and you know it. I gave you what you wanted about Tyler."

"And threatened me to recall a curse I may or may not have cast too, I might add."

"You know as well as I do, there's no need to witch the man. If you weren't already finished doing whatever it was you were doing to those bodies, we would have never found them. John would have never had a need to come clean about his part in it all. Knowing you, I'm willing to bet he somehow did you a favor in it all."

"And yet you've allowed him to live in terror of me. You know the curse. You know the fix. You could have ended it any time you liked."

He shrugged. "As cold as it sounds, it served a purpose."

"You mean giving you and that red-headed hussy a place to hide from them that might be looking for you?"

"Leave her out of it," Crane said, his voice little more than a growl.

Asherah leaned away from him, her eyes wide. "Oh..." She paused, looking him up and down in sudden understanding. "You know, don't you? Know that she's been marked? She's been—"

"I've suspected. And she's off limits, Ash. She's under my protection, and I'll see that no harm comes to her while she's in town." He let his words sink in before adding: "The Hag'll have to find another plaything, and so will you. Do we have an understanding?"

She repeated her previous pouty face and held up two hands in mock surrender. "I do," she said. "But you know as well as I that the *Mater Matris* won't be so easy to convince. Once she's set her mark on someone, there is no room for appeal."

"I'll deal with the Willow Hag when the time comes," he said, waving the notion away with a gesture. "Right now, we've got more important concerns. Now listen, I need you to—"

The parlor doors swung open again, and Vincent came in carrying a tray with two large glasses filled with ice, a pitcher of tea, and a bowl of sliced lemons. He placed the tray on the coffee table and looked down at his mistress with subservient, if not jealous, eyes.

"That'll be all, Vincent. Thank you," she said, leaning forward to fill a glass for Crane and then one for herself. She waited for the guard to leave the room and handed the drink to her guest. "You were saying?"

He took a sip of tea, then nodded. "I was just saying that I need—"

"Let's go away together," she interrupted, placing a hand on his leg and leaning into him. Her lips lightly brushed against his rough-shaven cheeks as she continued. "Why can't we just leave this place behind, travel the world, and see what sort of trouble we can get into together?" She smiled up at him. The smile of a hungry shark.

"Ash, please. This is a serious matter." He brushed her hand away and stood up.

"So was my suggestion."

"No, you're just trying to avoid everything."

"And why shouldn't I? *Leechers*, Ezekiel. Leechers."

"And apparently, the walking dead as well," he said, his eyes narrowing as he looked down at her. "Or rather, people who were proven clinically dead—people experimented on by you, I might add—who currently seem to be very much alive."

"I'm not concerned with them," she said, exploding from the couch to stare him square in the eyes. "It's the Leechers. Right now they might have another agenda…might be looking for someone else, but you know if *she* gets her hands on those bones again, they'll eventually turn their sights on you. Especially if you poke your nose into the Mother's business. Why can't we just leave? Now. While we still can."

"What exactly did you do to them, Asherah?" He ignored her questions, but couldn't resist the urge to draw closer to her. "The Leechers are after whoever brought the Kindred back to life.

Now, my guess is that means they're hunting the Willow Hag herself—only she'd be powerful enough for something like that —but I can't help thinking you're involved in all this somehow." Unconsciously, their bodies drew closer until they were nearly pressing together. "If I can make that leap of logic, then chances are, whoever's controlling the Leechers at the moment will too, Ash. Please. I want to help you with this, but you've got to tell me everything."

They stood inches apart for several long seconds, staring back at each other in silent, but equally desperate pleas. Whatever was going on, Crane knew that Asherah was scared. Very scared. And anything that worried someone like her was definitely worthy of respect. He also knew that she was fully aware that he would not back down from his inquiry, no matter how seductive she might be.

After nearly a minute of silence, she threw up her arms and spun around, giving a frustrated growl. "All right! Fine!" she said. "Believe it or not, I was trying to help you. I mean, with the experiments."

"What? How do you mean?"

"You know exactly how I mean."

"Humor me."

She glared at him, obviously tired of any games where she couldn't control the rules. "No."

"Okay. Then tell me why seven former cadavers you had been playing with are suddenly up and walking the streets of Boone Creek. Any theories?"

She turned away from him and moved over to the bookcase, pretending to peruse her selection of books in silence.

"Ash, if you know something…"

"Honestly, Crane, I don't know what to say!" She refused to turn around to look him in the face as she said it. "Yes, I experimented on them. Tried some tricks I'd learned from the Mother and even a few new ones certain recent business partners have been dabbling with...hoping to fulfill my old promise to you. But it all failed miserably. I'm telling you now, you're asking the wrong person."

"Then who should I ask? The *Mater*? Is she behind it all?"

More hesitation.

"Ash, I'm not looking to point blame here. But if I can figure out who the Leechers are searching for, I'll have a much better chance of discovering who is controlling them. If I can do that, then I can stop the Leechers once and for all. So tell me...did the Hag raise the Kindred?"

Asherah shook her head slowly. "I don't believe so...at least, not directly anyway."

"What do you mean, *not directly*?"

She let out a sigh, and with a shrug, she told him of her encounter with the Willow Hag the day before. Told him about the unwitting 'apprentice' the woman had alluded to and the Hag's desire for the Leechers to turn their sights to both Asherah and Crane.

"And she didn't give any clue as to who this apprentice might be?"

Asherah shook her head. "No. She was too giddy with delight over the prospect of the Witchhunter and his haints coming after me. Once she'd revealed that, our discussion was pretty much over. I blacked out, and when I woke up, I was home. In my own bed, with no further discussion."

"Then who, Ash? If it's not the Hag, who should I be talking to?"

Slowly, she turned around from the bookcase and stared at him for several uncomfortable seconds. "Ezekiel, I need to tell you..."

Crane's cell phone suddenly rang. Holding up his index finger to silently ask Asherah to hold on, he looked down at the phone's display where it read: BEAR BOONE. Pressing the

TALK button, he brought the phone up and spoke. "Bear, how are thing going on your end?"

"Zeke, we got trouble," the forest ranger said, before explaining what had happened at the Devil's Teeth. When he got to where Thornton's thugs shoved Kili into the back of the cult leader's Jeep, he nearly choked up. "I'm so sorry, buddy. I screwed up big time."

Crane's heart raced as he absorbed this new chain of events. "It's okay, Bear. I'll be right there. Hang on." The words felt hollow as soon as he spoke them, but there was little more he could say. He hung up and glanced at Asherah. "Thornton's taken Kili Brennan."

As expected, the island-born witch showed little concern. "I told you, Ezekiel…she's been marked by the Mater. The curse is surely already upon her…but then, you already knew that, didn't you? Something in the way your eyes glared when I mentioned it before. Already she's begun having the Sight, hasn't she?"

"I have to go to the Willow Grove," he said, ignoring her accusations.

"It's folly, Ezekiel," she said plaintively. "There's nothing you can do for her now. And you showing up at the Grove unbidden will only insult the Willow Hag even more. She'll take it out on your friend."

"Will you help me find it?"

She looked up at him in surprise. "You can't honestly ask that of me. Not after what we went through the last time. Not after all I've given up for you. I'm not going to let you throw your life away."

"And I can't let my friend suffer the fate I left vacant, Ash," he said. "I just can't."

Asherah nodded at this, before shrugging. "I can't help you in this. After all, I was the one who helped you to vacate said fate. I won't let you throw it away." After that, she walked up to him, leaned forward for one last kiss, then gestured toward the door.

Understanding the silent request, he obeyed and left the mansion without another word.

ASHERAH RICHARDSON WATCHED as Crane's truck melted into the winding vegetation of the estate's driveway. The meeting had not gone exactly as she'd hoped, though she didn't know why she'd expected anything different from the infernally stubborn man.

Why? Why wouldn't you listen? she thought, pouring a glass of bourbon and setting the decanter back on its metal tray. They both knew what was coming. Both had been involved in the Willow Hag's summons so many years before. Both had defied her. But Crane had received the worst end of the deal. While she'd merely been shunned by her former teacher and mentor, Crane had been cursed. He'd been marked—in a similar way as the Brennan woman was now. A mark that would drive the woman to the verge of insanity for one particularly distasteful reason.

Crane had been strong enough to resist. Strong enough to learn to utilize the curse in such a way that it actually became a blessing. Asherah doubted the redheaded FBI woman could handle the strain for very long.

She sighed and downed the glass of Kentucky's finest. She wasn't sure which was worse: Crane running headlong into the lion's den of the Willow Grove or those accursed Leechers. No matter who their current master was targeting, they would eventually turn their malicious eyes upon their eternal mission. The Witchhunter's mission. The mission that was sure to end with the death of the man she loved.

As she turned back to the window, staring up into the noon-day sky, the old nursery rhyme she'd learned so long ago came back to her. The words formed on the tip of her tongue, beckoning for a release. Reluctantly...nervously...she relented and gave the words voice:

That ol' Mother Leary, who spurned things less dreary
Ne'er knew the right thing to do.
She cottoned the haints and witched the saints
'Til her head, the Leechers did hew.

Now ol' Lady Fanny, nary anyone's granny
Had just settled down for a stew.
She'd ground the bones, of childrens with stones
'Til her head, the Leechers did hew.

When ol' Bonnie Mary stood a'hexin' her quarry
The blood of yan goozler did spew.
The witch whooped and she hollered, and young men they all follered
'Til her head, the Leechers did hew.

Now the Leechers, they came for the witches to hang
'Til the Willow Hag did come along.
And now they all pray for that glorious day
When her head, the Leechers will hew.

A shiver washed down Asherah's spine as she reflected on the old verse. The Leechers' axes were swinging again, and Ezekiel Crane's head would soon be on the chopping block along with anyone else the haints deemed a target.

"God help us all," she muttered to herself, as grief threatened to overwhelm her. "Please."

CHAPTER
FIFTEEN

Briarsnare Marsh
April 28
5:00 PM

The rusted-out, mud-caked Jeep Cherokee Kili had been stuffed into, rolled to a stop, followed immediately by the sound of car doors opening and footsteps trudging around the side of the vehicle. She had no idea where she was or how far they'd traveled from the Devil's Teeth. After being taken by Tom Thornton and his cultists, she'd been bound by zip ties and her face was covered by a sweat-stained pillow case. Then she had been shoved into the cargo area of the Jeep. She'd tried to keep track of time as best she could, but the terrain was so rugged and she'd been jostled about so roughly, she'd been unable to keep up her concentration for long.

Before she had a chance to recover her bearings, the Jeep's rear hatch flew open and a pair of rough, calloused hands grabbed hold of her ankles and yanked her out. She'd half-expected they'd let her fall to the ground, but at the last minute, another pair of hands took hold of her arms, just below the armpits, and eased her to her feet. Seconds later, the pillow case was whipped from her head, and she found herself blinking back at Reverend Thornton's scowling face.

"Welcome to Briarsnare Marsh," he said, gesturing to the swampy landscape around them.

She looked around, still blinking away the harsh light after being blindfolded for so long. Eventually, she took in her surroundings with a mixture of awe and dread. It was indeed a marsh, as far as she could tell...or rather, the remnants of an ancient lake that once covered the land for miles all around. She was surrounded by high grass, as tall as her waist, for as far as her eye could see. Stocks of cattails and reeds jutted up from the mud, some as high as her own head. And though the water that blanketed the area now appeared to be only ankle to knee-high in places, the pungent smell of algae and decay permeated the stagnant air with its oppressive rankness.

"Okay, so what happens now?" Kili asked, half-expecting him to put a bullet in her head and leave her in the marsh for scavengers to pick clean.

In response, he nodded to someone standing behind her, and she felt the cold touch of steel, as a knife sliced through her bonds. She pulled her arms forward, rubbing at her abraded wrists, while keeping her eyes fixed on her captor.

"Simple, Ms. Brennan," Thornton said with an amused sneer. He nodded to the goon once more, who reached into the Jeep, pulled out an old, rusted machete, and handed it to him. Kili felt her throat tighten as she stared at the ugly looking blade. "You're gonna follow that trail right there." He pointed to a small, indistinct path to her right. "You're gonna keep to the trail no matter what. No veering left or right now, understand?" He waited for her nod before continuing. "Then, eventually, you're gonna come upon a grove of old weeping willow trees. When you do, I reckon the rest will become pretty evident in time."

"And what are you going to do with that machete?" she asked anxiously.

At its mention, he gave it a careful once over, felt the tip of the blade with the flat of his thumb, and grinned. "They don't call it Briars*nare* for no reason. It ain't an easy path to get through. Plus, there's some mighty nasty critters—copperheads, rattlers, and the like—lurking in those fields of cattails, I can tell ya that. The Willow Hag wants you safe 'til she can have her own fun with ya. The machete is to make sure you can take care of business in there, if ya need to."

He held out the blade hesitantly, then pulled it back the moment she reached for it. "Uh-uh…just don't get no funny ideas," he said with his snaggle-toothed grin. "Terrance there will shoot you dead, right where you are, if you decide to use that thing on me."

Kili considered it, then nodded her assent. Thornton then handed her the machete and stepped back. "What if I decide to wait until you guys leave and then backtrack out of here?" Kili asked. "What if I decide I don't want to talk to this *hag* of yours?"

The Reverend glanced over her shoulder, presumably at Terrence, and they both started giggling uncontrollably. The whole thing was eerie as all get out. Two grown men, giggling like little kids who'd just heard the word 'boobies.'

"I was being serious," she said, the machete tucked under her arm as she pulled her hair back and tied it into a ponytail, before turning her attention back to her two captors.

After several unsettling seconds, Thornton composed himself, hitched his blue jeans up against his beer belly, and sniffed the air with a derisive snort. "Well, honey pie, that wouldn't be the brightest thing you might do," he said finally. "First of all, the Willow Hag will see who the Willow Hag chooses to see. No one can escape her attention, if she so wills it. Second, you're in the furthest end of the Dark Hollows. The sun will be setting in about..." He glanced up at the sky, "...two and a half hours. And you know just as good as me that wanderin' the hollars at night can be deadly dangerous. No ma'am, I'd wager you wouldn't last through the night if ya decided to go it on yer own."

"Okay," she said, absorbing his explanation. Only two hours until dusk? How long had they been driving? It had been morning when they'd taken her. But she decided to pass on that question for something a little more pressing. "Then how do I get back? I mean, after the Willow Hag and I have had this little chat she's gone to such trouble to have."

More snickering from the two cultists, but Thornton managed an answer nonetheless. "Well, I reckon that all depends on *what* she wants to chat with you about. But fear not, pretty lady...if the Mother Hag wants to let you go home, she'll see to it that it happens. You can mark my words on that."

Unable to argue with his logic, she opened her mouth to ask another question.

"Ms. Brennan, yer losin' daylight," he said. "Best you get movin'."

"But one more thing...Mr. Davenport and Bear."

"That's a question?"

She shook her head. "I mean, are they okay? Will they be okay?"

"Other than tresspassin' on our place of worship, I got no beef with either of 'em. Johnny and Clint are at the Devil's Teeth watchin' 'em even as we speak. The moment I get word the Mother's through with you, those two will be let go." He stepped toward her, leaned in close, and smiled. "I promise."

Kili took a step back, gripping the machete tightly in her hand, in case the creepy older man decided to surprise her with an unexpected move, but he backed off and walked over to the driver's side of the Jeep without another word. A minute later, the vehicle was fishtailing its way through the muck, leaving her alone to fend for herself in the stagnant mire all around her.

Once the Jeep was out of sight, she let out a sigh, turned around to eye the trail, and started walking.

THE LAST VESTIGES of the sun had just dipped over the horizon when Kili found the Willow Grove, which was fortuitous considering that buffoon Thornton hadn't thought to give her a flashlight for her trek through the marsh. Of course, she'd been stupid enough not to even consider asking for one, so who was the real buffoon anyway?

The journey had been every bit as harrowing as she'd anticipated. She'd had to use the machete at least twice to avoid being struck by the vipers that called the godforsaken place 'home.' And it had certainly been handy as a trailblazing tool. A quarter of a mile on the path, Kili had become painfully aware of just how apt the name *Briarsnare Marsh* was. The entire 'path,' as Thornton had generously called it, was overgrown with thickets and brambles that tore at her skin and clothing with every step she took. All the while, she'd been forced to trudge through numerous mud pits that came up to her calves. In all, she estimated the distance from where she'd started to the grove had been no more than a mile or two...yet it had taken the full two and a half hours Thornton had estimated to traverse the rugged terrain.

Then, there'd been the otherworldly glow hovering just below the clouds. A cold, ghostly green and purple light that blanketed the sky above as it grew darker. She'd seen pictures of the Aurora Borealis up north, though she'd never seen it in person. The luminescent haze above her head reminded her of that, though it was far less beautiful. As a matter of fact, the strange lights had weighed heavily upon her soul, as she'd scrambled through the mire. Of course, she knew what it was. She'd seen enough Discovery Channel to recognize the telltale signs of swamp gas. Though knowing something and being able to deal with its emotional effects were two entirely different things.

If the swamp gas and the rugged terrain weren't bad enough, she was fairly certain she'd been stalked during her journey as well. She never saw what it was, but she'd caught movement from her periphery on more than one occasion. Felt, more than saw, the graceful gliding of a predator through the underbrush. She had a pretty good idea what it was, and the thought unnerved her more than she imagined it should.

The Tailypo.

She wasn't certain and she would never have wagered on it, but for some reason, she just knew what it was. The strange cat-like creature she'd seen in the mortuary's garden the night before...still searching for its spectral tail. The one she still concealed in the pocket of her jacket.

But the Tailypo wasn't the most ominous of visitations she'd encountered during the trek. For that matter, she'd probably never experienced anything more unsettling...more gut-wrenching than the return of the unearthly dirge she'd first encountered at the picnic the day before. It had flitted on the pungent air around her, and at first, she'd believed the noise was simply the wind itself, until that notion was quickly dismissed upon realizing that the air was still. Almost suffocating and stagnant.

As she'd strained to listen, she'd been unable to discern the direction from which the song was coming. Nor could she tell whether it was a choir or a single singer, or whether the voice was male or female. And though the words themselves were just as indecipherable as they'd been at the picnic, the song had been dreadfully morose, and Kili soon found herself overwhelmed with hopeless despair. As the *a cappella* elegy reached its distressing crescendo, she'd been brought to her knees with the memories of every love lost, every failed moment, and every crushed dream flooding her mind's eye. But worst of all, she was left with the gut-wrenching sensation that someone—someone she was close to—was about to die. The song, after all, was a dirge for the dead. In many ways, the song had been little more than a great mournful wail over the loss of someone dear, though unlike with Elizabeth Crawford, she could not discern for whom the song was sung. This, of course, was even more maddening to her. After all, if she couldn't figure out who was about to die this time, then how on Earth could she do anything to prevent it? This question invariably led to an even more ominous one: "Is the death even possible to prevent?" This question sent her spiraling into even further despair. It had been nearly unbearable, and she wondered if she would have ever made it out of the marsh alive, if the chanting had not stopped as suddenly as it had begun.

As she stepped out onto the suddenly lush, emerald lawn underneath a grove of sprawling willow trees, she silently prayed to whatever being might watch over humanity, that she would never have to experience the song again.

The lawn…

That's when her new discovery finally hit home, and the tribulations she'd endured in the marsh suddenly evaporated. Perhaps 'lawn' wasn't exactly the right word for the perfectly round patch of rich green grass and moss that blanketed the land around her for an acre in all directions, but it was the best she could come up with at that moment. After all, wasn't the definition of a lawn, a manicured parcel of property that is usually occupied by a house or domicile of some kind? And wasn't there, in the center of the land, surrounded by a perfectly circular grove of weeping willows, a small, dilapidated shack that leaned to one side, as if ready to fall over with the slightest geological tremor?

Kili took another step, but reeled back when she noticed the strange, multi-colored, luminous mushrooms that littered the property in massive clusters—mushrooms that were all too familiar to her. It was, without question, the same genus of fungus that had created the One-Eyed Jack myth...that had ripped away her brother's sanity and had transformed him into a grotesque, homicidal giant.

She shouldn't move any closer. It was too dangerous. Crane had believed the mushrooms all destroyed in the purging of the Devil's Teeth, but here they were...in the Willow Hag's grove.

"Come in, come in," came a wizened female voice from inside the shack. It was a pleasant voice. A soothing voice. One that Kili could imagine bringing great comfort to those who suffer. "No need to fret none. I promise you. No need to fear nothin' within this grove. Vow my solemn word on that, Daughter Mine."

"But the mushrooms," Kili protested. "The spores..."

"Will not hurt you here, bonnie lass," the woman said. "Come in. Rest yourself. I reckon the dirge has taken quite a toll on you, eh?"

Warily, Kili stepped forward once more, slowly inching her way to the door of the strange little house, while keeping her distance from the crop of mushrooms. No need taking any chances, despite the woman's assurances.

"The dirge," Kili said as she drew nearer. "Was that you singing?"

A soft chuckling echoed from inside the hut. "No, dearie," the woman said. "T'weren't me. What you heard was the Yunwi Tsunsdi. They've been singin' that tune for goin' on a fortnight now. Mighty troubled, they are...but I fathom you already know that. Been hearin' it a bit yourself lately, eh? Felt the unbearable sadness of it all?"

Kili found herself at the door, her hand reaching for the old wooden handle, but she stopped herself from opening it and let her hand hover there.

"But Ezekiel said the Little People have all but disappeared," Kili said. "Ever since those...those Leecher things showed up in Boone Creek."

"Tsk, tsk, child. Ezekiel don't know everythin'. Besides, the wee folk don't exactly cotton to him much. Not like they do you... Oh, they've taken quite a shine to you." The woman's voice paused for a moment, as if trying to decide how best to proceed. "But he's right in his own way, I reckon. They have been in hiding since those nasty lil' haints have reared their ugly bird heads in our fine community. That's why the Yunwi Tsunsdi have chosen this place to sing their songs of mourning...'cause the haints ain't welcome here. They can't pass through the marsh —the water, you see—makin' this the safest place on Earth." Another pause. "Now what you waitin' for, Daughter Mine? Come in, come in. I've been expectin' you for a might long time now."

Kili decided to let that last statement go for the moment, and although an overwhelming desire to open the door swept over her in a nauseating wave, she resisted. If the sweat pouring down her brow was any indication, her resistance to the strange draw was taking its toll.

"Why are they sad?" Kili suddenly asked. "The Yunwi Tsunsdi, I mean...what could cause them that much suffering? So much torment?"

She heard a resigned sigh from just behind the door, as if her hostess was pressed against its wood while speaking to her.

"Because they mourn, darlin' child. They know someone is about to die."

"People die all the time," Kili argued. "Especially in this place."

"Ah, but this time's different...they sense that ol' specter, Death, is creepin' up on the good people of Boone Creek, and he aims to collect himself a few mighty fine souls 'fore he departs again. The wee folk mourn the losses yet to come."

Kili shuddered with a sudden rush of dread. The Little People had been singing their song to her. For some reason, only she'd been able to hear it. But wait…that made no sense. Obviously, the woman on the other side of the door had heard it too. After all, she'd brought the dirge up on her own. Still, Kili couldn't shake the anxiety building up within her soul over the haunting melody that even now played out in her mind.

Had the Yunwi Tsunsdi been mourning her loss? By being forced to come to the Willow Grove, had she been led to her own doom?

"Who…whose death are they mourning?"

"You don't know?"

Absently, Kili shook her head, belatedly realizing that the woman wouldn't be able to see the gesture through the door.

"I'm honestly not sure myself," she said with a warm chuckle. "Though I do have my suspicions. Horrible, ghastly suspicions."

"What? Please…tell me."

"Come inside, and I will."

"But I'm not sure I…"

"I vowed your safety, Daughter Mine," the old woman said. "I keep my vows. Just come inside if'n you want yer precious answers. But if you don't come in, I don't know what you'll do. It's pitch black out there, and nighttime ain't no time to be traipsin' through the marsh to get home." Suddenly, the door to the shack flew open, revealing a dark expanse inside. So dark, in fact, that Kili was unable to see past the threshold. "Now, welcome home, dear one…welcome home."

Almost as if her limbs were propelled by marionette strings, Kili found herself stepping into the shack against her will, and the door slammed shut behind her.

CHAPTER
SIXTEEN

"**M**s. Kili!" came a voice from the darkness. It seemed distant. So very distant. But then again, in the darkened void in which she hovered, everything in the universe was far away. Forever away. Yet, somehow, the voice was able to reach out from the unfathomable distances to her. "Ms. Kili! Are you okay?"

She tried to move. She willed the muscles of her body to work, but for every ounce of effort she put into it, she felt some unseen force holding her back. The voice calling her name wasn't the only one she heard in the darkness either. She could also hear that torturous song...the dirge of the Yunwi Tsunsdi, lamenting the loss yet to come. The melody...the rhythm...the gut-wrenching undecipherable lyrics threatened to overwhelm her, to break her down to a facsimile of her former self. She wanted nothing more than to burst into a torrent of tears, but she couldn't find strength enough even for that.

"Breathe, Kili! Breathe!" Another voice. Such a kind, sweet voice, this one. There was genuine concern there. Concern for her. Concern for many others too, if she had to guess. No, the owner of that voice was good. Compassionate. Gentle. A good man.

A man? she thought. Her mind spun a whirlwind of confusion. *But when I stepped into the darkness, I was going to meet a woman. Wasn't I? A—*

"...don't know what the Hag has done to you, but you've got to breathe, Ms. Kili! Come on!" It was the first voice again. A male voice also...melodiously sweet, yet in some ways, callous. Hardened. Even potentially cruel.

Shivering, she turned her attention back to the second, kinder voice. There was great desperation in it. Just as desperate as the chorus of voices singing that hauntingly heinous, but deceptively lovely song in her mind. And there was something else there too. Fear. Fear for her.

Without warning, something powerful slammed into her chest. And again. And again. Then, strangely, a great wind rushed into her lungs, filling them to the bursting point. The pounding against her chest resumed again soon after.

What's happening? she thought. *Is someone attacking me?* In the darkness, she couldn't see a blessed thing. Couldn't sense anyone remotely near her, yet the powerful force pushed down on her torso again.

"Come on, Kili! Don't do this to me!" The second voice was screaming now. Panicked. "Wake up!"

But the darkness was beginning to grow quite comfortable; like a warm quilt wrapped tightly around her on a cold, February morning. Why on Earth would she want to ever leave it? If not for that black song constantly reverberating through the void around her, it would be near perfect here.

Another burst of gale-force wind rushed through her lungs, followed immediately by a fit of hacking coughs. She was coughing in the darkness. Only, now, it wasn't quite so dark. It was a bit gray, like the gloom just before dawn. And as she continued to cough, she felt an arm underneath her, lifting her up into a sitting position. The gray rapidly shifted to a haze of yellow, blue, and green. Light was beginning to invade her void of comfortable darkness, and inexplicably, she welcomed it.

Even more welcome than the light was the undeniable fact that she could no longer hear the Dirge. No longer hear the anguish of the Little People, and thus, her own heavily-burdened heart was instantly lightened.

"Oh, thank God!" she heard the second voice say, relief evident in the tone. She felt someone wrap their arms tightly around her torso. "Thank God, you're alive."

Slowly, warily, she opened her eyes. As her vision grew into focus, so too did the beaming smile of Alex Davenport, as he laughed joyfully at her return to the conscious world. He was holding her up; his arms were underneath her and keeping her head elevated. She glanced around to get her bearings. It was night, though the moon was bright, casting a ghostly halo through the strange swamp lights above. The stars blinked back at her from their heavenly perches.

In the dim light, she could see Ezekiel Crane's concerned face hovering just over Davenport's shoulder. Bear stood a few feet off, biting his lower lip while wringing his hands nervously. He gave a gentle wave and a nod, when he noticed her looking his way. She smiled weakly back at him before continuing her quick surveillance. Another man—vaguely familiar, and wearing a white collar of a clergyman—stood even farther back from the crowd. His head was bowed as if in prayer. Where had she seen him before? She couldn't quite place him, but she didn't get the same unnerving vibe from him as she did Tom Thornton.

Deciding he was no threat, she continued her assessment of the surroundings. She lay on the bank of a dank marsh. Cattails towered above her, and a forest of dark green conifers leading back into the Dark Hollows loomed a short distance away. She'd obviously just barely made it out of Briarsnare Marsh alive.

Wait. Briarsnare Marsh? How do I know that name? She glanced up at the night sky again in deep thought. Last thing she remembered, it had been nearly noon. Bear, Alex, and she had just entered the Devil's Teeth to see if contact could be made with—a cold shiver ran through her as the Yunwi Tsunsdi and their cold, dark song of death sprang to mind.

Shoving the thought aside, she was immediately bombarded with a whole series of other questions. *How could it be dark now? How long have I been unconscious? What happened to me? How...*

"...did I get here?" she asked weakly. Her voice seemed distant. Hoarse.

"I was hoping you could tell me," the reporter said, placing two fingers along the curvature of her neck to check her pulse. He gave her a quick wink to show how pleased he was with the results. "When that weird cult guy took you away, his goons pretty much let Bear and me go. We started searching for you right away, but couldn't find a trace. So, we did the only thing we could think of...we called Mr. Crane."

Kili looked at the mountain man, who was now crouching beside the two of them. "It was actually Reverend Lorrie over there who found you," Crane said, nodding back to the older man with the cleric's collar. "He has sort of a sixth sense when it comes to the Hag's evil doings. Knew you were in trouble even before Bear called me." Crane's calloused hand reached out and felt her forehead for a moment, then he smiled. "Looks like you'll be okay now, though," he reported. "A mild fever, but I see no injuries or anything *physically* traumatic to cause us concern."

She eyed him warily. She didn't like the way he'd said the word 'physically'...as if there might be something else wrong with her, invisible to the naked eye. She decided to ignore it for now.

She looked over at the man Delores had called the Preacher at the picnic the other day. "Thank you," she said. "Thank you for looking for me."

Reverend Lorrie gave her a sad smile, and nodded without a word. He then looked over at Crane, gave him an enigmatic look, then turned around and melted into the woods.

"You know, for a *preacher*, that man sure doesn't talk much," Davenport said.

"So what happened to me?" she asked, ignoring the reporter's attempt at levity. She looked over at Davenport, who was merely staring at her curiously. Ordinarily, she might have been flattered by his undue attention. Now, in these circumstances, she simply found it unsettling. "You mentioned some cult guy?"

"You don't remember?" Davenport asked, as if suddenly snapping out of a deep trance. His eyes jerked away the moment he realized he'd been caught staring. "Any of it?"

She shook her head. "Nothing since you and I walked into the Teeth and set up that offering. After that, it's just a blank."

The reporter glanced over at Crane nervously, then back to her, before proceeding to fill her in on her kidnapping.

"The Willow Hag? I was taken to see the Willow Hag?"

"You seriously remember nothing about it?"

She shook her head, a lump slowly forming in her throat. Had she really been in the presence of some immortal witch? A real, honest-to-goodness hag? What had happened when they met? What had they discussed? What did it all mean?

One look at Crane told her he was silently asking the exact same questions.

Again, she was in no hurry to discover the dark thoughts running through her friend's head, so she changed the subject. "Okay. So what's next?" she asked. "I mean, after I head back to my hotel room for a shower and a change of clothes. This marsh water stinks to high heaven."

Crane pursed his lips at that, but nodded. "Good idea. It's nearly midnight. Go get cleaned up, and get some sleep," he said. "We'll meet at Granny's in the morning. Should be pretty safe for us to meet in the open by then. We'll have breakfast and work out our next move." He turned away from them and started heading toward the tree line. "Bear will see to it you get back safely. Right now, I have something I need to check out."

"Wait," Kili said. "What's going on? Where are you going?"

He turned to look at her, his face even more grave than it had been since she awoke. His cold blue eyes seemed heavy. Sad even. Then, he pointed at her arms. "It's a message to me," he said. "A little nudge in the right direction, if you will."

She held up her arms and gasped. They were covered completely, up to her short sleeves, in dark red ink. Problem was, she knew in her heart it wasn't ink she was staring at. Only blood—fresh blood—could make the perfect shade of crimson that marked her arms. A virtual Rosetta Stone of blood-stained symbols had been scrawled over the surface of both of her arms, and it was all she could do to keep herself from running back to the marsh and washing the filth away.

"What is this?" She heaved for breath, while tears streamed down her face. "What has she done to me?"

Crane stepped toward her and took her by the hand. "Don't fret none, Ms. Kili. And before you look at yourself in the mirror, you need to know...the same sigils have been drawn on your face and neck as well. I suspect over your entire body, if truth be told. We managed to wipe a lot of it—pig's blood if I had to guess—away during your resuscitation, but not all of it."

"And what exactly *is* it?" she repeated. She was getting frustrated. She was in no mood for Ezekiel Crane's enigmatic platitudes and evasive riddles. "Tell me. Now."

Nodding, he lifted her arm and pointed to one of the symbols. A strange, but familiar looking spider-like doodle hovered over a rectangular box. "Recognize it?"

She shook her head, though she was pretty sure she'd seen it before. Recently, as a matter of fact.

"What about this one?" he asked, indicating what looked like a serpent coiled around the body of a struggling bird. He waited until he saw the recognition in her eye. "Yes. They're exactly what you described seeing on the support beams in Overturf's cellar. I think the Willow Hag is telling me we missed something there."

Kili's mouth hung open, unable to formulate words to express the horror now threatening to overwhelm her. Then, something in her mind clicked. Something even more mind-numbingly terrible than being tattooed in blood. The sheer number of symbols. She remembered the support beams well now, and the symbols etched into the stones at the Devil's Teeth. There'd only been a handful of carvings on either of them...there were many more scrawled over her body, which she was unable to recognize.

"W-what about the others, Crane?" she said, her arms held out at her side. They were stiff, unwilling to make contact with the rest of her body. "What do these other symbols mean?"

Gently, he placed both hands on her shoulders and looked into her eyes as if plunging into the depths of her very soul. "You've heard the Dirge, haven't you?" He frowned.

She suddenly felt stifled. Bound in place. As she struggled desperately to catch her breath, she groped at the fur-covered tail still secured in her jacket pocket.

"Thought so," he said. "Regular contact with the Yunwi Tsunsdi is fine. There've been people for generations back that could speak regular with 'em, like Granny. And apparently, like you. But when you caught sight of the Tailypo, I knew something was off. Something dark was shaping itself around you. But I prayed—oh, Ms. Kili, you've no idea how much I prayed—that it wasn't what I thought it was." He paused to stare down at his mud-caked boots while he collected his thoughts. "You hearing the Dirge of Briarsnare Marsh is the key, though. It confirms my worst fears."

"And those are?" Davenport cut in. He'd moved up to Kili

and was gripping her hand, squeezing it gently to let her know he was there. That he would be there for her no matter what.

Hesitating, Crane turned away, his hands balled up into frustrated fists.

"Don't you dare keep this from me," Kili spat. "Don't you dare give me the run-around on this. If you care anything for me, you'll tell me the truth. Now."

"Yeah, Zeke." It was Bear's turn to put his two cents in. During the conversation, he'd quietly sidled up behind Kili, lending the weight of his shadow as a bastion of support and comfort. She'd felt him there, more than seen him…but the small gesture meant the world to her. "She deserves to know the truth. I reckon she's strong enough to handle anythin' that ol' hag throws at her."

Crane, his back still turned to them, shook his head slowly. "You don't understand," he said. "No one alive can possibly understand what this means…no one but me." He turned around and let out a beleaguered sigh. "I know better than anyone what she's in for…what she'll have to endure for the rest of her life if I don't find some way to stop it. I know better than anyone the emotional torment she'll be bombarded with every day until she dies." His eyes locked onto hers once more. "It's my curse, Kili. The death curse I've denied for so long. The Willow Hag has marked you, and she's used the same hellacious curse she cast on me to do it."

CHAPTER
SEVENTEEN

Morriston, Kentucky
April 29
2:15 AM

E zekiel Crane glanced down at his watch, after slipping in through the window he'd jimmied open on the Kilner Avenue side of Overturf and Sons. A little after three in the morning. He estimated he'd have about an hour and a half to snoop around in the cellar before the first, more stalwart employees started popping in. Of course, that all depended on whether they'd upped their security since Kili and Davenport's unfortunate break-in the other night.

A pang of guilt lashed out at him, as he conjured Kili to mind. He hated how he'd had to leave things between the two of them. Hated how cold he'd been toward her and her current predicament. She was scared. Naturally so, and he'd all but turned his back and wished her a not-so-fond *adieu* while he was at it. It was all for show, of course. But no one else—especially Kili—knew that. The truth of the matter was, the sooner he'd dealt with the Leecher problem, the sooner he could turn his attention to the Willow Hag and that damnable curse she'd used to mark Kili. For now, however, it was essential that the vile witch believed he simply would not get involved. After all, the curse could only be cast on one person at any given time. The more it took hold of Kili, the more he would be rid its burden. In effect, once the curse was firmly in place in Kili's life, Crane would finally be free. Any sane man who learned he was about to expunge the mark from his life and break free of the bondage the Hag had tricked him into, would certainly steer clear of anything that might pull him right back in.

Fortunately, he'd long since given up trying to maintain anything remotely resembling sanity when it came to the Willow Hag and her coven. He just had to make sure no one else knew that, or Kili was doomed for certain. So, he'd sent the devastated woman on her way to deal with the horrors she'd soon endure on her own. His only consolation was that the reporter, Davenport, seemed to truly care for her. He'd look out for her as long as he could. Of course, this broke Crane's heart as well, for he knew that as long as the curse was bonded to her, she could never truly experience the beauty of a real relationship. She'd never be able to know love again, for that matter. After all, how can you fall in love with another human being knowing exactly when—and often, how—they will die?

As he glided silently through Carl Overturf's office, he shoved the morose thoughts to the back of his mind, focused on the task at hand, and crept over to the desk. After a quick search of the desk's contents, he moved over to the security panel on the southeast wall, punched in the code he'd discovered in the appointment calendar on the desktop, and watched the monitors as they faded quickly to black.

The interior IR cameras had been a new addition to security since the other night's break-in. *Awfully quick precautionary installation for a backwoods funeral home with nothing to hide*, he thought. Still, at least now, he wouldn't have to worry about any electronic eyes watching over his shoulder while he dug around a bit in the proverbial trash of the business.

Having done everything he could think of within Overturf's office, he stole over to the door, cracked it open about an inch, and peered into the empty, first floor hallway to survey the lay of the land. Only problem was, it wasn't empty. Apparently, the cameras weren't the only precaution the funeral home had recently added. They'd also hired a security guard. The single antique lamp, resting on the mahogany table in the foyer, revealed an old man in a rumpled Pinkerton uniform, leaning back in a rusted folding chair in the lobby.

Not exactly a murder of crow-masked haints, Crane thought. *But a problem nonetheless.*

He reached around and pulled open the messenger bag strapped over his shoulder. Prior to driving to the funeral home, he'd made a few stops to pick up a handful of odds and ends that might be useful. One such oddity squirmed wildly in the largest pocket, and Crane had to be cautious as he rummaged through its more benign contents.

Fortunately, the security guard, well into his sixties, was looking painfully bored. When not preoccupied with sipping on a tepid thermos of coffee, which now rested on a TV dinner tray beside his chair, the old man's eyes would invariably drift down to glance at his watch. And though Crane couldn't see his face from this angle, he couldn't help notice the guard's head lingering longer and longer…as if his eyelids were simply getting too heavy to keep aloft for much longer.

Sorry, my friend. Crane smiled. A few more seconds of rifling through his pack and he found what he needed. Withdrawing a glass container of a yellow-gray powder, he gave a furtive glance in the opposite direction to make sure no one else was lurking nearby, then he slipped into the shadowed hallway. He slowly made his way toward the unwary security guard. *You're probably going to need to find a new job after tonight.*

Once within arm's reach of the old man's coffee mug, he poured a handful of the strange powder into his palm, and transferred the pile into the coffee, before inching his way back to Overturf's office to wait for the inevitable.

He didn't have to wait long. Within five minutes and two sips, the guard's snoring echoed down the hall. Of course, the result hadn't surprised Crane. His special blend of valerian root, persimmon bark, mugwort, and a few other singular ingredients would put a perfectly alert person to sleep in minutes. But because the sedative wasn't a benzodiazepine, as many are, the restful state would be far more natural, with far fewer side effects. Unfortunately, it would also be relatively easy to wake the man up, should Crane make any noise.

Confident the guard would sleep the rest of the night away and that his burglary had gone unnoticed, he slid once more into the hallway and made for the Preparation Room. Once in, he bypassed the morgue drawers that had drawn Kili's and Davenport's attention the other night and sped straight to the rickety old staircase. Reluctant to turn on the overhead light, which might draw unwanted attention, he cupped a hand over his flashlight to minimize glare and made his way down into the dank cellar of the old Victorian house.

Once on solid ground, he paused and listened to the dehumidifier hum within the tightly confined space; the sound was augmented by the stone masonry used to construct the cellar. The *drip-drip-drip* of water striking plastic told him that someone had been down here and replaced the bucket Kili had used against the Leecher that had attacked her.

Allowing a brief smile at the thought of Kili's resilience, he moved over to the support beams Kili had told him about and scrutinized the enigmatic carvings cut into the wood. The photos they'd taken with a cell phone had been grainy. Almost unreadable. So, he was thankful her description had been quite accurate. The only detail she'd left out was just how fresh the carvings appeared to be. He could still make out the reddish wood where the rough bark had been sliced away for the pictograms. They'd been made fairly recently.

Upon inspecting the symbols in their proper habitat, Crane knew his original assessment that they had been used as sigils to channel magical properties, was entirely correct. If he was reading them correctly, this particular series would have been used to promote, if not accelerate healing of some type. Maybe a better interpretation was 'growth'.

Growth? In the cellar of a funeral home? he thought. *Intriguing.*

Satisfied he'd seen everything the pillars could illuminate, he moved over to the two doors on the far end of the chamber. Both were once again closed, though now they each came complete with a digital keypad lock; the state-of-the-art security device was a stark contrast with the rustic, wooden door it was used to secure.

And still even more *intriguing.*

When they'd been there earlier, Kili and Davenport had taken the door on the left because Davenport had believed the roots had sprung up to bar entry into the right one. Crane, however, suspected it had been a simple locking mechanism disguised to look like natural blockage to the unwary interloper. Of course, all pretenses had now been dropped since the high-tech PIN pad had been installed. Fortunately, it wouldn't prove much of an obstacle for Crane.

Pulling a thin, but sturdy stick out of his pack, he carved a single name into the wood, wrapped a piece of jet black hair around it, and tied it off. The dowsing rod was an instrument taught to him by Granny when he was just a boy, just as she'd been taught by her own grandmother, and on and on for genera-tions. Crane descended from a very long line of what the Appalachian people called 'Water Witches'...people skilled at divining the location of deep wells of water in even the most desolate of areas. To most people, it was seen as magic...unless, of course, you were given the secrets to how it really worked. Then, it was just a simple matter of subatomic physics.

He smiled at the thought. No matter how many times he'd insisted it was all about science, not a single person had ever believed him when they saw it in action. When he honestly considered it, he could understand why...especially when he considered what he was about to attempt at that moment. Something he'd never even considered before, in fact. It was very different from trying to locate a subterranean source of water. Infinitely more complex than using the rod to track down a missing person. No, if he pulled this off, he'd have to admit it was something bordering on the miraculous. But then, Crane never had a problem with believing in miracles.

Quieting his thoughts, he turned the rod toward the keypad on the right-hand door and focused on the strand of hair he'd managed to nab on his way to the funeral home—another 'oddity' he'd taken from the driver's seat of Dr. Maher's BMW. Hair that had probably entered this cellar on a number of occasions before...hair that had been present, as the digits on the keypad were pressed time and again. Hair that would undoubtedly reveal—

Ah, Crane thought as the thin piece of wood tugged against his fingers. *There it is.* Relaxing the muscles of his arm, he allowed the dowsing rod free reign to seek out the combination to open the door. Slowly, imperceptibly, the wood thrummed within his grip. Vibrations so subtle...so faint, they'd be unnoticeable to anyone other than an expert Water Witch.

Crane watched as the tip of the stick veered slightly to the right, hovering just beyond the numeral nine. It then slowly dipped, hesitating on the six before moving over to the one and up to seven. When the rod didn't seem to want to move any more, Crane punched the numbers into the pad and was rewarded with the click of the lock disengaging.

Well, how 'bout that? Miracles do happen after all, Crane

thought, while pulling the door ajar and peeking through the crack. As he suspected, the door opened into a dark hallway. But unlike the rest of the cellar, the floor, walls, and ceiling were anti-septically clean. The black and white checked linoleum that lined the floor gleamed against Crane's flashlight. The smell of mildew and grime was immediately replaced with pure oxygen, which seemed to be coming through the rows of ventilation units near the ceiling. *What in the name of Heaven is going on here?*

Kili had, of course, told him about the other chamber they'd discovered by going through the left door. An immaculately clean laboratory, complete with specimen jars containing the most singular of oddities—strange round growths containing eyes, hair, and teeth, which made him most curious indeed. The description sounded a great deal to Crane like Teratoma tumors —growths quite common in a large number of people and rela-tively benign. Teratomas typically grew in the reproductive areas of the human body and contained tissue and under-developed organic matter resembling eyes, teeth, and hair. If the specimens were indeed these tumors, oversized as described, it would go a long way in explaining the mystery of the Kindred.

The fact that Kili had said the jars themselves were all labeled with the company logo of AION PHARMACEUTICALS was even more unsettling. The company name had sounded familiar to Crane, but he couldn't place where he'd heard it before. Certainly not from anyone around Boone Creek. He'd merely assumed he'd picked up the name while on his sojourn of world exploration. Still, it seemed the pharmaceutical company had some part to play in the dark goings-on of late, and he resolved to have Davenport do a little digging tomorrow, to see what he could turn up on them.

For now, however, he needed to push forward and see where this new, unexplored tunnel would lead. He was just about to pull the door fully open when a creak from above grabbed his attention—the sound of a footstep on the old wood floors on the first floor. More footfalls followed soon after, more rapidly than the ones preceding it. Had someone discovered the drugged guard? Had his break-in been noticed?

Holding his breath, he cocked his head to one side and strained to listen. There were muffled voices. At least two, and both sounded excited. Flustered even. He couldn't make out specific words, but he could assume he'd been found out. His explorations could not be prolonged any longer. He'd need to get moving before they realized where he was.

Exhaling, he moved into the darkened hallway and closed the old wooden door behind him, making sure not to let it lock. Though the other tunnel had an emergency exit that led into the mortuary's tranquility garden, he couldn't be certain the same would be true for this branch of the cellar. The last thing he needed was to bar his only way of escape. As an added precaution, he removed the strand of hair from the divining rod and wedged the stick into the crack in the door to prevent it from completely closing when his back was turned. After placing Maher's hair back into his shirt pocket—he didn't know when it might come in handy again—he crept down the hallway as quickly as he dared.

One hundred yards in, he gasped and came to an abrupt halt. The cone of his flashlight zoomed across a rather large hospital room. There was currently no patient occupying the modern hospital bed, still neatly made with crisp folds of bedding covering all four corners of the mattress. A bank of computer monitors lined one wall, while state-of-the-art medical electronics hummed throughout the room—useless without a patient to treat.

Crane let out a soft whistle as he scrutinized each of the devices. Every piece was cutting-edge. Not a single device was older than a year, if he wasn't mistaken. The cost for the equipment alone would have been more than the entire county of Jasper would see in a year. Maybe even two. So the question was... Who was paying the bills? Well, that much he could guess. But the other question would then be "Why?"

Shoving the problem aside for now, he walked over to the nightstand next to the bed and examined its contents: a glass vase containing a single wilting lily, a disposable ink pen, thirty-five cents in loose change, a copy of the King James Bible, and an old dog-eared copy of Tarzan of the Apes. A single brown hair clung to the linen doily covering the surface of the night stand. Carefully, Crane removed the strand and placed it securely in a plastic baggie.

Someone had been here. From the condition of the flower, not to mention the complete lack of dust on any of the equipment, he guessed it had been pretty recently too. The literature on the nightstand gave him a few clues to help identify the patient as well. He was probably a male. Possibly young. A child maybe, with dark brown hair. And finally, Crane guessed that he, or his parents/caretakers, were somewhat spiritual in nature.

So who was it? What does all this have to do with the Kindred or the Leechers? And finally, why would the Willow Hag lead me here to begin with? Crane gave the room another once over. *None of this is adding up.*

But even as the questions were asked, one name kept popping up in his mind as the most likely person to provide the answers. He figured it was high time he paid a proper visit to Dr. Ruth Maher—

The sound of the door opening from the Prep Room staircase echoed through the cellar. Crane spun around, searching for a way out. His light flashed high and low for an escape route, but he already knew there was no other way out but the way from which he'd entered.

"And I'm tellin' ya, it's yer imagination," said a gruff male voice from above, followed immediately by the creaking of the steps, as someone descended into the basement. "There ain't no one down here."

Someone huffed irritably. "Well, how on Earth could you possibly know that?" said someone else. Crane recognized the voice instantly as belonging to Carl Overturf. "After all, you were sawin' away at them logs, when I walked in on ya. Anybody could've walked right past ya, and you'd never know." From the sound of it, the two had made their way down to the dirt floor and were now scurrying around looking for telltale signs of any intruders. "Grady, that lady doctor is payin' us both a pretty penny to keep her laboratory secure, and we owe it to her to make sure we double check for intruders, right?"

"I reckon yer right," said the security guard, Grady. "It's just I've been doin' this kind of work for goin' on a quarter of a century. Just hurts my feelings, is all, when you go around accusin' me of doin' a poor job of it."

"You were *sleepin'* on the job, Grady!" Overturf's frustration over his employee laced his words with venom. "Ain't no way you can put a good spin on...uh...what is that?"

Knowing what he was going to have to do, Crane stalked back into the hallway and made his way toward the door.

"What's what?" Grady growled.

"The door, you coonswaggle. The door. It's open."

There was an awkward pause. Crane could imagine each of the two older men inching closer to the door with wide eyes and dry mouths. He genuinely regretted what was about to happen. Neither of these two men deserved what was coming, but there was no way around it. He only hoped neither had a heart condition.

In one fluid motion, Ezekiel Crane shoved the door open, reached down to scoop up his stick, and stepped boldly into the cellar proper, before either intruder had time to react. His eyes burned harshly at the two men, who leapt back with a start upon seeing him.

"Ah, dear Lord in Heaven!" Overturf cringed.

Crane's eyes continued to glare at the duo as he stepped

toward them silently, pulled out his pocket knife, and began whittling nonchalantly at the stick.

"W-what are y-you d-doin' here?" the funeral director asked, taking another step back.

Grady's trembling hand moved down toward the sidearm holstered on his belt, but Crane raised the stick in the air and waved it back and forth at him.

"I wouldn't do that if I were you, Grady."

The old security guard's eyes bulged when he heard his name used. Crane had never met the old man before, so like many other Appalachians, he feared any stranger bandying his name about so frivolously. Names, after all, have power. And the fact that Crane seemed to supernaturally know his, was something the old man didn't even want to think about.

As soon as Grady held up his arms in submission, Crane, still cutting away at the piece of wood in his hand, turned his attention back to the mortician. "Carl Overturf." He made sure to pronounce each syllable of the name perfectly. Menacingly. He was finding it exceedingly difficult not to smile. "You know who I am," Crane hissed. "*What* I am."

Crane was well aware that his notoriety hadn't merely been confined to just the Boone Creek community. Stories about the cursed seventh son of a seventh son had long spread throughout the entire county. Some as far north as Harlan County had even heard a few stories about him. So when the mortician swallowed and nodded silently before taking another step back, it wasn't much of a surprise.

"Then you know what I'm capable of?"

Overturf nodded again.

"Good." Crane grinned devilishly at the two men. "That'll make our next few minutes far more productive, I'd say. You see, I have a question for you, Mr. Overturf, as well as a message." He paused, allowing the men to absorb the severity of their current predicament in light of their own superstitions. "First the question...who was Ruth Maher treating in that room back there?" He thumbed backwards toward the left hand door through which he'd just walked.

"I-I don't know." Overturf didn't even hesitate, a good sign he was telling the truth. "N-never saw him. Transport crew brought him in the middle of the night, about a month or so ago. They moved him out after the office was closed last night...after another break-in we had."

"And you never saw this patient?"

The mortician shook his head emphatically. "Just rented out the space to Dr. Maher. None of my staff were allowed down here."

"Wait, Carl," Grady said, holding up a hand to him. "Why are we talkin' to this guy? We caught him breakin' into a federally controlled facility, right? We should be callin' the Sheriff."

"Federally controlled?" Crane asked.

"Dr. Maher is with the CDC," the security guard said, sucking in his gut and valiantly attempting to stoke up his courage. "One word from her and..."

"Grady, shut up!" Overturf said, taking another step back. His eyes looked placatingly over at Crane. "Don't you know who this is? It's Ezekiel Crane, for Pete's sake!"

The old man looked him up and down and shrugged. "Don't look so special to me." Crane watched with bemused fascination. The security guard's false bravado seemed to be fed by his employer's lack of courage, rallying him to the verge of a brainless act of heroism...or utter stupidity. And Crane knew the man was going to choose the latter when his hand inched once more to the hilt of his sidearm. "Way I see it, all we got to do is hold him here 'til the feds show up."

"Grady, what are you doing?" Carl Overturf pled vainly.

But his employee could not be swayed. The gun was out from its holster the second after the question was asked, and it was now pointed nervously in Crane's general direction.

The mountain man just stood there, casually glancing at the .38 caliber revolver held in the guard's sweaty hands. The old man reminded him so much of Don Knotts in his Mayberry deputy uniform...drawing down on the town hoodlum with quaking limbs. The smile threatened to return at the mental picture, but he knew it would be a mistake. He only needed to maintain the menacing act for a little while longer.

Reining in his amusement, he turned back to the mortician. "Well now," he said. "Seems we have a bit of a problem here." Crane took a single step forward. Overturf gulped and plaintively tried talking sense into Grady.

"Lower the gun, man! Lower the gun!"

The old man looked to his boss, then to Crane several times; each glance caused the gun to shake even more uncontrollably. Crane would have to end this soon, or someone might unintentionally get hurt.

"I said I had a question for you, Mr. Overturf, and a message." He took another step forward, brandishing the newly carved stick into the air with one hand, while deftly reaching into the messenger bag at his side with the other, without anyone noticing. "I've asked my question." Theatrically, he twirled the stick between his fingers and held it up for the two men to get a better look. While talking to them, he'd casually whittled away at the long piece of wood, cutting line after line of concentric circles all around to give it the most unsettling impression of a...

"Is that a snake?" Overturf asked, stepping back once more and wiping a stream of sweat from his brow. The heel of his boot was now up against the first step of the staircase leading into the Prep Room. Though Grady still clutched the sidearm, it was all but forgotten, as his eyes were now following every movement the stick made.

"Of course not, Mr. Overturf. It's a stick," Crane whispered, pushing forward with another step. "But it *can* be. A snake, that is...if I want it to be. And that, Mr. Overturf is my message.

What I can do with this stick, I can also do to you. Or Mr. Grady here. Or anyone I choose." Crane's eyes burned at the two men, as he slowly waved the piece of wood in front of them while closing in. "Such is the power of a seventh son of a seventh son, right?"

There was a pause. No one moved. Crane wondered if the two men even allowed themselves to breathe for the disquieting fifteen seconds each of them stood there. Only the constant hum of the dehumidifier could be heard above the men's heartbeats.

"Remember this message, Mr. Overturf, and tell no one I was here this morning," Crane said. "It would behoove the both of you to not tell a living soul."

And with that, he flicked his wrist, sending the stick flying through the air toward them. They watched in abject terror as the object landed on the ground, a mere two feet away from each of them, and suddenly coiled into the hissing form of a red, yellow, and black striped snake.

With a high pitched cry, the mortician and the security guard turned around and fled immediately up the stairs. Crane listened as two pairs of fast moving feet pounded across the wooden floors above and made their way to the funeral home lobby. Less than a minute later, the front door slammed shut, and Crane finally allowed himself a satisfied chuckle.

Confident the men were gone—at least for a little while—he slowly walked over to the two-foot-long king snake, picked it up, and placed it carefully once more in his bag. He then shook his right arm and watched as the carved stick fell from his shirt sleeve into his palm. *I'm going to regret that little trick*, he thought, as he trotted up the stairs to the funeral home's first floor. He had worked so tirelessly to abate the irrational fear the people had of him. Had worked so hard to convince everyone that he wasn't of the Devil. And then he goes and pulls a stunt like that. *They'll be talking about this for months.*

He rolled his eyes as he strode confidently through the

funeral home and toward the front door. It was as he reached for the knob that he willed his mind to focus on what was truly important and the challenges that lay ahead. He'd managed to gain quite a few pieces of the puzzle with this latest excursion. Now, he just needed to talk to the woman who'd be able to share how those pieces fit together.

And something told him that Dr. Ruth Maher wouldn't be nearly as impressed with a slight-of-hand magic trick as Carl Overturf and his aging security guard. He knew he might have to resort to even stronger methods for her.

CHAPTER EIGHTEEN

The Crane Homestead
April 29
5:45 AM

E sther Crane was near exhaustion. She couldn't remember the last time she'd managed to get any semblance of restful sleep. Three days? Four? And here it was, dawn approaching within the hour, and she'd spent the entire night tending mercifully to her patients.

Not that she'd ever complain. These people were her friends. Her family. They were helpless. Some were dying. There was nothing she could do to fix what was wrong with most of them, but she was determined to see each and every one of them through it, until the bitter end. She owed them that much. She could, of course, sleep when everything settled down. Or when she was dead, whatever came first.

But at that very minute, there was an entire house full of the Leechers' victims—at least eight more had arrived since the day of the county picnic—and that was the only thing that mattered to her.

For now, she busied herself preparing the morning's medicine. An iron cauldron hung over the low burning embers in the fireplace; its contents simmered slowly as she stirred. She'd decided today to add a touch more snapdragon to the mix, to elevate relief for those with severe burns, as well as to fight off infection. Another addition to this particular batch was the dried leaves of perennial foxglove, a plant well known to regulate heart rhythm. Though those afflicted by the Leechers' Trials all demonstrated varying ailments, they had one thing in common —tachycardia, or the speeding up of one's heart to over one hundred beats per minute. Prolonged tachycardia could lead to heart failure, and Granny was determined to do whatever she could to prevent that from happening. The foxglove should assist with that little problem.

Granny sighed. A little more stirring and the potion would be ready to go.

"How goes it?"

The sudden question startled her. She turned to see Delores McCrary, rubbing at her eyes as she walked into the living room. Her hair was a tangled mess from where she'd fallen asleep in the recliner, next to her boyfriend Max.

"About the same," she replied. "No change...though I fear Wallace Biggs ain't got much longer on this Earth."

"I'd say none of 'em do," Delores said, looking back at Max, who was finally sleeping peacefully on his cot. The old man had had a pretty rough night. His entire body was covered in festering boils, and no matter what they'd tried, the poor man just could not get comfortable. He'd finally passed out around two in the morning, from exhaustion. "I'm about to make coffee. Want some?"

"Wake Jimmy first," Granny said. "It's gonna be a long day, and I need him to take care of some chores 'fore he heads off to school."

Her friend's nose crinkled at this, obvious annoyance on the apprentice's face.

"Now don't get started on this again," Granny scolded. "I need his help. It ain't doin' him a bit of good if we just coddle him all the time."

"But he's been through so much. Seen so much death," Dee said. "He needs his mama."

"His mama is dead, Dee! What am I supposed to do?"

Her friend simply smiled at her.

"And for the last time, no, Delores. I ain't gonna help you raise Candace Staples from the grave. Someone's already been experimentin' with that kind of thing, and you can see how that's all turnin' out."

"But it's not the Kindred's fault, Granny. They're not responsible for all these sick people. The Leechers are." Delores's sad eyes pleaded silently to her friend. "The Kindred were dead. Gone. Their families devastated. But now…now, they're back together again. They're…"

"They're barely human," Esther Crane growled. "What they have is *not* life, Dee. They sit around all day, staring up at nothin'. They hardly ever speak. Heck, seems the only thing they do well is eat. They all eat more food in a day than what any of 'em would have eaten in a week 'fore they died. Now somethin' strange is goin' on with them. Somethin' dark." She paused, her face softening slightly, as she placed a hand on her friend's shoulder. "Look, Dee. I know you mean well. You love that boy more than Ezekiel or I ever could. I know you'd do anything in the world for him. But no good can come from *any* resurrection spells. Ever."

Delores looked down at the ground and nodded. "Yeah, I reckon yer right, but I just wish…"

A frantic pounding at the front door interrupted her train of thought. Simultaneously, both women looked over to the clock resting on the fireplace mantle. It was just approaching six in the morning.

"Who on Earth could *that* be, at this hour?" Delores asked, turning toward the foyer.

Granny merely shrugged and made her way to the door. Unlocking the deadbolt, she cracked open the door and peered outside to see a battered and bruised Helen Stillwell. Tears streaked her face, as her left hand clamped desperately around her right forearm, blood oozing between her fingers.

"Help me," she said in ragged gasps. She would have collapsed had Granny not deftly reached out for her and prevented the woman from falling.

Quickly, she and Delores hefted both of the forty-five-year-old housewife's arms onto their shoulders and led her to the only unoccupied chair in the room. They eased her into the recliner and began systematically tending to the woman's injuries.

When Delores brought a pail of water, Granny began washing away the blood staining the woman's arms, and gasped when she saw a chunk of flesh missing.

"Lord have mercy! What happened to you, sweet child?"

Helen shuddered, her teeth chattering inside her skull from shock and fright. "I-it w-was foolish of me," she stammered. She closed her eyes as Granny worked at bandaging the arm up as best she could. "Should've known better, really."

"Should have known what?" Delores asked, wiping the steady flow of sweat from the woman's face.

"Carl. He'd gotten so hungry lately, and I'd just ignored him," she said, wincing in pain as the bandage was pulled tighter around her forearm. "B-but he's so quiet all the time. Never complains about nothin'. Just sits there mostly. I got caught up doin' my chores last night before bed. Forgot to make sure Carl was taken care of." Tears began rolling down her cheeks as she confronted the memory. "I woke up just a little while ago, with him on top of me. He'd started gnawin' on my arm." She let out a horrified sob. "Oh God! I managed to pull away, but he grabbed me again and started hittin' me. Only reason I escaped was 'cause I managed to grab hold of the baseball bat we have for burglars, and I hit him upside the head with it."

Gravely, Granny held up Helen's arm and pointed to the bandage. "You're tellin' me he didn't just bite you then?"

Helen Stillwell shook her head. "Uh-uh. He was literally gnawin' on it. Like he was trying to eat my arm off."

"Was he lucid? Did he say anything to you while this was going on?"

"Just that he was so hungry. That's all he kept sayin'. Just that he was hungry."

Granny turned to Delores, an eyebrow raised in a silent rebuke.

"Yeah, yeah," Delores said. "I get your meaning."

"Well, while I take care of Mrs. Stillwell here, I need you to call Sheriff Slate. Have 'im go and check on Carl."

Delores nodded and turned to go find the phone when—

SLAM!

Something powerful crashed against the front door. Helen screamed at the sound, curling up into a defensive fetal position. "It's him! It's him!"

Granny shushed the terrified woman and quietly instructed her apprentice to stay and watch over her, while she went to check on the noise. Stealthily, she moved through the house, weaving around the minefield of cot-bound patients. She made her way to the front door. Just as her hand stretched out to grasp the knob, there was a crash from the other side of the house. Then a third coming from the master bedroom down the hall.

That's when she heard it...the subtle, almost imperceptible whispering coming from the other side of the door.

Quickly, she dead-bolted the door and dashed back into the

living room with a shout. "It's the Leechers!" She bound past Delores and Helen, and moved straight for the gun case in the corner of the room. Uncertain what she'd done with the key, she grabbed a nearby lamp, smashed it into the glass case, and withdrew a 12-gauge pump-action shotgun.

SLAM!

The crash was on all sides of the house simultaneously. They were trying to force their way in. She glanced around the room to see all of her patients—victims of the strange creatures just outside these very walls—squirming unconsciously in their cots. Each patient's mouth opened and closed in sync with the whispers outside. They were being unwillingly drawn in to the haints' wicked incantations. Their power was being added to that of the Leechers.

"Dee, catch!" Granny tossed the gun to Delores and sped off toward the nearby closet. Pulling it open, she reached in, grabbed three old brooms, and carefully laid the first diagonally across the front door's threshold. She did the same with the back door, before moving to the center of the living room, brandishing the third with both hands gripping the handle.

"W-what's goin' on?" little Jimmy Staples asked, coming out into the living room with a yawn.

"Jimmy, go to Delores," Granny commanded. "Stand behind her and do everything she says. Is that understood?"

SLAM!

The whispers were getting louder. Less hushed and more desperate. She was able to now clearly make out the words, and it sent chills down her spine.

Daeh rehekat ot de nommus!

SLAM!

Neebeva hew swolliw!

SLAM!

E'htfogah eh't keesew! Nisutel! Nisutel!

SLAM!

They were running out of time. She wanted to call Ezekiel. She wanted him to come right away, but she knew it would be counterproductive. Not only would he be unable to arrive in time, it would distract him from doing what truly needed to be done—it would distract him from finding the bones of Eli Smith and putting a stop to this terror once and for all.

No, there was nothing Ezekiel could do. She was going to have to deal with this on her own.

Clutching the broom handle tighter, she moved to a nearby steamer trunk and flipped it open. She had one trick up her sleeve. One deplorable—if not outright blasphemous—little trick that would send the Leechers scurrying on their way. She was, of course, loathe to do it... She had no idea how such a conjuring would tarnish her soul. But she was out of options, unless she was willing to sacrifice all those she'd brought into her home for refuge. As a place of hospice. Grabbing a vicious looking dagger from the trunk, she moved back into the living room to set the ritual up.

But the sudden crunch and the sound of splintering wood at the front door told her she was out of time. The Leechers had breached the threshold.

CHAPTER NINETEEN

The Crane Homestead
April 29
6:20 AM

T he purple-orange haze of the sun could just barely be seen making its way over the hills, as Davenport pulled into the Crane driveway. Kili leaned back in the plush leather seat of the reporter's Audi, ran her fingers through her hair, and sighed.

"I see you didn't have any trouble getting your car back from Morriston," she said, truly disinterested, but in desperate need to turn her attention to anything mundane.

The reporter let out a bemused chuckle. "Actually, it wasn't as easy as you'd think. Seems the good Sheriff felt that it had been abandoned. Had it towed. You should have seen the paperwork I had to fill out just to get out of the impound yard."

Figures, Kili thought. *So much for 'mundane.' And after the night I've had…*

To say it had been a very long night would have been a major understatement. But she'd managed to get through it, and tired as she felt, she was ready to face a new day and tackle the problems that battered her at every side—the worst being the supreme irritation she was now feeling for Ezekiel Crane. He dropped such an enormous bombshell on her and had simply walked away, leaving her to absorb it all by herself.

Though she would never admit it, she was supremely thankful for the new friendship she had developed with Davenport. Once they'd escaped the Dark Hollows and driven back to her hotel room, he'd not left her side the entire evening. After she'd cleaned herself up, they'd spent the remainder of the night just talking, dealing with her abduction by the Willow Hag, this curse Crane had alluded to, and even to a lesser extent, the loss of her brother. The tabloid reporter had genuinely been interested in what she had to say and in how she was feeling. And so, he'd simply sat in that horribly uncomfortable hotel room chair and listened to her vent against the whole rotten world until they drifted off to sleep from pure exhaustion. Their slumber had only lasted an hour or so, but she now felt at least a little refreshed from her trials of the night before.

She glanced over at him now, as he steered his overpriced sports car down the winding, gravel driveway. Not a single blonde hair seemed out of place, and though he hadn't shaved in a few days, the stubble was starting to really give his face that rugged quality that was always so appealing to her.

Cool it, Kili, she thought, turning her attention back to the driveway. *As if you don't already have problems enough. Romance is the last thing you need to worry about at the moment.*

Davenport cleared his throat, breaking the silence.

"Um, so you think it's going to be too early for Granny to have breakfast ready?" he asked. The look on his face told her that he knew the question was completely inane, but she figured he'd do or say anything to alleviate the tension that had been building in the car ride over here. Tension directed toward Ezekiel.

She smiled at his awkward attempt to lighten the mood. "How long have you been staying here, exactly?"

"Well, it's just that I rarely wake up before noon." He threw her a lopsided grin. "How am I supposed to know what time she prepares breakfast?" Turning the steering wheel, he pulled the car in directly behind Granny's shiny black Hummer and put it in park. "Bear told me to expect grits. Never had grits before. Don't even know what grits are, actually. Are they any good?"

Rolling her eyes, she opened the door and climbed out, just as a loud boom thundered from inside the Crane homestead.

"That sounded like a gunshot," he said, spinning around to look, once he climbed out of the driver's seat.

A second crack rang out.

"More like a shotgun," Kili corrected, already running toward the house. "Come on!"

The two sprinted toward the white picket fence that lined the property. Alex struggled to keep up, nearly tripping twice if not for his cane. Reaching the gate first, Kili threw it open and ran toward the porch. As they approached, the front door burst open, and a young boy—Jimmy Staples, if Kili wasn't mistaken —tumbled out onto the porch in a clumsy sprawl. Quickly getting to his feet again, he leapt the two porch steps and dashed toward them, as fast as he could. When he saw Kili, he ran straight to her and grabbed her around the waist with racking sobs.

"Jimmy? What's wrong?" Kili asked. "What's happening?"

Before he could answer, Granny backed out of the door, her shotgun still pointed inside. "Come on, Delores!" she screamed. "You gotta get outta there. Now!"

Prying Jimmy away, Kili knelt down to look him in the face. "I need you to be brave for a few minutes, okay? I need you to get in Alex's car over there and sit tight while we go help Granny. Lock the doors. Don't let anyone in until you see one of us. Will you do that?"

Wiping a stream of tears from his eyes, the boy nodded and did as he was told. Ten seconds later, they were at the front porch.

"What's happening?" Davenport asked, leaning heavily on his cane.

If Granny was surprised by their sudden appearance, she didn't show it. Her eyes remained fixed on the house's interior, as she anxiously clutched the shotgun and an empty burlap sack. "You can't be here," she said, calmly. "It's too dangerous. I'm tryin' to get Delores out of the house too, but she won't leave Max."

"But what is it?" Kili asked. "What's attacking you in there?"

Granny's eyes narrowed. Her jaw set hard, and she ground her teeth with apprehension. "Leechers," she said. "Three of 'em, and they seem to have their eyes fixed on Dee."

The reporter looked from Granny to Kili and back again. "Well, um, what... What can we do to help?" His voice was a few octaves higher than normal. Kili knew he didn't savor the idea of going up against the Leechers again—of possibly experiencing their drowning Trial again. "I'm pretty handy with a shotgun." He nodded to the twelve gauge in Granny's hand.

She merely shook her head. "Shotgun's useless against them," she said. "All it does is slow 'em down a bit. But if you want to help, I've got an idea I want to try. I just need some time to fetch somethin'...." A loud crash erupted from somewhere in the house, followed by a shout. A female shout. "Delores!"

Granny moved for the door, but Davenport grabbed her wrist to hold her back. "Wait. Go get what you need," he said. "I'll go in and get her. I'll be able to carry her out if I have to."

"On a bum leg?" Kili asked, nodding at the cane.

Another scream exploded from down the hallway to their left, only this was not from a woman. It sounded animalistic. Bestial.

"Don't have time to argue," he said, pushing his way into the house. Kili watched him round the corner before she gave Granny a quick nod. She handed Kili the shotgun grimly. Kili then turned toward the front door and followed the reporter inside.

"What the heck are you doing?" he asked her, once he realized she was right behind him.

"Backup." She hefted the gun into view. "After all, you rushed in without a weapon."

He rolled his eyes, lifted his cane and yanked on the handle. A gleaming steel blade eased its way out of the wooden casing. "Granny already said the shotgun wouldn't work, but everything I know about supernatural nasties and spooks say they're not too fond of iron or steel. I'm hoping this will..." His words caught at the back of his throat as they came into view of the living room. Several rows of wooden cots lined the floor, each filled with unconscious people. In the opposite corner of the room, huddled between another cot—containing the comatose form of a man—and the far wall was the elderly woman Kili had gotten to know at the town meeting. Delores McCrary. And though she couldn't see the comatose man's face, she imagined it was more than likely Max.

But the old woman was only part of what had arrested Davenport's attention. The other was the three nightmarish liches now standing over the pleading woman with raised axes. The moment Davenport entered the room, however, they swiveled their bird-like faces in his direction and began shrieking with a banshee's wail.

Without giving them a moment to react, the reporter raised his cane sword up over his head and, with a battle cry, charged at the three bewildered haints.

"Alex, what are you doing?" Kili cried, but he was already in full swing at the nearest creature.

Unable to move in time, the blade sliced through the fabric of the Leecher's voluminous cloak, eliciting an ear-piercing scream that caused Kili's fillings to vibrate.

"Ah-ha!" Davenport yelled, twirling the sword in the air like a two-bit swashbuckler in a B-movie. He turned to look at her, a wild grin on his face. "See? Iron!"

But he'd taken his eyes off his adversaries one second too long, and while the first writhed in agony, its brethren lunged toward him.

"Alex, look out!"

As if anticipating the move, Davenport met the Leechers' attack with the swipe of his blade across the second haint's arm. The blade bit fiercely through the cloak's sleeve, but failed to make contact with whatever constituted its body. It yanked free when the lich jerked its arm away. Not allowing a reprieve, the reporter spun, swinging the sword once more, this time aiming directly for the Leecher's head. But the haint was incredibly fast. Before the sword's arc was complete, the beak-faced monster swept to one side, threw up one booted foot, and kicked Davenport to the ground.

Delores McCrary, watching the entire encounter from across the room, screamed while her would-be rescuer's head slammed against the hardwood floor. The cry quite possibly saved his life, as both uninjured creatures swept their heads around to locate the screaming woman.

"HHHAAAGGG!" they cried in unison, momentarily forgetting the reporter.

The distraction was all that was needed. Davenport, regaining his composure faster than Kili would have thought reasonable for the Ivy Leaguer, flew to his feet and swung the blade toward the back of the nearest creature's head. With one blow, it sunk deeply into the Leecher's wide-brimmed hat, to where its skull should have been. Without a sound, the creature crashed immobilized to the floor.

"Now, Kili! Get her out now!" he yelled, levering the blade

back and forth, trying to free it from the thing's head before its comrade had enough time to take out its revenge.

Without arguing, Kili darted past, well out of range of the remaining Leecher's axe, and took the older woman by the hand. "Come on," she said. "We need to go."

But Delores shook her head emphatically amid mournful sobs. "N-no, no! I can't. I can't leave my Max. Not with th-those things still in here."

"Delores, everything's going to be okay," Kili said, patting the woman on the back. "Granny's working on something right now that'll take care of everything. She can't do that with us in here so—"

"Holy crap!" Davenport cried, cutting off Kili's words. She turned to see both Leechers the reporter had downed climbing to their feet and rejoining the third. "They're still alive! They're still freakin' alive!"

KILI LOOKED up to see the nearly decapitated Leecher struggling to rise up off the floor, fending off more sweeps of Davenport's sword with its arms. The blade sliced through air in a blur, but the other two blocked each parry with their axe handles, to protect their injured comrade.

"You need to get her out of here now!" the reporter screamed.

Without protest, she grabbed Delores's wrist and pulled her away from the cot of her boyfriend.

"No!" Delores cried, trying desperately to break free. But Kili's grip held, and she pulled the older woman past Davenport and the monsters, who were slowly regaining the offensive. Once they'd rounded the corner, Kili handed Delores off to Granny, who was just now returning with a burlap sack in hand. When she was sure both women were safe, Kili turned to run back into the living room, but was stopped by Granny's surprisingly strong hand on her arm.

"It's my turn now, sweetie," Granny Crane said. The older woman smiled before turning her malevolent gaze at the foul creatures invading her home. "STOP!"

Everything grew perfectly still. At the command, all three Leechers instantly arrested their advance and turned to look at the elder Crane. Davenport, who'd been knocked on his back with his attackers looming over him, struggled to back away with the momentary reprieve.

"Cursed Ones of Eli Smith!" Granny continued. She set the burlap sack down. Something wiggled inside the bag, struggling to free itself and crying out in sharp, high-pitched shrieks. Satisfied the creature wouldn't escape the bag, Granny withdrew a fierce looking dagger from the back pocket of her jeans and pointed it at the haints. "You'uns ain't welcome in my home. In the home of my children." She raised her right hand in the air and dragged the dagger's blade across her palm, allowing the blood to pour out onto the hardwood floor in a wide circle around her. "In the home of my Pappy and in the home of my kin!"

By now, Davenport had managed to scramble away and was sidling up to Kili, who was just as transfixed with what Granny was doing as the Leechers were.

"The Clan of Crane don't abide hellish critters like you," Granny shouted as she reached her blood-soaked hand for the sack, opened it, and withdrew one of the largest black birds Kili had ever seen. She wasn't sure if it was a crow or a raven. The bird's wings flapped madly, as it struggled to break free, but the old woman's grip around its neck held firm. The piteous animal cawed pleadingly, but it was powerless to escape its captor's grasp.

Kili stifled the impulse to cry out at the sight. "What are you going to do?" she asked.

Granny shrugged, keeping her eyes fixed on the Leechers. "Something darker than I've ever tried. Not quite sure it'll work," she said. "Only a handful of people in the world know about this. Been passed down for generations in my family, but as far as I reckon, the knowledge would have died with me, since Ezekiel..." She glanced over Kili with a wink. "Well, Ezekiel don't cotton none to this type of magic. Says it ain't natural. But then again, *they* ain't exactly what I'd call natural neither." She nodded to the haints, before addressing them once more. "I don't want to do what I'm about to do! Leave now, so I don't have to."

The three Leechers turned to one another for an unnerving number of seconds before shaking their heads. "The HHHAAAAAGGGGG!" They spoke as one in a unified whisper. "We've cooommee fooor the Hhhhaaaggg! Gggiiiivvve hhheeerrr tooo uuussss aaannndd wwweee ssshhhaaalll dddeepppaaarrrttt."

"The Willow Hag ain't here," Granny growled.

"The wwwooommmaannn," they said, still inexplicably held in place. "The oooollldddd wwwooommmaaannnn..."

"...is my apprentice, and she's under my protection. She's no more the Willow Hag than I am."

One of the creatures pointed straight at Kili. "Yyyooouuu wwwooouuulllddd llleettt hhheeerrrr hhhaaavvveee ttthhheee fffiiirrreee hhhaaaiiirrred wwwooommmaaann?"

Kili's heart leapt into her throat at its words. It knew about her mark?

But Granny didn't seem to take notice. "You'uns are barkin' up the wrong tree here, and yer not gonna lay a cursed finger on Dee's head. Now, last chance!" Gripping the bird by the back of the neck, she raised it in the air in warning. When they failed to obey, Esther Crane let out a resigned sigh, brought the dagger slowly up toward the raven's head and belted out a slow, steady chant in a tongue Kili found vaguely familiar. As the dagger drew closer to the bird's head, Granny's chanting boomed throughout the house, echoing wildly in the confined space. It sounded so desperate. Angry. Then, in one fell swipe of the blade, the bird's head sprang loose from the rest of its body. Blood spewed from the gaping wound, raining down on the circle of blood Granny had drained from her own hand. She poured it in a crisscrossing pattern inside the circle.

"Begone, foul Children of Scratch!" Granny shouted, binding the dead bird with a piece of twine and casting it toward the spectral trio. *"Emohym ni emoclewt t'nias nuuoy! Nerdlihcym foemoh emoh ehtni! Nikym foemoh ehtni'd nayp papym foemoh ehtni!* Go back to whenst you came!"

Without warning, the creatures' cloaks flared up in an ethereal silvery fire, consuming them completely from view. The conflagration blazed brilliantly for no more than five seconds, then disappeared completely—along with the three Leechers.

"...the heck was that?" Davenport said, rushing over to Granny, who nearly collapsed to the floor in a swoon. When he helped her over to the nearby couch and saw that she seemed to be fine, he continued. "That was awesome!"

"Never you mind what I did," she said weakly. "Just do me a favor and don't utter a word of it to Ezekiel. He wouldn't understand."

"Wouldn't understand? But... It. Was. Awesome!"

"Alex, shut up," Kili said, giving him a reproving glare. "I think it's just that the ritual she used wasn't exactly the *'magic is only science we haven't understood yet'* variety that Ezekiel preaches all the time. Everything he does...all the crazy magic-like stuff he does? There's always some Earth-science twist to it." Kili paused, looking down at the dead bird lying on the floor where the Leechers had only recently stood. "But this... This is something not of this world, was it?"

The old woman nodded silently, as if shame threatened to consume her.

"Still, not too shabby," Davenport said. "I mean you killed the monsters, right? That's a *good* thing."

"They ain't dead. Make no mistake about that." She let out another sigh. "I merely bound 'em to my will for a time. Find somethin' to represent your target, mix that somethin's blood with yer own, and you can take control of your victim temporarily."

"So a crow represented the Leechers," Davenport said.

She nodded. "A raven actually."

The reporter beamed at Kili. "See? Awesome. I'll stand by my assessment."

"But such rituals come at a price, dear boy," Esther Crane said. "This kind of magic always does."

"What kind of price?" Kili asked.

Granny looked up from the pile of ash—all that was left of the unholy intruders' clothing—and gave her a sad, weary smile. "You needn't worry your bonnie lil' head about it, sweetie," she said. "You've got problems of your own to worry about, I fathom. The Hag's laid her mark on you, ain't she?"

"H-how did you know? Is it because of what that Leecher said or did Ezekiel already tell you?"

"No one needed to tell me anything. I know the look all too well," she said enigmatically. "And I'm truly sorry."

"Please," Kili said. "Tell me. What does it all mean? Ezekiel refused to tell me...but I have to know!"

Granny leaned back on the couch and stared up at the ceiling with a sadness Kili had not seen in her before. "I imagine he wouldn't," she said. "It's a wonder he'd even acknowledge you'd been marked, to begin with."

Kili knelt down beside the old woman, taking a First Aid kit resting by a nearby table. She started bandaging the old woman's bleeding hand. "Please. I *need* to know. What is this Death Curse? How exactly am I marked? What does it all mean?"

After a minute or so, Granny pulled her eyes away from the ceiling and turned to Davenport. "Do me a favor, dear," she said with a warm smile. "Go out and find Dee and Jimmy for me, will you? I need to have a little chat with Ms. Kili here, but I want to make sure my friends are okay."

Davenport looked at Kili, who nodded that she was okay. "All right," he said, moving toward the foyer. "Be back soon."

Several heartbeats later, Esther Crane turned to Kili and sighed. "I reckon if I'm gonna do this right, I ought to start from the beginning."

CHAPTER
TWENTY

AION Pharmaceuticals
Lexington Branch Office
April 29
6:30 AM

D r. Ruth Maher walked into her lab as if on a mission. The moment she unlocked the door and walked through, she flicked the lights on and clip-clopped across the glaring tile floor toward her computer terminal, careful not to drop an ounce of the steaming coffee that slogged around her mug as she walked. Her eyes never wavered from the dormant computer screen until she reached it, and even then, she diverted her gaze only long enough to find the power button and press it. Her foot tapped impatiently at the floor, as the computer ran through the boot-up process. She cursed when it had to go through a routine disk scan, before allowing her entry into the operating system.

Once in, she started the e-mail program, checked a single e-mail among thousands, and was efficiently typing away at a reply within minutes.

"Having troubles?" Ezekiel Crane asked, sitting casually on a stool on the other side of the room.

The woman jumped with a shout, before spinning around to glare at him. Surprisingly, not a single drop of coffee was spilled, even with the sudden start. Say what you would about her, the woman was disciplined to the core.

"You're not authorized to be here," she said, quickly resuming her frigid composure. "Leave now, or I will be forced to call security."

Crane smiled, slid nonchalantly from the stool, and walked toward her with crossed arms over his chest. "Funny. You don't even seem surprised that I found you here, and not at the CDC building in Atlanta."

"I, uh…" Her mouth hung open, unable to respond.

"It's okay, Dr. Maher. I completely understand. I've known since the first week you showed up in Boone Creek that you didn't work for them," he said, drawing even closer. "Took me a bit longer to pinpoint Aion Pharmaceuticals as your true employer, though. Your cover story was exceptionally done. The paper trail very professional. Which makes me very curious…" He paused before leaning against the table directly opposite her, taking a pinch of tobacco, and stuffing it inside his bottom lip. "Why go to all the trouble? Why the deception?

"Oh, don't worry. I don't expect you to answer those things. I've pretty much worked a lot of it out in my head, as I've waited for you to show up today. There's really only one loose end I need answered before the picture will be complete."

"Security it is, then." Maher's hand shot for the nearby phone, but Crane struck with the speed of a viper, grabbing her wrist and whirling her around to look him square in the eyes.

"Not yet, Dr. Maher. Not quite yet. You still haven't told me what I want to know."

"And you expect me to? Just because you flash those spooky eyes of yours at me?" She belted out a contemptuous laugh, while jerking her arm out from his grasp. "I'm not one of those ridiculous hicks in your town, Mr. Crane. I don't swoon at the sheer mention of your name or tremble in fear if your shadow happens to touch my own. I'm a scientist. Parlor tricks like you used last night on Overturf and the security guard won't work on me quite so easily."

For a brief second, Crane wondered if the two had actually reported his break-in, but he thought better of it. The more likely scenario would be a secondary security system, independent of the one controlled from Overturf's office. She must have seen his little stick-to-snake sleight of hand on a discreet security feed. Not that it would matter much. He was already prepared to show her the part of him he never let anyone see...the part of him he'd kept hidden for nearly a quarter of a century. Frankly, he was tired of playing the games. People were dying in *his* town, and he was determined to put a stop to the Leechers as quickly as he could.

Opting to ignore her last comment, Crane continued. "The way I see it, they're all connected. The Kindred, the Leechers, and the Willow Hag...they're all linked somehow. And your mysterious patient in the funeral home's cellar is smack dab in the center of it all. So my question is... Who is he, and how does he fit in?"

"Seriously? Do you really think I'm just going to fold and answer your questions, Mr. Crane? I've already told you... I'm not scared of you or your little David Copperfield hocus pocus. There's nothing you can say or do that'll get me to betray the confidences my employer has placed in me."

Suddenly, Crane sprang from where he'd been leaning and drew within inches of the woman's stern face. "Dr. Maher, are you familiar with why those...*hicks*...as you so ineloquently put it, are so afraid of me?"

She rolled her eyes in a scowl. "Superstitious nonsense. Nothing more. Something to do with you being the seventh male progeny of a seventh male progeny, I believe."

"And you've heard nothing about my curse?"

She laughed again. "Oh, the curse. The *Death* Curse, I believe they call it. Yes, my employer filled me in on that as well."

Her employer told her about his curse? That was most intriguing. Very few people knew the specifics of the curse. Even fewer who lived outside the borders of Jasper County.

Putting the question aside, he continued. "And what did this employer tell you about it?"

Maher shrugged indifferently. "That anyone you grow close to always seems to die. That death follows you around like a jealous lover, destroying anyone that you grow too fond of. And because of that, people shun you like some diseased vermin just waiting to infect them."

"That's it? That's all they told you?" Crane's smile broadened mischievously.

"Oh, she told me quite a bit more, but I immediately chalked it all up as simply too preposterous to even concern myself with."

Ah, so her employer is a woman. The plot thickens. Though to be honest, it really didn't matter. In less than five minutes, she would be groveling at his feet, spilling everything she knew without a second's hesitation. When he thought of it, his heart broke for the poor woman. As severe and hard-nosed as she was, he sensed that although possibly misguided, she wasn't an evil person, per se. She certainly didn't deserve what was coming, but he could see no other way around it. No. The only way he could fathom to loosen her lips would be for her to experience— if only for a few moments—the horror of what it was like to be him.

"Do you believe in ghosts, Dr. Maher?" Slowly, he turned his back to her as he stared absently at the pristinely white tile floor.

"Excuse me?"

"Simple question. Do you believe in ghosts?"

"Of course not," she said. The contempt in her voice oozed

freely.

He nodded. "And, in a way, you'd be right. As the Good Book says, 'Absence from the body is presence with the Lord.' Know what that means, Dr. Maher?" He paused briefly, but not enough to allow her to answer. "Quite simply, when a person dies, their spirit goes immediately to their reward. If'n they were called God's Children, well then, I reckon they go on to Heaven. If not...well, you get the idea."

"What does this possibly have to do with..."

"Bear with me, ma'am. I'm getting there," he said, still staring down at the floor. He didn't want to look at her. Didn't want to see her eyes when they were finally opened. "Point is, if a man's spirit goes on to his reward at the moment of death, there can't be any ghosts, right?"

"Well, I'm not one to even believe that man has anything like a spirit at all, actually."

"So, the question is..." He ignored her comment. "...if there are no ghosts, what has been haunting me since that dreadful day the Willow Hag placed her hex on me? What have I been seeing all around me, my entire life? What am I seeing right now...in this very room...all around us, for that matter?"

He heard the doctor fidget anxiously where she stood, just before she cleared her throat. "Uh, well... I... What?"

"The Death Curse is *very* real, Dr. Maher. Deadly real," Crane said in a low whisper as he dug both hands into his pockets with a nervous shrug. "I won't go into all the particulars...won't tell you the darkest facet of the curse itself, but I will tell you that the stories you've heard about me...about how I can see the spirits of the Dead, are very true. Every second of every day, I'm surrounded by them. Only, they're not 'ghosts' in the classic meaning of the word, since those have gone on to their respective rewards.

"I guess the best way to explain it is similar to what happened with the shadows that burned into the ground and walls at Hiroshima. The brilliant light and intense heat of the atomic blast literally burned images of the dying into the various objects around at the point of impact. Same thing happens when someone dies violently. Tragically. A part of that person's soul is burned into our reality...like an after-image from a flashbulb. The ancients referred to these kinds of 'ghosts' as *shades* for that very reason. Some might have vestiges of the person's consciousness—might actually recall elements of their lives for a time—but most are mindless and simply mill around the living, repeating the menial tasks they performed during life."

Maher laughed. "Why on Earth are you telling me this? Do you really think these ghost stories will get me to tell you what you want to know?"

With that, he slowly turned around to face her; his eyes were dark and mournful. "The reason I'm telling you all this? Remember when we first began this conversation I told you that I pretty much figured everything out from the moment I walked into your lab? Didn't you find that statement curious at all?"

"I... I didn't really pay too much attention actually. After all, you were trespass—"

"I can't explain how it happens, Dr. Maher, but it's true. I literally spend every moment of my life surrounded by the dead. I see them everywhere I go, though I rarely am able to communicate with them. So imagine my surprise, when I stepped into your lab this morning and was greeted by the spectral visages of people I knew, all too well. People I grew up with. Neighbors. People I went to church with. Imagine my surprise when I walked in to find all seven Shades of Boone Creek's Kindred."

"But that's not possible! They're... They're..."

"Supposed to be alive? Resurrected? Yeah. My thoughts exactly. After all, if the Kindred were truly returned to the living, then why in Sam Hill would their shades be lingering?" Crane took a single step forward. His fists clenching into tight balls, he growled his next few words. "But the biggest question of all is...

Why would they be lingering in the research laboratories of Aion Pharmaceuticals to begin with? After all, I found them buried in the shadow of the Devil's Teeth in the Dark Hollows. I thought they'd died in Jasper County. Thought they were just a few more victims of ol' One-Eyed Jack." Suddenly, without warning, he slammed his fist down on a nearby table and roared. "What did you do to them, Maher? How did they die?"

"I... I don't know what you're talking about," she stammered. "This whole thing is ridiculous anyway. You're just... You're just trying to frighten me...trick me...into telling you what you want to know. I don't believe in ghosts. I don't believe in curses or magic, and I'm calling security right now!"

She turned to snatch the phone from its cradle again, but before she could, Crane flew at her, grabbed the phone, and yanked it wildly from its cord.

"You will listen to me, woman." His six-foot frame loomed over her, as the rage of what he'd recently witnessed threatened to overwhelm him. His former compassion for the scientist had all but evaporated, and a large part of him found the justice that was about to occur here most satisfying. As was so often the case when becoming emotional, he found himself losing control of the eloquence and exquisite diction he'd worked to perfect over the years. "There's an old Appalachian custom...a Granny Magic trick, I reckon, that really works. If'n a friend you're with happens to spy a ghost or a spook, and you have the hankerin' to see it for yourself, the old legend goes, all you got to do is take a look over his left shoulder." He tapped the designated shoulder with his right hand. "Go ahead. Have a gander."

The grin spreading across his face appeared positively maniacal.

"No, I don't want..." She averted her eyes, not daring to look at him.

"What's the matter, Dr. Maher? You don't believe in ghosts, remember?"

"But I..."

"Look and witness the work of thine own hands!" he shouted.

The fierce authority of his words compelled her, and before she knew what she was doing, her eyes lifted. Anticipating the move, Crane had positioned himself perfectly, making it impossible for her to avoid gazing across his left shoulder and into...

Instantly, the woman's eyes grew as round as the beakers lining the lab tables around her. She tried to scream, but her vocal cords seized up, paralyzed by the inability to draw in a single breath. After several seconds of wide-eyed wheezing, her mouth opened, and she let out a volley of ear-splitting screams.

"No! No! No!" she shouted. "It's not possible! They can't be real!"

The woman was finally beginning to understand. Finally realizing the consequences of her actions. Her eyes had quite literally been opened to the horrors of her scientific malpractice, and it would change her life from this moment forward.

"Now, I believe you're finally ready," Crane said coolly. "So tell me... Who was the patient in the cellar? What kind of experiments are you and Aion working on?" He paused momentarily, his teeth grinding with both fear and rage. "And what, in the name of Heaven, are the Kindred?"

"I-I don't know...don't know every...everything," she screamed pathetically, amid horrified sobs. "Don't know h-how the Kindred came to be anyway. But I'll t-t-tell you whatever I can! Anything I can! P-please...just m-make it stop."

With a knowing smile, Crane stepped out of her line of sight and helped her into a nearby chair. "Good," he said, his old southern charm once more reasserting itself. "Now after we sit a spell and let you gather your wits, we'll have ourselves a nice, calm chat, and everything will be okay."

But he knew better. Both of them did. After seeing what she'd just seen, Ruth Maher would never be 'okay' again.

CHAPTER
TWENTY-ONE

The Crane Homestead
April 29
9:05 AM

G ranny Crane sat in her rocker, her gnarled old hands anxiously wringing as she looked around the living room at her comatose patients. It had been nearly an hour and a half since Mr. Davenport had run back into the house to report that Delores and Jimmy were both missing. An hour since she'd sent both Kili and the reporter on their way to search for them.

Poor Ms. Kili, Granny thought, as she let out a weary sigh. *Such a sensitive child. Already devastated by what I told her about the curse.* She had broken down in tears at what Granny had told her, but it was essential that she knew the truth—as horrible as it all was. But there'd been good news as well. She'd also told her that the curse hadn't fully taken hold of her yet. There was still time to reverse it. Still time to slip past its horrific web. Granny wasn't quite certain how to do that at the moment, but she certainly intended to find out before it was too late.

Unfortunately, she couldn't worry about the FBI woman now.

There were far more pressing matters to concern herself with. As dire as Kili's situation was, the fate of all the people in Boone Creek were at stake. Countless souls were now depending on her. And though she was loathe to put the poor girl's situation on the backburner, she had to focus her full attention on the meaning behind the Leechers' sudden assault on her homestead, as well as what had happened to Dee and the boy. Though she didn't know how, she understood that the answer to those questions would be the final piece of the puzzle.

She glanced over at the phone. No word at all. She didn't know if her old friend was alive or dead. Worse, she wasn't sure how she felt about that. After all, there was only one logical explanation for this morning's attack that made any kind of sense. Delores had betrayed them all. Somehow, she'd done what no mortal soul should be able to do. She'd figured out how to raise the dead to life. She was responsible for the Kindred and their strange resurrection, and by default, she was indirectly responsible for the carnage the Leechers had released upon the town during their fevered search for the Hag.

Granny quietly lit her corncob pipe, as she considered the logic of her assessment. Try as she might, she could find no flaw in her analysis.

Over the past year, Delores McCrary had grown quite fond of Jimmy Staples, whose mom had been killed during the One-Eyed Jack ordeal. Jimmy, as most eight year olds often do, refused to accept his mother's senseless death. He knew all too well that Granny herself had powerful magic, and time and again, he'd pleaded with her to bring Candy back to him. Naturally, she'd refused. Even if Esther Crane had the knowledge to do such a thing, it was simply too dangerous, not to mention blasphemous. No matter how much she cared for the boy, she could never cross that line. After all, had she not refused the same request from her own grandson when all but two of his siblings had died in that horrible car crash so many years before?

So, as children often do, Jimmy had taken his supplications to the next authority figure in his life. Dee. Only she had never shared the same concerns about the consequences such an act would bring. After all, wasn't it their job to heal? To extend life? Didn't they have the obligation to see just how far they could take their doctorin'?

The topic had led to quite a few heated discussions over the course of several months. But one day, inexplicably, Delores just stopped bringing the subject up. Oh, sure, every now and then, she'd hint at it like she'd done earlier that morning, but for the most part, she seemed to have finally come to grips with the fact that Granny would never agree to do it.

So what had happened? Had she gone to the Willow Hag for help? Lord knows that most people believed the Hag was the only being around who had power enough to raise the dead. Ezekiel himself had believed exactly that, hadn't he? Had that not been why he'd sought her out so many years ago? Wasn't that why Asherah Richardson had convinced him to make that hellish bargain with the woman?

But no matter how it happened, it appeared that Dee had somehow managed to do the impossible. She had managed to bring the dead back to life, and because of that, whoever controlled Eli Smith's bones believed her to be the Hag.

"Oh, Dee," Granny said with another sigh. "What in tarnation have you done?"

She could only hope that Kili and Davenport would find her before the Leechers did, so she'd have the opportunity to explain.

Shoving the dark thoughts aside, Granny looked around the room once more to take in her patients. In the time since Kili and Davenport had left her house, she'd busied herself with cleaning up the mess the Leechers had made during their attack, as well as with checking on each patient to ensure they'd sustained no injuries. If there was any good that had come from tonight's encounter though, it was that her patients all seemed to show marked improvement. Fevers had dropped considerably. Boils and burns were showing the first signs of healing. And for the first time in days, it appeared that most of the patients were finally able to sleep soundly and without pain.

This, of course, made sense. The Trials had been used to track down the Willow Hag. Now that the Leechers believed they knew who it was, there was no longer any need to keep their dark hold over the innocents. They'd relinquished their control, which meant that those who survived the next twenty-four hours would be able to make a full recovery.

Silently praising God for the small miracle, she climbed out of the rocker and ambled into the kitchen. The sun was now quickly rising above the mountains, and bright yellow rays were shining through the quaint bay windows of the kitchen. Though later than usual, she decided it was finally time she put a pot of coffee on and wait out news of the search for Delores and Jimmy. Surely, it wouldn't be much longer.

She set to work on the coffee maker—practically salivating over the thought of the much needed caffeine—and as the dark liquid slowly began to percolate, she moved over to the kitchen table and sat down. Her muscles ached, and the pounding inside her skull was only just now subsiding. The spell she'd used to banish the haints had taken quite a bit out of her. Heck, if she'd only be honest with herself, she'd admit that it took more out of her than she could afford. There would most certainly be a consequence to such dark magic. One only had to look at the Willow Hag to see what becomes of those who choose to use the *Black*, as it was called by followers of the nameless Ancient Ones.

The thought of the Hag set Granny's nerves on edge. She'd been the bane of so many in Boone Creek through the years— through the centuries, actually. She was the cause of so much grief and pain. There was not a doubt in Granny's mind that the Willow Hag had her withered, leathery hands smack dab in the middle of all that was currently unfolding in their sleepy little hamlet, though she couldn't fathom for the life of her what that role might be.

Of course, it was easy to see that the Leechers' puppet master believed the exact same thing. He or she had gone to an awful lot of trouble to steal the Witchhunter's bones. Even more trouble learning how to harness them to summon and control the thirteen haints. Know-how wouldn't have been enough either. Such a feat would require a great deal of emotional energy—more than likely hate. Hate, after all, is one of the most powerful of emotions. Or rather, it was the most powerful emotion that elicited the quickest results.

The fragrant odor of freshly made brew permeated the air inside the Crane home, but Granny didn't move to fix herself a cup. Her mind was cycling through a series of connected thoughts. Ideas. Small fragments of memory and observations she'd made in recent months, and a picture was slowly starting to emerge. A picture of the one behind the Leechers' return.

They, or someone they loved dearly, would have been personally assaulted by the Hag. More than likely, they would be riddled with scars—either physical or emotional. Their family, Granny realized, would more than likely have been decimated at some point, or at least, the culprit more than likely didn't have anyone to help him differentiate right from wrong.

A lump slowly began to form in her throat, as the picture became more and more in focus. Part of her didn't want to proceed. Didn't want to peer too closely into the veil, for fear of what she'd discover. Still, she had no choice but to press on.

Such hatred as was used to summon the Leechers could not have been weak. It would require a great deal of force, and that can come only from old hurts. Old wounds, which would suggest that the Witchhunter's puppet-master would have probably been rather young when the Hag's atrocities had happened. They would have been...

Oh, dear Lord, no, she thought, as she jumped to her feet, grabbed her cell phone off the table near the door, and ran out into the fresh morning sun. As she ran to the Hummer, she put a call in to Bear, explaining that she needed to go on an unexpected trip. She asked him to come to her place to watch the patients while she was away. Racing down the gravel driveway toward the highway, she called Kili's phone, but it went straight to voicemail. She left a quick message, imploring her to call the moment they had news about Delores and Jimmy, then turned her attention to the road and the confrontation she was now driving toward. A confrontation she'd dreaded for almost two decades.

CHAPTER
TWENTY-TWO

The Dark Hollows
April 29
11:38 AM

Kili wasn't sure how long she'd been running through the thick, dead brambles of the hollows, but she knew without question that she wouldn't be able to continue much longer. If her body betrayed her...if she was forced to rest...it would be over. The thing chasing her would catch up. It would ravage her and pull her back to its mistress, like a house cat dragging a dead bird to its owner's front porch.

She shuddered as the memories bombarded her mind's eye. She wasn't exactly sure where it had all gone so wrong. Davenport had been driving the bumpy dirt roads along Ryder Bluff, searching for the fleeing Delores McCrary and little Jimmy. At first, things had been tricky. The rising sun coming up over the eastern ridge had played havoc with their field of vision, blinding them wherever there was a break in the tree line. But as the sun swept higher, the going became easier, and they made quick time, circling back and forth in a sweeping search pattern.

In her panicked haste, Delores had left her old beat up pickup in Granny's driveway. They knew that the elderly woman wouldn't have been able to make it far on foot, so at first, they'd kept within close proximity to the Crane estate. But after nearly an hour and a half of their search, Davenport had decided to expand their perimeter, moving out into nearby farm land.

Tractors busied themselves in the fields, plowing up earth for the year's upcoming tobacco crop. A handful of rusted-out coal trucks zoomed past them, in their rush to the nearby strip mine. But no matter where Kili and Davenport took their search, they saw no sign of Delores or Jimmy.

The last thing she remembered was driving over a short bridge along County Road 43. Once they crossed it, something black, lithe, and deadly darted out of the trees and leapt in front of the expensive sports car. Next thing she knew, she found herself hanging upside down, strapped into the passenger seat. There'd been a crash. There must have been. When she'd pulled herself from the wreckage, she remembered seeing nothing but a twisted mass of metal and fiberglass. Davenport was nowhere to be seen, but he'd not put his seatbelt on when they'd left Granny's, and Kili suspected he'd been ejected—from the looks of it, probably from the driver's side window when the luxury car had overturned.

Panicking, she'd scoured the thickly wooded area in search of him, but there'd been no trace. Slowly, three nerve-rattling realizations dawned on her, as she searched for her friend. The first was that the woods around her were dead. The vegetation surrounding her was made of dried, thorny branches that clawed viciously at her face with every turn. Additionally, there were no signs of life anywhere. No animals scurrying away from the alien presence that had invaded their territory. No bird song flitting through the Spring morning air. Not even the sound of cars zipping by on their way to work. All of these things together could mean only one thing—she was as far removed from civilization as she could be. And in this region of eastern Kentucky, that meant she must have been in the very heart of the Dark Hollows.

The second realization came immediately upon the heels of the first. If she was indeed in the Hollows, then by geographic definition, she was literally miles away from the nearest road. She'd glanced around the wreckage of the car and found no trail. No trace of the bridge or the creek it loomed over. No indication of where exactly Davenport's vehicle had entered its final resting place. It was as if some giant had plucked the car up while it had been speeding down County Road 43, and tossed it haphazardly in the direction of the Hollows.

The final thing that had dawned on the bewildered Kili Brennan, as her mind reeled over her current predicament was that she was by no means alone.

She hadn't seen what was lurking in the dark woods with her, but she'd known it was there. She could sense, more than see or hear its presence. And her instincts reacted with one decisive move—she had run for all she was worth.

And she'd been running pretty much the entire morning, racing past the gnarled branches that slashed at her face and clothing. Ducking beneath low-lying tree limbs. Glancing over her shoulder for the slightest peek at who or what was now chasing her, though there really was no need. She pretty much knew exactly what it was. And worse, she imagined its dark purpose.

It would soon be over. Her lungs, as well as her legs, were failing her. Soon, she'd be doubled over—lying in a fetal position underneath some ancient rotten husk of a tree and waiting for fate to claim her.

But not quite yet. Not while she still had some inkling of hope. There was no way she'd make it that easy on the predator now stalking her. She was determined to make it work for its kill.

A grim smile spread across her face, as she took a deep breath and turned on the speed once more.

———————

"KILI!" Alex Davenport shouted, as he hobbled through the dense foliage around him. He'd lost his walking cane in the crash—well, technically, he'd actually managed to lose the crash as well, or rather the crash site. He could remember it. Could remember something dark and large, almost feline in its grace, dart out in front of his car, just after the bridge on County Road 43. He could remember losing control and seeing the stand of trees racing toward them in the chaos. Then, there'd been nothing.

According to his watch, he'd awakened a few good hours later, and though the thick canopy of vegetation above him blocked out the sky entirely, he was sure the sun was already high overhead. The fact that he was surrounded on all sides by walls of dead trees, the stark absence of bird calls, and a swelling sense of dread in the pit of his stomach, told him he'd awakened smack dab in the middle of the Dark Hollows.

But that made no sense. By his estimation, the highway on which he'd been traveling was miles away from the haunted cluster of valleys. How had he gotten here? At the moment, he figured, it really didn't matter. His first priority was to find Kili and get the heck as far from the insanity of Boone Creek as he could.

Fortunately, he'd found his phone in his jacket pocket... undamaged and miraculously enough, with three bars. The first thing he tried was calling Kili, but it had gone straight to voicemail. He'd then tried calling Granny, then Bear Boone and John Tyler, but had received the same response. Alex had a feeling no help would come from anyone he'd gotten to know since coming to this crazy town. It was just the kind of day he was having.

He chided himself for not getting Crane's phone number when he'd had the chance. To be fair though, he'd always figured that if they needed to get a hold of the strange mountain man, Kili would have been there to do it for him.

So, with no idea who he could call, he found a sturdy piece of hickory to use as an impromptu walking stick, took a look at his phone's global positioning app, and headed due east. Back toward town. He hoped that he'd run into Kili on his journey. Better yet, maybe she'd already made it back. But he wouldn't give up until he knew she was safe.

"Kili! Where are you!" he shouted again.

"You won't find her that way, sweetie pie," someone to his left suddenly said, causing him to stumble over a jutting root.

Once he regained his balance, he spun around to see a woman—a most stunning woman—of ethereal elegance and beauty. At first glance, Davenport could have believed she had grown out of the very forest from which he now struggled to escape. There was something primal about her presence...something visceral about her light caramel skin and long, kinky black hair. A wreath of dandelions adorned her head, and she wore a sun dress of soft linen that was almost sheer against the dim light now peeking through the trees above. The woman's bare feet strode over the rugged terrain with graceful ease, as she moved seductively toward him with the most provocative smile on her face.

"Um, excuse me?" Davenport managed. He couldn't pull his eyes away from the vision before him, even though he'd already guessed the strange woman's identity and the danger she represented.

"Ms. Brennan," Asherah said, drawing so close to him he could feel the fibers of her dress against his bare arm. "She's not going to hear you. She's gone."

"I, uh… I mean…"

Asherah's smile widened at the reporter's discomfort as she

drew even closer. Her soft hands reached up to stroke the stubble on his face, and she leaned in toward his ear. "What's the matter?" she whispered. "Cat got your tongue?"

Her breath against his face smelled of honeysuckle, and Davenport found himself transfixed by the stimuli overload the woman was causing his system. But a sudden flash of Kili— possibly in danger somewhere nearby—broke the spell that was being cast on him.

"W-where i-is she?" he stammered, backing away from her. "Where's Kili?"

Frowning, Asherah took another step forward, but he held out a hand, forcing her away. "Uh-uh," he said. "I'm on to your games, Toots. Now tell me where she is."

Rolling her eyes, Asherah shrugged with an exasperated sigh. "New boy in town's been warned about me, I see." She was still grinning devilishly, albeit with considerably less enjoyment in her eyes. "Fine. Truth is, I'm not sure where she is. But a little bird told me she'd been taken."

"Who? Who told you?"

Asherah glanced around as if looking for the Candid Camera crew that must have been hiding in the woods nearby. "A little bird," she said. "Seriously."

Davenport didn't know if she was toying with him or not. In this town, it honestly wouldn't surprise him if she was telling the truth.

"Well, did Tweety tell you *who* took her?"

"Didn't have to," she said, her face turning serious. "It's obvious, isn't it? The Willow Hag."

Hearing the name, the reporter's grip tightened around the hickory stick. "Okay then," he said. "Take me to her."

The beautiful witch tilted her head back and guffawed at the impetuous command. "Even if I knew where she was, why should I do such a foolish thing, you gorgeous idiot, you?"

"B-because y-you—"

His words were cut short by the abrupt thrum of his cell phone vibrating in his pocket. Nearly jumping, he reached into his pocket and pulled the phone out. 606 area code…local…but he didn't recognize the number.

"Hello?" he asked after accepting the call.

"Mr. Davenport? I'm lookin' for Granny," the smooth, honey-like voice of Ezekiel Crane echoed in the earpiece. He sounded unnerved. On edge, which did little for Davenport's own nerves. "She doesn't seem to be home. Is she with you?"

"Crane! Thank God, it's you!" He noticed Asherah back away two steps at the mention of the man's name. He couldn't help smile over it, but pushed his amusement aside long enough to tell Crane everything that had happened to them since arriving at Granny's house early that morning. About the Leecher attack, their strange interest in Delores McCrary, and the woman's subsequent disappearance. About his and Kili's mission to find the old woman and the car crash that separated him from Kili. "So now I'm somewhere in the Dark Hollows, and I have no idea what to do. Don't know where Kili is or how to find her." He looked over at the dark-skinned woman and added, "But I'm with your friend…Asherah…right now. She said that the Willow Hag has taken Kili."

There was an uncomfortably long pause on the other end. Cautiously, Davenport checked to be sure he hadn't dropped the call. Satisfied they were still connected, he brought the phone back to his ear. "Crane? Did you hear me?"

The mountain man cleared his throat before answering. "Yes, I heard. And Ash is with you right now? At this very moment?"

"Yep. I'm looking at her exceptionally large green eyes, even now."

"Let me talk to her," Crane demanded.

Without hesitation, the reporter held the phone out. "He wants to speak with you," he said quietly, but with a certain sense of satisfaction. Like a little brother handing a phone over to an older sibling, whose wrathful parent was on the other line.

Tentatively, she reached out and took the phone. "Ezekiel, Dear," she said. "How good it is to hear—"

There was a pause while Crane cut her off. Davenport heard the soft Kentucky drawl murmuring from the ear piece, but couldn't make out what was said.

"But I—" Asherah looked in Davenport's direction while Crane interrupted again.

Davenport wasn't entirely sure who this Ezekiel Crane guy was, but he was really starting to respect the fear of God the man could put in people.

"I already checked the Grove," she said. "No one was there, and I left some, um, warning charms there to alert me if they showed up."

More silence while Crane replied.

"Delores? But I thought... No, that doesn't make any... The Kindred? Oh, come now, how could I possibly know..." The beautiful woman bit at her lower lip, as she listened intently to what she was being told. "Yes," she said. "Yes, yes... I will... Yes, I will look out for him... Crane, I said I'd watch over—"

Crane mumbled something else before she handed the phone back to Davenport, who immediately accepted.

"Crane?"

"Alex, listen to me. Things have never been more dire. Ms. Kili is in grave danger."

"Tell me something I don't know," Davenport said.

"You misunderstand me. It's not a physical danger I'm worried about for the moment. I can't explain everything right now, but in a nutshell... She is an unwitting knot in a spiritual game of tug of war at the moment. A choice is currently being put before her...one with no winning prospects.

"Now listen to me closely. Your life, and that of Ms Kili's depends on it. I'm on my way to Somerset right now, and I won't be able to help you. Ms. Kili doesn't have much time left, so I've convinced Ash to take you to the Devil's Teeth. That's where you'll find Kili and the Willow Hag as well, if I'm not mistaken."

"Okay, but what are we supposed to do once we get there?" Davenport asked. "I imagine this hag woman won't exactly welcome us with open arms or anything."

"Not a woman," Crane said. "No matter what you see there, remember that point. The Willow Hag is not a woman. Not anymore, anyway. She ceased to be human when she started feeding on the souls of the living, and it is from that very fate that we must race to save Kili." There was a short pause, but no explanation to the strange declaration. "Now go! The dirge is growing stronger. We're running out of time."

And with that, the phone went dead. Confused, Davenport looked up at Asherah. "What a weird dude," he said, while tucking the phone back into his pocket.

"You've no idea," she replied. Then abruptly, with no warning, she walked up to him, pressed the palms of both hands against his chest, and shoved him to the ground. Once he was on his back, she crouched down and reached for his belt. "Now, sweetie pie. Let's get those pants off you."

"What..." he slapped her hand away with a squeal of surprise, "...the heck are you doing, you crazy broad?"

"Ooooooh, Mr. Davenport, I assure you... My intentions are quite noble," she said with a smile. "It's just that we have quite a hike ahead of us, and unless I mend that injured hip of yours, it'll take us all day to get there."

Sitting up, he eyed her suspiciously. "Wait a minute. Mend my hip? You can do that? I mean...I mean, fix it for good?"

Her teeth shone brightly at his question. "Of course, you dimwitted, sexy buffoon," she said, standing to her feet and wiping her hands on her dress. "Now, get your pants off, and I'll go gather the necessary ingredients."

Without waiting for a response, she dashed off into the

woods and disappeared. Nervously, Davenport removed his left pant leg, but kept the other side on. After all, the witch didn't need him to strip down to his skivvies to fix his bum hip.

A few minutes later, Asherah returned, brandishing an armful of herbs and mushrooms, which she mashed into a disgusting smelling paste. Disappointed about the reporter's modesty, she whined as she spread the nasty stuff over his left waist, hip, and thigh. Then she hummed a few stanzas of some indecipherable chant. Three minutes later, he felt an intense heat shoot up his leg from his feet, and his leg grew instantly numb.

"My leg... I can't feel it!" he shouted.

"But it's still there, isn't it?" she said with a sly grin. "I said I'd mend the injury. I never promised to make your leg as good as new."

"I... You... But I don't..."

Once again, she tilted her head back and laughed delightedly at his confusion. "Relax, sweetie," she said. "The numbness will wear off soon. Your leg most definitely will be as good as new. But for now, we need to get moving." She reached a hand down and helped him to his feet. Cautiously, he tested the strength and balance of his left leg, and he was surprised to discover that his new companion had been telling the truth. He was already beginning to regain some sensation, but he couldn't detect even the slightest trace of pain where the broken hip had previously failed to mend properly. As a matter of fact, if he'd been in much better shape, he guessed that he'd be able to run a marathon on it with very little trouble.

"Wow," he said, stepping back and forth from one leg to the other before doing a quick jog in place. "Thank you so much."

Asherah merely shrugged. "Don't thank me yet," she said, as she turned to the south and started walking. "One day, I'll come to you to collect payment for my doctorin', and you might not like the cost. Now come on. Your girlfriend isn't going to save herself, now is she?"

A chill ran down his spine as he considered the witch's cryptic threat, but he couldn't worry about that now. He quickly pulled his pants back on and darted after her, traveling deeper into the Dark Hollows on his very first damsel-in-distress rescue mission. He decided very quickly that it was by no means as much fun as he'd always imagined it might be.

CHAPTER
TWENTY-THREE

I-75 South
April 29
1:00 PM

C rane glanced at the dashboard clock as he hung up with Davenport. 11:45 AM. His discussion with the reporter had not gone well. Of course, he'd honestly expected no less. After being unable to make contact with Granny, he feared something unexpected had happened. When he began to hear the unearthly dirge within the cab of his pickup, he knew things had suddenly turned disastrous. Davenport's declaration that Kili was missing had simply confirmed his worst fears.

But he couldn't think about her right now. He had to trust in Asherah and the reporter to find Kili in time, while he remained focused on the heavy burden he would soon have to endure. It was essential to keep his mind fixed on the problem he was about to face, or everything they'd worked for to this point—and the sacrifice his friend Kili had unknowingly made—would be for naught. No, he simply couldn't allow his mind and intellect to cloud over with emotion right now.

A quick look into the rearview mirror told him it was already too late. The constricting knot in his throat was testament to the fact that his emotions were already on edge. Though he wouldn't allow the Hag the pleasure of a tear—not yet anyway—he knew that he'd already accepted the inevitable. He was already beginning to mourn the loss that was to come.

The damnable curse! he thought, slamming a fist against the center console.

The cold hard fact was...someone was going to die today. The question he couldn't begin to answer was whether it would be Kili, Granny, Asherah, or even...

No, he couldn't even consider it. Couldn't afford to even entertain *that* possibility. Better by far for Crane himself to die than *him*. But the dirge he'd been hearing since leaving Maher's lab hadn't revealed anything specific to him, just that someone close to him was doomed to die soon, and that was enough to bring any man to his knees.

The Dirge. He let out a contemptible laugh as he pondered the word. The very notion that such a thing even existed was the epitome of irony, for as all the old-timers were aware, there is one thing that the spirits are incapable of doing. Whether ghost or angel, demon or spirit of the land, there is one thing among their vast and awesome powers that none of them can do.

Make music.

Most laugh when they're told this little fact, but it was absolutely true. No spirit has the ability to sing, for instance. No matter what the cartoons and bric-a-brac of popular culture might say about the choirs of angels, nowhere in the Bible did it describe them as such. A fierce army, yes. Stalwart messengers, certainly. But there was not a single verse of Scripture that described them as 'singing.' That was because they—as well as all other spirit beings—were literally incapable of song.

Because of this, spirits of all kinds are invariably attracted to music. It's why they congregate by the dozens in dance halls.

Why Christmas, with all its carols, is their favorite time of the year. It is why wind-chimes, flutes, or even radios can be used to draw them near. They literally *crave* song. They desperately desire music. But tragically, they are unable to make a single note of it for themselves.

The reason? Song comes from man's unique ability to be spiritually redeemed. Forgiven. Restored to his proper place in the universe. Since singing is one of the basest forms of emoting joy, sorrow, pain, euphoria, contentment, or desire, it is the ultimate expression of a redeemed soul. Spirits, being incapable of receiving grace, cannot possibly understand the joy that redemption brings. This inexperience makes it impossible for them to feel joy or sorrow the same way humans do, and therefore, makes them incapable of song.

With one soul-wrenching exception.

Death.

Though unable to truly know pain or sadness, spirits can grow attached to the living. They form bonds with them, even if the living person is unaware of their existence. When that person is soon to be taken from them, it rips an emotional hole in the spirit, causing them to be wracked with the closest thing to sorrow they will ever feel...and song escapes their ethereal lips. No mortal is ever supposed to hear such a mournful song. It has the potential to rip a human's soul to shreds upon hearing a single stanza of such a spirit dirge—which is precisely the reason the Willow Hag had incorporated it into her Death Curse. It was a kind of metaphysical tenderizer for her intended meal, so to speak.

All right, Crane thought, turning on the radio and flipping through the stations. He hoped a little Blue Grass or Country might help drown out the incessant song in his head. *Dwelling on it is not going to help anyone. Stay focused, and maybe, just maybe, you can prevent this from happening.* He stopped tuning the radio dial when he found a station blaring Willie and Elvis in a wonderfully haunting duet. For now, he would put all the anxiety away, soothe his weary soul with some of the most exquisite music around, and concentrate on the drive to Somerset.

Of course, his mind could not remain idle for long. Though he managed to put aside the horrible implications the Dirge represented, his thoughts quickly returned to the recent revelations imparted to him by Dr. Maher.

Strangely, the news she'd told him hadn't come as a complete surprise. He'd already pieced most of it together. Asherah, who had recently assumed control of the McGuffin drug empire, had been attempting to carve out a unique niche for herself among the international drug cartels. Undoubtedly, she'd been aware of the One-Eyed Jack spores long before Crane had discovered them. She'd probably been introduced to them by the Willow Hag, during Ash's apprenticeship with the undying witch. All too familiar with the spores' ability to quickly grow new cells, Ash had seen a perfect opportunity to approach Aion Pharmaceuticals with a potential new drug with amazing regenerative properties. That much, Crane had already deduced.

What had caught him completely off guard was to learn precisely who Ash had approached within the company—Crane's very own estranged sister, Jael. But once Maher had admitted that his sister was indeed her employer, he quickly surmised the rest.

Josiah. His brother and the mysterious patient in the cellar of Overturf's mortuary.

His illness had been part of the reason Jael had broken ties with Granny and Crane. She believed that they were responsible for Josiah's unfortunate condition...his supernaturally induced coma granted to him by the Hag herself, when he tried to prevent the Leechers from carrying out their vengeance against Crane. Jael had blamed him and Granny just as much, if not more, than the foul creature who'd hexed Josiah. Not that Crane could blame her. Not a day had gone by that he'd not cast blame against himself for the same thing.

So Asherah had specifically approached Jael, claiming the fungal spore could be the answer to reviving Crane's brother. His sister, so consumed with the thought of bringing Josiah back from the brink, had formed a cautious partnership with Ash, and the *experiments* began shortly after.

Maher swore that she and Jael had done everything they could to cure the seven victims that had eventually become the Kindred. Apparently, unknown to even Sheriff Tyler, they'd been found still alive by Ash's men, wandering aimlessly through the Dark Hollows, during the search for Cian Brennan and his assistant, Miles Marathe. They'd been taken immediately to Jael, and she and Maher had worked day and night, trying every conceivable treatment to combat the fungal infection that had begun to mutate them on the genetic level. And after a while, they came to believe they'd stumbled upon the answer.

The teratoma tumors Kili had seen in the specimen jars.

Every single one of them had the growths. Not just one growth. Or even two. But numerous, mutated tumors growing inside them. Crane, himself, had even seen similar aberrations during his autopsies of Marathe and Candace Staples, but he'd discounted them as being insignificant. Merely coincidence. But Jael and Maher had speculated that the teratomas were the byproduct of the accelerated cellular regeneration. Even they couldn't fathom the truth behind them. Now, Crane knew. Knew their meaning. Knew the horrible truth. He'd suspected it from the moment Kili had told them of the specimen jars—the weird blobs of tissue, hair, teeth, and eyes—though he hadn't been sure until this moment.

Maher insisted the last she or Jael had seen the victims of One-Eyed Jack, they had been thoroughly deceased. Crane, of course, believed her. The fact that their shades still haunted the labs of Aion was testimony of that. The seven people had come to a brutal end there, which had ingrained a portion of their psyche on the building's infrastructure.

And Crane now understood why. The Kindred were not the victims of One-Eyed Jack resurrected to new life. They were merely a fluke of nature, enhanced, possibly with a touch of dark magic. An abomination of mutated biology mixed with the arcane. The One-Eyed Jack spores had indeed begun changing each of their DNA. Changing them. Regenerating their flesh while simultaneously eating away at them. Digesting proteins and enzymes so that the spores could reassemble their genetic code in the form of the teratomas.

Teratomas that continued to grow. To change. Teratomas that thrived even within the rotting corpses of their hosts. Until one day, those vestigial eyes blinked. The hair began to grow. The teeth extended to form a mouth.

No, the Kindred were not a miracle of life after death, but genetics run amok. Spontaneous clones. Walking cancers with only minimal recollections of their former hosts' lives. What that meant for the Kindred and their family—what it meant for the people of Boone Creek—Crane couldn't be sure. At the moment, the mystery would have to wait. Now, his only task was hunting down the one who stole the Witchhunter's bones and putting an end to the Leechers' bloodthirsty crusade.

When he'd left the still-stammering Maher, Crane had been no closer to discovering the bone-thief than when he'd first broken into Aion. He'd been heading home from Lexington when everything fell into place…starting with his phone call to Davenport and the revelation that the Leechers had their sights set on Delores McCrary. That little tidbit of information told him everything he needed to know.

It told him that she was the one responsible for the Kindred's 'resurrections'. It told him that the Leechers had been sent on a mission to discover the identity of the one responsible, in hopes of drawing out the Willow Hag. And finally, by considering the individual who had the most reason to loathe the Hag, it told him precisely who was responsible for the Leechers' return to Boone Creek. So, upon this realization, Crane had made a forced U-turn to head back to I-75 and had begun making his way southeast toward Somerset.

Toward a lonely rehabilitation facility called Southwood, and his brother, Josiah.

CHAPTER
TWENTY-FOUR

The Dark Hollows
April 29
3:13 PM

K ili flinched as the talon-like branch of an old oak slashed across her face, just before she burst through a thick wall of trees. Whatever was chasing her was closing in quickly, and she was running out of steam. She'd been running for hours, though she had no idea how she'd not already collapsed into oblivion from pure exhaustion. Spasms of pain shot through almost every nerve in her body—whether from the car crash, the scrapes and bruises sustained from the chase, or oxygen deprivation, it made no difference. By this point, it was all the same. And it was wearing her down.

"*Kiiiiiilllllllliiiiiiibbbrrreennnaannn!*" taunted the raspy, disembodied voice from somewhere behind her. "*Whhyyy dooo yoouuu ruuuun?*"

That had been the second time she'd heard the voice, though she still couldn't pinpoint the source. The furtive glances she cast over her shoulder had been fruitless. Though she knew something was indeed hunting her through the Dark Hollows, and that whatever it was had upped the ante by hurling those haunting jeers, she still had been unable to identify exactly what *it* was.

"*Kiiiillllliiibbrrreeennnaannn! Whhhhy are yooouuu friiightened, little giiiirl?*"

Her pulse quickened at the taunt. The voice sounded inhuman. Horrifying. At first, she'd believed it might be one of the Leechers, who'd sounded eerily similar in Granny's house, a few hours before. But the more the thing spoke, the more she knew it wasn't a Leecher. This voice was too different. More mewling than the raspy demonic voices of the haints. And though the sound of the voice was terrifying, instinctively, she knew it meant her no real harm. Its questions were from genuine curiosity. Perhaps even concern.

Still, despite this intuition, Kili pressed on...running faster through the unimaginably dense woods. And suddenly, she broke free of the vegetation and found herself out in open air. The bright yellow light of the sun blazed its way over the mountainous horizon, momentarily blinding her to her surroundings.

The sudden blindness, as well as the introduction of open space, set her off-balance; her head and torso over-extended, causing her to tumble to the moist, moss-covered ground. Instantly, she clambered to her feet and brought her arms up in a defensive posture—awaiting her pursuer's inevitable pounce.

But it never came.

"*Kiiiillllliiiibbrrreeennnaannn!*" the voice hissed from somewhere in the shadows of the forest. "*Iiiiiitttt iiiisssss ttttiiii-immmeee!*"

The throaty greeting chilled her to the core. Her throat constricted, making it difficult to swallow, as she peered into the darkness for the source of the voice.

Then she saw it.

Slowly, weaving in and out of the trees, Kili caught sight of an all too familiar feline form. The shape was hazier than she'd seen in the past...more shrouded in shadows...but it was unmistakable. The long, upright ears. The sleek, lithe body and taut muscular legs. The stump, where a serpentine-like tail should have been. But there was something very different about the creature she'd never fully seen before. The Tailypo's two hazel-green, very human-like eyes—now clearly visible for the first time—were staring passively at her as it paced back and forth along the forest's edge.

Human eyes, she thought, willing her wobbling legs still. As hard as she tried, she was unable to break her gaze from those eyes. They, too, were familiar...though she wasn't sure how. But they elicited a horrid sense of loss, desperation, and angst that threatened to crush her soul with their familiarity.

Instinctively, she fumbled for the Tailypo talisman in her pocket and gripped it tightly as the creature continued to speak.

"*Iiiittt iiiiss nnnnoooowwww tttiiiimmmeee to ccchhoooossse, Kkkiilliiibbbrrreennnaaannn.*" Though there was no indication that the Tailypo's tooth-filled mouth even moved, Kili was sure the strange declaration had come from it. "*Chhhooossseee wwhhhoooo yyyooouu wwwiiillll bbbeeeee.*"

"W-what do you mean?" she asked, surprised at how her voice cracked with each syllable.

But the strange creature simply continued pacing back and forth, never venturing out past the tree line.

"Please," she said, taking a single step toward it. The Tailypo side-stepped once, keeping the distance equal between the two of them. "Help me. Tell me what I need to do."

"*Chhhooossseee.*"

"What? What am I supposed to choose?"

Several nerve-racking heartbeats went by before the creature spoke again. "*Bbbrrriiaarrrsssnnnaaarrre Mmmaaarrrsh,*" it said. "*Yyyooouu mmuuusstt eennnttteeerr aanndd ccchhhoooosse!*"

"But where is Briarsnare Marsh? I have no idea where—"

Instantly, the creature melted into the shadows without another word.

"Don't go!" she cried. "Please! I need your help!"

But there was no response. Frustrated and still feeling the sting of the inexplicable sadness the creature's eyes had provoked in her, she threw up her hands and yelled at the top of her lungs. It was a near-feral, growl-like scream that rose from the depths of her soul, and it felt so good. After all she'd been through...after all the things she'd endured... The ability to unleash all her fury at the world without fear of reprimand or social convention was a very welcome change.

So, she screamed again—this time more ferociously than the last. Vaguely, she was aware that as her voice echoed all around her, it was accompanied by something else. Something musical. A song of some kind. A terribly sad, angst-filled song. She screamed even more. Her voice reverberated in the clearing, as every ounce of grief, misery, terror, and murderous rage ebbed from her, like heat from a radiator.

She thought of Cian as she roared...at his misery under a reign of mental illness for most of his life. About the spores that had invaded his body and had transformed him—ripping and tearing away at his flesh as he'd grown into a thirteen-foot monster. She railed against the indifferent townspeople...about the way they'd treated her, when she first came to Boone Creek in search of her brother. How they'd threatened her and tried so hard to scare her away. She vowed in that deep, soul-releasing scream that they would one day regret their actions.

And the song continued to accompany her fury.

She thought of the curse placed on her by the mysterious Willow Hag and of Crane's seeming indifference to it. She'd believed the man to be a friend, and his heartless abandonment of her worked to fuel her rage, so she screamed even louder. And all the while, she knew...somehow in the pit of her stomach, she was sure...that they would all be sorry for how they'd treated her and Cian, in this horrible little town. Every last one of them.

She had no idea how long she did this, but it wasn't until the breath gave out in her lungs and the screams slowly died away, that Kili Brennan found herself smiling broader than she had in a very long time.

Of course, it wasn't fair to say she was becoming happy over Boone Creek's impending misfortune. After all, a few people— Granny, for instance—certainly didn't deserve such wrathful ire. But there was definitely a part of her that relished the thought of the fast-approaching disaster she inexplicably knew was coming.

A word materialized within her mind. A word she'd never heard before.

Ghostfeast.

She didn't know what the word meant. Nor did she understand how she even knew it. But she relished the sound of it within her mental ear. She laughed at how much comfort the word had given her and how much sadness it would bring to these horrid redneck hicks.

She paused for breath. She was acutely aware that something was happening to her. Something had changed. A mental breakdown, perhaps? Had she finally snapped? In the end, she didn't care. She enjoyed the freedom this newly born attitude she'd developed made her feel. She felt empowered by it. She laughed again, then stopped.

She was suddenly aware that all was silent. The song—the Dirge—had stopped. And for some reason, the realization struck her hard in the gut, wiping the mad grin off her face.

She felt sick. Unexpectedly, she was unsure of her own sanity. Unsure of what she was becoming. The darkness she'd just witnessed in the corners of her soul disturbed her more than shadowy cat spirits, zombie witchhunters, or evil hags combined. The vengeful joy she'd just allowed herself in the imaginary suffering of those who'd wronged her had come from nowhere. Only, that couldn't be true, could it? After all, it had come from inside her own heart. It must have been there all along, and if that was true, Kili couldn't help but wonder what else might be lurking in there as well.

"So now yer beginnin' to understand the Tailypo's choice, eh, deary?" The voice behind her was old. Grandmotherly. Kili vaguely recalled hearing it before. In a shack in the middle of a grove of willows. And somewhere else. Some place more recent.

Slowly, Kili turned around to find herself on the very edge of Briarsnare Marsh. It had not been there when she'd exploded from the woods at full speed. It had simply been acres of rolling hills and pasture. Now, as she stared out at the horizon, there was nothing but dead, flat marshland, a sky ablaze with blue-green fire swirling along the wind currents, and a shadowy figure of a wizened old woman who stooped over malformed shoulders.

The old woman, covered from head to foot in a ragged old burial shroud, inched closer to her.

"But don't you fret none 'bout it, deary," the Willow Hag said, just as two meaty hands stretched out from behind Kili and clamped a strange-smelling handkerchief over her nose and mouth. The odor...was it chloroform? Kili's vision quickly dimmed to little more than a single pinprick of light. The last thing she remembered before passing out was the shrill sound of a woman laughing and the old crone saying, "We'll just make that choice of yers a might easier for ya, shall we?"

CHAPTER
TWENTY-FIVE

Southwood Rehabilitation Center
Somerset, Kentucky
April 29
5:45 PM

T he hallway on the third floor of Southwood Rehabilitation Center was unusually quiet for a late afternoon. Even for a floor comprised of no one but the comatose or catatonic, Esther Crane would have expected there to be more activity—more of a buzz—especially since the early spring thunderstorm raging outside would have prevented the staff from taking patients out onto the facility's sprawling grounds for a bit of sun and fresh air. As it was, only three patients and the orderlies manhandling their wheelchairs could be seen meandering through the antiseptically clean hallway, as she strode purposefully from the elevator and headed to Room 321.

Good. The fewer people, the fewer complications. Granny wasn't sure if her confrontation was going to cause an unwanted commotion, but if so, better to have no one around to get in the way. To an outsider, what she was about to do wouldn't look very gentle, and she knew she'd have a difficult time explaining herself to any authorities that might happen to walk in on her during the ritual.

Walking past the nurse's station, manned by only one obviously sleep-deprived woman tapping mindlessly away at a computer terminal, Granny moved to the door, gave a quick glance over her shoulder, and turned the handle. Opening the door, she stepped in and closed it behind her. The lights were turned off, and only a sliver of light shone through the bottom of the navy blue curtains that covered the single window in the room. She stopped long enough to allow her eyes to adjust to the dim lighting in the room, then walked quietly over to the young man resting peacefully on the mechanical hospital bed and gently took hold of his hand.

"Josiah," she whispered, leaning in to kiss him on the cheek. "Josiah, my sweet, sweet boy." She felt her throat constrict as the words scraped past her vocal cords and tears welled at the corner of her eyes. It had been far too long since she'd last paid her grandson a visit. Of course, that wasn't entirely her fault. Jael had done a fair job of keeping his location secret from both her and Ezekiel. But as she'd demonstrated earlier that morning with the simple divining spell she'd whipped up, there weren't too many places her granddaughter could have hidden him if Granny had set her mind to finding him.

But the truth was, she'd secretly never faulted Jael for the blame she'd placed on her for Josiah's condition. If anyone was capable of stopping the Willow Hag on that horrible day...of putting an end to the horror the old crone had conjured...it would have been her. Only, she hadn't. She'd been too plagued by indecision. Too fearful of the consequences of such an act. And because of that, her youngest grandchild had suffered for years in a coma.

She looked down at the boy now—no, at twenty-seven years of age, he wasn't a boy any longer. He was a man. With an underdeveloped musculature from fifteen years of convalescence, he was physically weak. An invalid. And there was no telling whether Josiah had sustained any brain damage during his encounter with the Leechers that might cause even more debilitation. But the point was, no matter how much she wished he'd been able to have a normal childhood, those days were forever gone. He truly was a man now, and there was nothing she could do about it.

She glanced over at the EKG monitor to the left of Josiah's bed. His heart rate appeared strong. That was good news at least.

Or bad. She wasn't quite sure yet.

Disturbed by that thought, she wiped a tear from her eye and hefted the Gladstone doctor's bag she'd carried in with her, setting it on the bed next to her grandson. She quietly rummaged through it. A second later, she withdrew two sets of wind chimes and placed one carefully in the southeast corner of the room and other in the northwest. Once the chimes were secured, she pulled out two sticks, each a foot long and intricately carved with strange lettering and symbols handed down from her grandmother's grandmother. Moving back over to the door, she brought the sticks together to form a letter V, said a quick prayer, and relaxed her grip.

Instantly, she felt the dowsing rods begin to tremble within her palms. Relaxing her own will, she focused on the sticks' subtle pull and took a step forward. And another. And another. She couldn't believe it. The bones were here. Somewhere hidden within Josiah's very room. The rods were homing in on them just as easily as if she'd been trying to find clean water.

Not wanting to rush and risk losing the connection, she closed her eyes and concentrated on the subtle vibrations thrumming within the rods. A thousand questions raced through her mind, confounding the process. How could she have been right? How could her grandson have anything to do with this? He'd been in a coma all this time. How could he be behind the theft of the Witchhunter's bones? How could he have summoned the Leechers?

Her thoughts immediately drifted to Jael. Was she the one behind it? Surely, she would do anything to save her brother and would probably do just as much to punish the ones responsible. But Granny knew in her gut it wasn't her granddaughter. Knew that despite the animosity she had for the Willow Hag, Ezekiel, and everyone else in Boone Creek, Jael had adamantly renounced anything remotely supernatural in her life. She'd dedicated herself completely to science, and unlike Ezekiel, she had all but abandoned the ways of her ancestors out of sheer disgust with it all. No, Josiah's sister would never stoop to using magic to gain her revenge. Granny was confident she would use a much more direct approach, if the time ever came.

So, that left only her bedridden Josiah. The only one with enough natural talent to harness his hatred into something that could bind the Leechers to his will.

Speakin' of wills, you need to get a grip on yours, you ol' coot, Granny chastised herself, before returning to the task at hand. A little more concentration and she felt the tug of the rods once more leading her toward her grandson's bed. Three more steps and she was beside it. Oddly, the dowsing rods had completely stopped. No tug. No vibrations. They were now fully inert. *So what does that tell you, ya ol' biddy?*

It didn't take long to discern the answer. Kneeling, she peeked under the bed and saw what she'd been looking for—a wooden ossuary with carved symbols, similar to the ones on her rods, etched over its entire surface. Instinctively, she reached out to grab the box, but pulled her hands away at the last minute.

Something was wrong. This was all too easy. What's more, Josiah hadn't gotten up out of bed, trekked deep into the mountains to steal the bones, and returned here only to slip back into a coma. No. He'd needed help for that. Someone was working with him, and she had a hunch whoever it was wouldn't be leaving the boy out of their sight for long. What's more, she was certain that they wouldn't have left the box without certain protections either—a mistake Granny had made herself. She'd been too confident the hiding place in which she'd left Smith's bones would never be discovered. The thief would have obviously learned from Granny's own mistake. Would have erected charms to ward off any would-be sticky-fingers trying to snatch the powerful relics away.

Grabbing her Gladstone, she withdrew a small bottle of whiskey and a bag of M&Ms. She then slid under the bed, carefully placing pieces of candy around the ossuary in a tight circle, before pouring seven shot glasses and positioning them on the floor at the four corners of the box.

"My friends," she whispered. "I don't right know if you'uns is here or not. Ain't heard from none of you since those danged Leechers raised their ugly beaks in Boone Creek, but I need yer help in the worst way now. Oh, people of the Yunwi Tsunsdi, help me to set things right again. Help me to end the evil what's scourging the land. If'n we's ever been friends, help me break any wards what might be placed on this here box."

Ezekiel would have scolded her for sending so blatant a request, and she knew it. As benevolent as the Lil' Folk could be, they were still spirits nonetheless and not to be beseeched for anything. Sure, her grandson would honor them with an occasional peace offering from time to time to garner their favor, but he'd never request specific help from them. Spirits, after all, could never be truly trusted. They were all ornery in their own way. But Granny was running out of options. And time. If she didn't deal with this now...

"What do you think you're doing?" someone near the doorway asked. It was a female, but from her position under the bed, Granny couldn't see who it was.

Her brain kicked into overdrive, trying to come up with the

best answer to the question. "Oh dear," she said feebly as she began to crawl out from under the bed. "I'm so very sorry. I was here visitin' my grandson, and I dropped my glasses. I'd just climbed down to fetch 'em when you walked in." As she finished, she came to her full height and looked over at the door. Her son's pretty blonde nurse—Tiffany? Beth? *No, Heather*. Her name was Heather. The nurse stood scowling from the doorway, her arms crossed over her chest. Feigning relief, Granny threw the nurse a bright smile. "Ah, sweet Heather! It sure is good to see you after—"

"Don't lie to me," Heather said, stepping further into the room and closing the door behind her. "I know exactly what you were doing. Josiah called to me. Told me what you were up to. Told me you were here to take the bones away from him."

Called to her?

The sound of tinkling metal and glass arose near the southeast corner, drawing her attention away from the nurse. One of the chimes. Something was coming, but what it was, there was no way to tell.

"Your grandson is so much more than you ever imagined. Greater than you could believe. He's the one—even in this vegetative state—who figured out where you'd hidden Eli Smith's bones. Told me where to look. And even though it took some doing to get past your little booby traps you'd set, I finally managed to dig them up. Then, it was only a matter of time and patience for Josiah to teach me how to use them properly..."

What is she talking about? Granny thought. *How is all this possible?*

But the nurse, oblivious to the older woman's confusion, continued with her diatribe, "...and he might not have the guts to deal with his beloved *Granny*, but we've come just too far to let you screw everything up now," Heather spat, as she held up a single bone—a femur if Granny wasn't mistaken. "I've waited too long for this... Finally, after all this time, I see the light at the end of the tunnel. Josiah and I will soon be together. Forever! And I'm not about to let a decrepit old hag like you come between us."

Even with their distance, Granny could feel the femur begin to hum with energy, eliciting even more clatter from the wind chimes. Within seconds, the glass and metal fragments of the chimes whirled around in a cacophony of sound.

"Heather, dear, what have you done?" Granny asked, planting her feet firmly apart as if preparing for a fight.

"I've done exactly what needs to be done!"

Slowly, the sound of a thousand whispers began to flood the room, as a dark, swirling form began to take shape just past the nurse's left shoulder.

"Heather, stop! You ain't got no idea what yer doin'!"

"I know precisely what I'm doing. I'm doing what you didn't do. I'm saving the man I love. From the Willow Hag. And from you!" Heather paused, looking curiously at the comatose form of Josiah laying prone in bed. "But I have to. She's going to mess everything up." Another pause. Was she somehow communicating with him? Was Josiah somehow reaching out to her and actually speaking? "I know what you said…but this is for us. Once she's gone, there's nothing to stop us from killing that witch, McCrary!"

With that, Granny decided to step in. "But that's the problem," she shouted past the roar of whispers ripping through the room like a vocalized whirlwind. "Delores ain't the Hag! You've set Eli Smith's Leechers to find the one responsible for the Kindred, but you never considered whether the Willow Hag was the one to do it."

Without warning, something hard smacked up against her foot, breaking her concentration. She glanced down and saw the ossuary jutting out from under Josiah's bed. The Yunwi Tsunsdi! They'd heard her plea and had somehow gotten past the wards to shove the box into view. They were helping her! Fortunately, the move had gone unnoticed by Heather, whose attention was torn between the man she obviously loved and Granny's exhortations. Hoping to press the advantage, Granny ignored the box of bones and continued.

"Delores McCrary did, somehow, raise the dead. Heck, she might have even used the Hag to do it, but she's not who yer lookin' for, and a whole town of people are dyin' 'cause of it. You've got to stop this, Heather." She looked down at her grandson. "You've got to stop this, Josiah. It ain't right. Yer daddy most definitely wouldn't approve, and you know it."

She turned back to the nurse, who now stood motionless, transfixed with indecision. The chimes continued their merry dance, as the whispers still increased. Granny nodded to the bone in Heather's hand. "Give it to me, darlin'. We'll figure out a way to break this curse, I promise."

Heather glanced down at the sun-bleached bone in her hand, then back up at Granny before white-knuckling the bone even tighter. "No." Her voice was low. Determined. "Josiah's right. You've been too blinded by your friendship to see the truth in front of your face! The Willow Hag's been using you all this time, and you just can't see it. I won't let you strip us of all we've worked for!"

Just as the words left her lips, a black leather boot solidified from the amorphous mass materializing behind her, followed immediately by a dark robed figure with a bird-like mask. But unlike the other Leechers, this one wore no hat. Instead, a hood covered its head, shading most of the macabre face.

Dear Lord have mercy. Eli Smith, himself.

The lich's axe was already in its hand, as it stepped toward Esther Crane. Though she couldn't see past the shadowy mask, she couldn't help but get the sense that the thing was smiling maliciously at her. Enjoying the task it had been commanded to perform.

It raised the axe with its next step, bringing the whispers and the tinkling of the chimes to complete silence.

"Heather, I know you don't want to do this," Granny shouted. But the young blonde's blank stare told her all she needed to know—the mental strain of controlling the Witch-hunter had rendered her beyond the scope of hearing.

Smith lunged, bringing the felling axe down toward Granny's head. Though older than most would believe, she was still spry enough to dive from the mortal blow and scramble away from the bed, in hopes of protecting her grandson from a stray swing. Instantly, the Witchhunter whirled around, swinging the axe horizontally, attempting to strike her as she came to her feet. When it missed, the Leecher took two steps toward the bed and turned to face her again.

"Eli Smith, you are not welcome in this place!" Granny cried, clenching her hands into tightly bound fists. "I command you to be gone!"

The dark creature stared at her for several long moments before a deep rumble of laughter rolled out from behind its mask.

"I'm serious," she said, backing up into the wall behind her. "If you know what's good fer ya, you'll leave now and never return."

It was a bluff, of course, and the monster knew it. If she'd been dealing with a human, her idle threats might have been heeded. Heck, if it had been a creature of considerably less power and knowledge, the threat might have done the trick. But the Witchhunter had been around for too long and was full of such rancor and hatred, she doubted it even cared any longer about its own well-being, as long as its mission continued.

Granny risked a glance down at the Leecher's boots. They were within inches of the ossuary. If only she'd had enough time to grab it before the creature's attack, her situation might have been different. Even her medicine bag was now too far out of reach. No, as it stood now, she was a sitting duck. All she could do at the moment was wait for the final swing and the oblivion that would follow. She only regretted not being able to do more to help Josiah. Not being able to do anything to help him recover from the infernal curse that had destroyed his life.

"Josiah, son," she said, taking a deep breath and resigning herself to the inevitable. "I'm truly sorry. Ain't a day gone by what I ain't prayed for you. I love you with all my heart. What's more…I forgive you for doin' what you thought was right."

As if sensing Granny's last words were finished, the haint snarled as it began its final attack. It was just about to leap toward her, when a pair of hands exploded from the bed behind the creature and wrapped themselves around it.

"No!" Josiah Crane shouted as he pulled the creature back on top of him. The Leecher's legs sprawled as he tumbled backwards, dropping his axe to the floor with a clank.

Granny dashed forward, grabbing the ossuary off the floor and raising it into the air. Though Heather still possessed a single bone, the box contained many more still, giving the elder woman primary control of the creature.

"Eli Smith, I say again…be gone!" she shouted. "You're not welcome here!"

Suddenly, the chimes began to clang together once more, followed by the ethereal shriek of the creature writhing on top of her grandson, trying to regain its freedom. But with each movement of its limbs, the creature began to fade away, until after thirty seconds, it was gone.

She immediately turned her attention back to her grandson, expecting to see him smiling up at her, awakened after all these years. But when she looked at his face, it felt as if the Leecher's axe had cleaved her heart in two. Her grandson's eyes were closed, his heart rate on the monitor was steady, but low, as if he'd never awakened to save her from the Witchhunter at all.

"No, no, no!" she shouted, sitting the box down on the nightstand and reaching out to cradle his head in his arms. Tears rushed down her cheeks, as she burst out with an angst-ridden howl. For one moment—for one bitterly-sweet second in time—he'd come back to her. Saved her. Only to have it all ripped painfully away again. She lowered her head to his chest and cried, not caring what was happening around her. Her tears dampened Josiah's pajama top as she bawled over the second time she'd lost him.

Eventually, she was aware of the other presence in the room. Heather had slowly moved closer to the bed, invading her space.

"I'd be careful how close you get, missy," Granny said, still clutching her grandson tightly. She didn't even waste a glance in the blonde's direction. "Or you just might see what the wrath-filled love of a grandma is really like."

Heather cleared her throat, though now it sounded a bit farther away. "I'm...I'm sorry," she said. "I didn't know what to do. He...he pleaded with me not to send the Leecher after you, and I didn't listen. I...I just couldn't stand the thought of you taking his only means of revenge away."

"And how, pray tell, is revenge gonna bring him back to us?" Granny asked, just as she began running her fingers through his dark, curly hair.

"It...it wouldn't, I know," she said. Her voice sounded weak. Trembling. "But we also hoped that if the Willow Hag was dead, the curse would be lifted and..."

"You don't think I ain't thought of that?" Granny still refused to look over at the nurse. Her eyes were steadily fixed on Josiah, as if waiting for him to move again. "The curse's power is self-contained now. It will continue long after she's gone. The only way to break it is to get her to release him, ya bleached idjit!"

There was a pause as the nurse absorbed what she'd just been told. "We didn't know. We just thought..."

Granny heard the door creak open, just as the chimes began to clamor again.

"Well, my lands!" came a frighteningly familiar feminine voice. "If this don't beat all. I came here to steal the Witch-hunter's bones. Maybe tie up a few loose ends. But dang it all, if I don't get to kill two Cranes with one stone, while I'm at it. That's just butter on the bread, right there."

Slowly, Esther Crane raised her head and looked toward the door. When she saw the person standing just inside the doorway, it was as if the very floor she stood on was suddenly dropping away from her feet. The world had just turned upside down.

"It can't be!" she said, absently grabbing the bone box from the nightstand and clutching it tightly to her chest. "You're dead."

The figure let out a mewl of a laugh before stepping further into the room and closing the door. "Well, as you've no doubt noticed, there's a lot of that going around," Candace Staples said with a sneer. "And as I've already pointed out, the three of you will be joining me real soon."

CHAPTER
TWENTY-SIX

The Dark Hollows
April 29
6:05 PM

"We've been walking for hours," Alex Davenport said between ragged breaths. Asherah had been true to her word. His leg had held up very well during their lengthy hike, but it didn't change the fact that he was horribly out of shape. In his line of work, it was becoming self-evident that if he survived all this, he would need to reconsider his personal workout routine—which was to say, he needed to start one. "Crane said Kili was running out of time. How much farther?"

"We're close," the witch hissed without looking back at him. If she was winded from their journey, she certainly didn't show it—a fact made all the more impressive with her traversing the rugged terrain without shoes. "So that means from this point on, we need to keep as quiet as we can. The Mother has spies everywhere in these woods." She let the last sentence sink in for a bit before adding, "But if the redhead's situation is what I believe it to be, you shouldn't worry. Ritual magic tends to work better after sundown. Nothing will happen until then, and that's still a few hours away. We'll get there in less than thirty minutes, so for now, shush."

"*Ritual* magic?"

Asherah's glaring eyes discouraged any more discussion on the subject, so the two continued moving through the dense woodland, squeezing through in some places that would have barred anyone of thicker stature. Twigs lashed at Davenport's arms, neck, and face as they walked, bringing several reddened welts across his sun-bronzed skin. Though there was hardly any light within the woods to begin with, as they trudged forward, he began to develop an inescapable sensation that what little illumination made it through the branches above was growing dimmer with every step.

After close to forty-five minutes, Asherah suddenly stopped, holding up a hand to bring Davenport to a halt as well. She then crouched, rocking back and forth on her bare feet, and gestured for silence before pointing several yards in front of them. Davenport mimicked his guide, crouched, and followed her finger in silence.

He nearly yelped at what he saw. Not more than fifty yards away, the one-and-a-half-foot long beak of a Leecher's mask was staring off blankly in their direction. The tall, bulky figure stood unmoving, between them and the ancient megalith of the Devil's Teeth. Its dead, black eyes watched them with contemptible indifference. The reporter's heart pounded madly against his chest, as memories of the Leechers' strange attack on him a few nights before came vividly back to him. He supposed that the incident would forever scar his psyche, and he had resigned himself to being struck paralyzed with fear whenever he'd see any bird larger than a sparrow flitting about. How he'd managed to overcome the fear at Granny's house that morning was beyond him. It had certainly not been courage that had fueled his action. He didn't relish the thought of going up against them again, and a small part of him wanted to turn tail and run before it was too late. He just wasn't sure he'd be able to survive another attack.

"What's that thing doing here?" he whispered. "Why's it just staring at us like that?"

"Because," Asherah answered, "he's not interested in us. At least, not yet."

"If he's not after us, then who? The Willow Hag?"

She looked over at him, her eyes darkened. "Technically, yes. But as you know, they're confused as to who, or rather what, she is. Their eyes are set on only one person...but they are biding their time. They have to make absolutely sure her mantle of power hasn't passed on to another or they will continue to remain in this realm for as long as she lives."

Davenport cocked his head. "Um, passed on? What?"

"It's rather difficult to explain."

"Try me. If what you said about sundown is true, we still have some time, and I'm not taking another step until I find out what you're not telling me."

She glared at him for a few excruciatingly slow seconds, then shrugged submissively. "Fine. Ezekiel has told you about Eli Smith?"

"Yeah," he said. "He told us he was a physician-turned-witchhunter back in the day. Said he eventually ended up settling near here and raising a family."

"And did he tell you what the Willow Hag did to him?"

"About his son? Yeah. Kidnapped him. Sacrificed him to her gods and left the kid's body out in the town square for all to see the next morning." Davenport paused, trying his best to recollect Crane's story. "Apparently the townspeople wouldn't do anything to help him, so he went to kill the Willow Hag on his own. She ended up killing him and..."

"And the town's fathers ended up being cursed by Smith with his dying breath," Asherah said. "Yes. Yes. Most everyone around here knows the story. What most people do not know—including Ezekiel, by the way—is that the Leechers are intrinsically linked to the Mother. Their essences are woven to her own.

"But no matter what people think, the Mater Matris is *not* immortal. Yes, it is true that she was born centuries ago and has been kept alive all this time by the darkest of magic…as well as by feeding from the life-forces of others. But eventually, even her magic cannot sustain the continual decomposition of her body. Eventually, it will wither away, and she will be lost to this world, unless…"

"Unless she finds another body to transfer her essence into," Davenport said, following along surprisingly well. "Oh my God! Is that what Kili's been marked for?"

"Are you really this dense? You haven't figured out what's going on with your little girlfriend yet?"

"Um, no?"

The witch shook her head mockingly. "You poor thing. How, pray tell, do you ever make a living with your job? It's really quite simple. What kinds of things do people normally brand?"

The reporter considered the question and decided against answering with sarcasm. There was just too much at stake to play games now. "You mean, like cattle?"

The witch nodded. "And what do people usually do with cattle?"

Asherah's earlier words rushed back to him an instant. "The Hag's going to feed off her?"

The nearby Leecher shifted disconcertingly at Davenport's sudden outburst.

"Shhh," Asherah hissed. "But that's not all. Typically, the Mother feeds regularly off hikers, hunters, anyone foolish enough to wander into the Hollows. She feeds from their essence, but it rarely leaves them dead. Just drained. But Kili has been chosen for an entirely different kind of feeding, and to do that, her spirit must be broken completely. It's why the Death

Curse has been placed on her. To break her spirit. To shatter the inner strength that she has. But I fear the curse isn't enough, and the Mother knows that. I have a feeling she will do something else to your friend, from which there will be no coming back."

"Hence, the ritual magic you mentioned."

"Precisely," Asherah nodded. "Which brings us back to the passing on of her mantle. I believe the Mother senses her own demise. I think she has found someone—a new apprentice—whose body will be used to receive her essence, and this new Hag will be the one to consume Kili.

"But the problem I cannot work out is how. The Mother could not just choose any old person to transfer her mind and powers to. It would have to be an exceptional body...one capable of enduring the centuries without eroding. For the life of me, I can't fathom how she plans to do it."

Davenport shook his head after letting all this new information process. "Hold on a second. Let's forget about this 'apprentice' for a sec and go back to something else you just said...about the Leechers and the death of the Hag." He pointed to the Leecher. "Those things are after the Hag now. Are you saying that if they kill her, they'll cease to exist?"

Asherah nodded. "In their state, they have no free will. Not really. They are controlled by the one who possesses Eli Smith's bones. However, I'd wager, they'd gladly cut the Mater Matris's head off anyway if given the chance—simply as a means to escape their curse if nothing else."

"So what if we gave them a little help? What if we kill her—now that she's weakened to the point where she's looking for a new body anyway? We'd be killing two birds with one stone." Davenport looked over at the Leecher's bird mask and winced at the unintended pun.

"I wouldn't put it so simply. It would be no easy feat, no matter how weakened she is, and I daresay that there is little you or I could—"

A bone-chilling scream suddenly ripped through the forest, cutting off her words.

"That was Kili!" Davenport shouted, leaping to his feet and running toward the sound before he realized what he was doing. When the sudden foolishness of his actions finally registered, he was already committed and running straight for the Leecher that stood between him and the Devil's Teeth.

The sudden movement had the undesired effect of drawing the bird-masked creature's attention directly toward him. Instantly, as if coming out of a trance, the creature brought its arms up in a defensive stance, with its felling axe gripped tightly in its gloved fists.

"Don't provoke it!" Asherah shouted from behind. "Just run past! It shouldn't bother with you unless it perceives you as a threat!"

Well, of course, I'm not gonna provoke it, he thought while weaving his way through the trees. *The thing's got a freakin' axe for crying out loud.* Although, the real question was: how was he going to avoid the Leecher? It was, after all, blocking his path. In hindsight, he needn't have worried.

Without warning, two streaks of silver shot past him, burrowing themselves deeply into the Leecher's robes. In the brief few seconds that the objects were in his line of sight, Davenport could make out the carved wooden handles of knives. Knives that could have been thrown only by his new companion.

The Leecher sent out an ear-splitting screech and turned its crimson-eyed gaze past the reporter's shoulders.

"Go on without me!" Asherah yelled, just as he shot past the spectral sentry. "I'll catch up to you!"

From what he'd seen of the Leechers before and of even Crane's inability to deal with them, he doubted it very much, but he said nothing. His only goal was to reach Kili in time. Nothing else mattered at that point. He was having a hard time comprehending all that was going on between Kili, this mysterious apprentice, and the Hag, but then, it didn't take a lot of understanding to do whatever he could to kill the witch, save the day, and if he was very lucky—kiss the girl.

He was just beginning to smile at that thought when another scream erupted just ahead. The woods were beginning to thin, and the silhouettes of the moss-coated megaliths had become easier to see. Within ten seconds, he burst through the trees into the clearing, into the blood-red rays of the descending sun. Asherah had been right. It was still daylight, which meant that they still had time to save Kili, despite how her previous screams sounded.

The Devil's Teeth were just as he remembered. Perched on a small, moss carpeted earthen mound like some monolithic crown...thirteen stones jutted up toward the sky. His eyes immediately began scanning for his target while slowly ascending the hill.

His heart immediately caught in his throat when he saw Kili. He couldn't quite grasp what he was seeing. She was hovering over a figure resting supine on a large, stone slab in the center of the circle. He couldn't make out who it was, but he could see that she had bare feet, like Asherah. Only instead of a dark, shapely ankle with a charm anklet like Asherah wore, this leg was pale, swollen with edema, and old. As a matter of fact, from his position now on the edge of the stone circle, the skin tone looked almost gray. Mottled. Cadaverous. The impression was only intensified by the dark red liquid streaming over the edge of the slab onto the moss under his friend's feet.

Without a word, he took another step forward, then paused— afraid to startle her. His eyes took in every detail of her quivering body. Her copper-colored hair shook as she sobbed violently at the sight before her. Her jeans and t-shirt were soaked in blood. And clutched tightly in her right hand was the nine-inch gleam of a knife blade, now stained red as well.

"Kili?" he whispered, inching his way over to her. "Are you all right?"

If she heard him, she didn't show it. Instead, she merely stood there, staring down at whoever rested on the stone slab and sobbing uncontrollably. Her grip on the knife never loosened as he moved even closer to her.

"Careful," Asherah whispered from behind. He turned to see her standing at the entrance of the Teeth, but not entering. A nasty gash split the skin at her shoulder, and the bruises that were beginning to form across her cheek and jaw-line gave the impression that she'd been in a slugfest with a jackhammer and lost. The fact that she was standing there at all seemed to indicate that there must have been some victory against the Leecher she'd faced, though. Despite his misgivings toward her, he couldn't help be glad she'd somehow survived the encounter. "Don't get too close. She might not be who you think she is."

"What are you talking about?" he asked, just as Kili wheeled around on him with a mournful keen. He gasped involuntarily at the ragged tatters of her clothing and the sheer amount of blood that covered her. He'd known there had been some, but now that he was getting his first full glimpse of her, he couldn't help but wonder if she'd been swimming in a pool of the stuff. The crimson liquid even trickled down the bridge of her nose as she stood there, shaking helplessly.

She dropped the knife to the ground and stumbled over to him. His arms embraced her, pulling her trembling body to him. At that moment, her torment was fully unleashed, and the keening swelled into a full blown wail against his chest.

"Shhhhh", he said calmly, rubbing her back as he spoke. "Everything's going to be okay. I swear. Everything is going to be..."

His words caught in his throat as he peered past Kili's heaving shoulder to see the corpse sprawled against the altar stone. It was Delores McCrary. She lay nude on the slab, a jagged incision eviscerating her torso, her entrails hanging from the chest cavity. Though the corpse was obviously fresh, thousands of fat, gyrating maggots swarmed the woman's interior as if they'd been glutting on her insides for months instead of minutes.

A flurry of feathers flapping above arrested his attention. He glanced up to see a wake of buzzards perched on the branches of several gnarled trees surrounding the megalith. Their heads were bowed, almost in reverence, even as their beaks gleamed with ravenous hunger. How they'd already gathered over their awaiting buffet, so soon after her death, Davenport couldn't fathom. In the end, it didn't matter. Right now, all that he cared about was Kili.

"Kili," he whispered in her ear. "What happened?"

"I-I..." she stammered, but couldn't get the words to come before bursting into another fit of tears.

"Mr. Davenport, I suggest we take your friend there and leave as soon as possible," Asherah said quietly from her position outside the stone ring. "Things are going to get worse before they get better, and we shouldn't be near this place when they do."

He craned his head to look over at her and glared. He was overly conscious of Kili heaving for breath against his chest. Whatever happened here, she'd been torn apart emotionally, and he didn't want to rush her away unless it was absolutely necessary.

A sudden thought struck him. Asherah had said the Hag would have to break her spirit. Was this how she planned to do it? Was this how Kili's essence would be tenderized for the Willow Hag's consumption? A sudden flash of rage shot through the reporter, and he spun around to face Asherah. "What else do you know about what's going on? You've been holding something back from the beginning, and I want to know what it is. Now!"

"We haven't the time for this," she said. "We really need to…"

"No! Tell me now or get lost." The words spilled from his lips before he knew he'd said them. It was a dangerous gambit. He had no idea how to get Kili back into town from where they were, which meant Asherah was his best hope for a guide. Send her away and he and Kili could be stuck in the Dark Hollows 'til Kingdom come. On the other hand, he was reasonably certain she wouldn't intentionally do anything to stoke Ezekiel Crane's wrath either—which meant she wouldn't be as apt to abandon them.

"You are asking a great deal more than you realize," the woman said, her eyes burning. "Something odd is happening to the Leechers. I can't explain what exactly…only that I didn't win my fight with the one back there. It merely disappeared. But there is more to this place than the haints. There are more things lurking within these woods—and especially the Devil's Teeth—than what you've encountered so far, and they'll be drawn to the blood that pools upon the ground. I, for one, am in no way capable of dealing with whatever calls this place home, and neither are you."

"Okay, fine. But answer this…just this," Davenport said, pulling his right arm away from Kili's back and pointing at the mutilated body in front of him. "Who killed Delores and why?"

Asherah's head tilted to the side as if not understanding the question.

"Don't give me that look," he growled. "There's no way on God's green Earth that Kili did this to her. Even if she had the capacity to murder anyone, Delores had been nothing but kind to her. Sweet. She was Granny's friend, for crying out loud! There's no way Kili would have murdered—"

"She could have, if controlled by the Willow Hag," Asherah said quietly. "The Mother can, under certain conditions, be quite convincing. I'm not sure how, but Ezekiel figured all this out. As for who...you found her with the bloody knife in her hand. You're the reporter. You tell me what that usually means."

He cast his glance back at the horrifying tableau on the altar, then back to Asherah. "Uh-uh, no way. It's a trick. Part of that 'breaking her spirit' thing you mentioned."

Asherah nodded her response. "Undoubtedly. But that doesn't mean that Delores McCrary didn't die by your friend's blood-covered hands. If it makes you feel any better, this is what the Mother does. She corrupts everyone she sets her eye upon. Kili truly had no power to overcome the Willow Hag's will."

Kili nestled tighter against Davenport's chest, her weight getting heavier and heavier with each breath. He could sense that her exhaustion was getting the better of her. She was quickly falling asleep between sobs, which meant this was probably a good time to do what Asherah had been saying all along and get out of there. There'd be time for more questions later. He hoped.

"Okay," he said quietly, absently stroking his friend's back as he held her. "Let's go. We need to get her back to town, and then we'll figure out a way to stop all this."

"Please, do not get your hopes up on that," Asherah said, sadly. "No one has ever broken free from the Mater Matris, once they have been marked." The witch paused for a second and shrugged. "Well, perhaps I should say no one but Ezekiel Crane, that is."

He wasn't sure why, but the revelation didn't surprise him in the least. "Fine," he said, picking Kili up into his arms and walking toward the treeline. "Then we'll get Crane to show us how he managed it, and we'll do the same thing."

Asherah, who was walking ahead to clear a path for them, sighed. "That, I'm afraid, might prove more costly than any of us —including Ms. Kili—are willing to pay." Without another word, the three of them slipped into the woods and began making their way toward town, unaware that a pair of green feline eyes watched them pass with cold, calculating interest.

CHAPTER
TWENTY-SEVEN

Southwood Rehabilitation Center
Somerset, Kentucky
April 29
6:33 PM

"How is this possible?" Granny asked, casually slipping between Candace and her comatose grandson. She wasn't sure what she was dealing with at the moment, but she certainly wasn't going to make it easy for the undead hussy to hurt him. "I've seen the Kindred. Treated a few of them, even. They ain't got the brain capacity of a turnip. They're nothin' like you."

As the words spilled from her lips, Esther Crane suddenly realized just how true the statement was. In fact, not only was this Candace Staples as far removed from Delores McCrary's seven other resurrection experiments, the cold intelligence and confidence she held within her eyes was nothing like the booze-addled Candy that died over a year earlier at the hands of One-Eyed Jack. Whatever this woman was, she certainly wasn't merely the revived corpse of Jimmy Staples' mother.

The woman laughed merrily at Granny's confusion. Her short-cropped blonde hair swayed back and forth with each boisterous laugh, partially obscuring her frigid gray eyes, which beamed with unreserved malevolence.

"Oh, sweet Mother…this really is a sight to see," Candace mocked. "The great Esther Crane is as flummoxed as a polecat in a perfume aisle. You really ain't figured it out yet, have you?" She paused, cocking her head mischievously. "Not even that devil of a grandson of yers either, I suppose." She let out another cackle as she waved her arms victoriously in the air. "Oh, this is gonna be sweeter than I ever imagined. I'm gonna really enjoy watchin' that accursed boy as he spirals helplessly down the path of hopelessness. Gonna revel as every ounce of his uppity pride is stripped away, and he finally gets what's a'comin' to him…when the Mater Matris finally gets to feast on that rotten ol' soul of his."

The Mater Matris? Granny thought. *The Hag? So Candy's resurrection wasn't Dee's doin', after all. What in tarnation is goin' on here?*

But Candace's tirade was far from over. "She'll grind his bones into powder and feed on him 'til there ain't a speck left, and I'll be there every second to watch it happen too. I'll see that smug smile ripped straight off his face, as the Mother strips him of everything he holds dear." She took a single step forward and leaned in conspiratorially. "And guess what, old woman. Yer gonna be the first step in makin' that happen."

The elder Crane didn't need to guess what the crazed woman meant. The Hag could only feed on those with broken psyches. It was the whole point of the Death Curse, after all. And the quickest way to break a man like Ezekiel was simple…take away those he loved most.

"What do you want from us?" Heather asked, breaking Granny's train of thought. The moment Candace had entered the room, the amorous nurse had followed Granny's lead and dutifully moved over to Josiah's side. *Say what you will about the misguided lil' tart, she's definitely loyal to the man she loves.* "Just take the bones if you want them and go. We don't want any more trouble."

"Ah, but see, sweetie...they're not exactly yours to give now, are they?" Candace said, her right eyebrow raised provocatively. "The water witch has them now, and I highly doubt she aims to give 'em up as easily as you."

Granny felt, more than observed, both pairs of eyes falling on her as Candace's words struck home. But unlike Heather, who merely stared at the aged woman, Candace took another step forward. As she did so, the sound of growling filled the room, just as three large coyote-like creatures materialized from behind her. They were larger than any coyote Granny had ever seen in nature—at least a head taller—and covered with bristling black and gray fur. Their snouts curled up into sneers, as two rows of sharp canine fangs glistened in the fluorescent light of the hospital room. As she stared into the animals' cold, black eyes, an overwhelming sense of dread iced down Granny's spine.

She has the Coyote familiar? But that's not possible... That would mean... A sudden thought gripped her, chilling her to the bone. The only other possibility was that she was really...

"Oh my God!" Heather shouted, pointing to the canines. "Where did those things come from? How did you get them in here?"

But if Candace heard the nurse's frantic questions, she ignored them. Instead, a cold gleam shown brightly in her eyes, as they locked murderously on Granny.

Then, everything fell into place. The Kindred. The Hag's deception and Delores's role in the resurrections. Heather had been right. She'd been blinded by her love for an old friend—a friend who'd most certainly been dead for quite some time before the Kindred had returned to life. She even understood why Kili had been marked and what the Hag had in store for her. And ultimately, how it all tied to Ezekiel. As the last piece of the puzzle finally fell into place, the Crane matriarch could only grit her teeth in defiance, as the beasts now padded their way around their master in a protective circle.

"Ah, so it finally begins to make sense to you, old woman," Candace giggled, clapping her hands gleefully. Oddly, her voice seemed to be changing with each shrill cackle. It sounded strained. Almost brittle…like that of an old crone. "The three familiars of the Dark Hollows. Raven, cat, and…" She bent down to scratch one of the animals behind its ear before looking back at Granny. "Coyote. We already have the one. The other two will be ours soon enough and then, the Ghostfeast will begin. Oh, don't fret none, though. There ain't a blessed thing you'll be able to do to stop it. The good news is that you won't be around to see it happen. Nor how your beloved grandson will be meetin' his maker."

Instinctively, Granny reached down to pick up the ossuary and held it close to her chest.

"Whatever happens to me, Witch, you ain't getting' yer demon-spawned hands on these bones," Granny said. Defiantly, she spat at one of the dog-like beasts, then turned her determined gaze back to Candace. "Eli Smith once had yer number, and I daresay he'll be more than happy to have you in his sights again. And another thing, you ain't got the totems yet, so yer not fully merged. Yer still weak. Vulnerable. A might good target, I'd say.

"As fer Ezekiel, I think you two have underestimated that boy, and it'll be yer undoin'." The slight, nearly inaudible, tinkle of the wind chimes began to echo around the room. With each passing second, the chimes began to clang harder and harder upon each other, raising into a melodious cacophony all around them.

Candace and her coyotes glanced around to the northeast, then the southwest corners of the room, eyeing the wind chimes nervously. Granny smiled mischievously at the undead woman in front of her. "And if I ain't mistaken, those chimes are for you."

Candace whipped her head around to face Granny. Panic filled her overly dark eyes. "Why do you say that? They're just wind chimes. At the very least, it just means a few harmless spirits are nearby...nothing that I need to worry about."

Granny's smile broadened as she hugged the bone box tighter against her chest. She'd been sorely tempted to use the bones to summon the Witchhunter and his Leechers to end this confrontation once and for all. But she knew better. The timing just wasn't right, and that would prove ultimately disastrous. Besides, the chimes provided her a source of hope far superior to those unholy liches.

"But oddly, you are worried, aren't you? Those chimes are unnervin' you somethin' fierce," Granny countered. "And no wonder. I can rightly understand why they should." Now it was her turn to step ominously toward Candace and her phantom coyotes. "You see, it's the funniest thing. On that horrible day yer mistress cursed my grandson, an odd thing started happenin' whenever he'd start headin' toward home. The chimes on my front porch would start a'playin' the pertiest sounds you ever did hear. Not the hodgepodge clatter of glass and metal strikin' each other all chaotic like...but rather, some-thin' quite melodic. Comforting. Heavenly even." She nodded toward the nearest set of chimes. "Somethin' similar to that, as a matter of fact."

The coyotes growled angrily, their tails tucked tightly between their hind legs as they simultaneously bared their teeth at her; they were clearly agitated by the sudden melodious tune filling the room. The song, if it could truly be called that, was otherworldly. Pure. And radiating hope for Granny and more than likely, even for young Heather, who would have no idea why her heart was being so lightened. But from Granny's experi-ence, no mortal could possibly resist the song's bold, yet soothing chords, haunting harmonies that wafted through the air as if spun on fiddle strings made of pure silk.

Granny's mind flooded with memories of young Ezekiel and the ethereal song of the chimes upon his approach to the ancestral homestead. He'd hated it, of course. Even demanded she take the wind chimes down from the porch, claiming it was a constant reminder of the curse he had to endure. After all, for generations, chimes had been used to detect the presence of ghosts and spirits, and there weren't no one 'round Boone Creek that had more ghosts congregating around him than poor Ezekiel. Naturally, he'd always despised his gifts—both those of the seventh son, as well as those endowed to him by the Hag's wicked magic—which was why he'd always clung so passionately to science and the natural order of things. Over time, he'd learned to incorporate a little of both into his life, including the wind chimes, but when he was younger, they were a blatant symbol of all that he loathed about his own special place in the world.

As she allowed herself to be enthralled by the tune now clinking its way throughout the room, Granny couldn't help but be thankful to the odd side effect produced by the Hag's curse. For there was no doubt in her mind at that moment, her grandson was near. Even more importantly, the Staples-thing and her attack dogs knew it too, and Granny highly doubted they were strong enough yet to deal with him effectively.

Candace stood transfixed for several moments, indecision evident on her face. Then, she turned back to face the elder Crane, and her malevolent smile abruptly reappeared.

"Well, then," she said. The words were little more than a snarl. "We best make this quick."

Without further warning, the three coyote-creatures pounced.

CHAPTER
TWENTY-EIGHT

Southwood Rehabilitation Center
Somerset, Kentucky
April 29
6:45 PM

S omething was horribly wrong. The Dirge had stopped. Ezekiel Crane couldn't so much as hear an echo of it in the recesses of his mind, and that terrified him. As he ran up the three flights of stairs and burst through the stairwell door at Southwood Institute, his fears only intensified.

Things weren't just horribly wrong. They were downright nightmarish. As he half-walked, half-jogged down the long winding hallway of the third floor, the electric charge of something malevolent permeated the air, raising every hair on the back of his arms and neck. Even more unsettling, as he moved toward his brother's room, he watched as the residents and rehab staff moved here and there, their eyes glazed over as if their conscious minds had been stripped away and their ambulation was merely the product of a puppeteer manipulating ethereal strings.

The strange behavior brought Crane to a standstill, just as an orderly walked past, slowly pushing an empty wheelchair in concentric circles around him. To his right, a nurse huddled at her desk, phone tucked under her chin. Crane could hear the person on the other end of the line questioning if he'd been disconnected, but the nurse stared silently off into space. Crane's eyes moved to the left, to see a patient wearing nothing more than a robe and a pair of boxers, shuffling along at a brisk pace down the hall, his eyes rolled unnervingly back in his head.

Wherever he looked, Crane saw more of the same. Everyone in the building was dazed. Seemed stuck in some sort of trance-like state, as if the switches to their minds had simply been flicked off.

"This," he said to himself, "is not a good sign."

That's when he heard it. The snarling growls coming from just down the hall. Instantly, he was moving again, running at a full sprint and nearly knocking a clueless orderly to the ground, as he made his way toward the howls now coming from the other side of his brother's door. Without knocking, he barreled through and skidded to a stop at the most gruesome sight of his entire life.

For a split second, all he could do was stand there, watching the scene unfold. Unable to move. Unable to scream. Unable to think. Unable to blink.

The first thing he saw was his brother, lying motionless in bed; his chest was rising and falling normally. A blonde woman —Dr. Maher's nurse, if he wasn't mistaken—lay sprawled out on top of him as if protecting him with her own body. From his vantage point, Josiah appeared fine, but something was off. Something just wasn't quite right. It was the bed linens. The normally pristinely white sheets were a different color now. Maroon? No, red. Crimson. And wet.

Crane's eyes analyzed the red liquid. The angle of the blood spatter—a long tail capped with a short round ball. The blood wasn't trickling from the top of the bed down, but rather was moving up. Spraying up was perhaps a better term, as there appeared to be a massive amount of arterial spurting.

Absently, almost as if his spirit had escaped the snug confines of his own flesh, his eyes followed the trail of blood down to the floor next to his brother's bed. Down to where Granny laid struggling, face down. Her arms were covering something protectively, as three monstrous coyotes ripped and tore at her fragile skin with fangs and claws. The back of her shirt was in tatters, and scraps of her flesh hung loosely around the base of her neck. Blood sprayed from the wound, not only coating the bed, but covering the canines' fur with crimson stains. Despite the struggle...despite the obvious pain she was enduring, she still held valiantly to the thing beneath her as she mumbled a desperate prayer to ward off the attack.

The world threatened to spin out of control, as he watched the gruesome spectacle. So why couldn't he move? Act? Why wasn't he rushing forward to save his grandmother from being ravaged by these feral dogs?

He felt numb. Detached. Cold. Frigidly cold. His limbs were stiff. Unyielding. Defiantly rebelling against every mental command to act. Just like...

Just like the people in the hallway! I'm being witched!

A surge of anger flooded his veins, fueling just enough willpower to focus more on the room. Slowly, his eyes began to stab through the mental gloom—the shadows that shouldn't otherwise be present—and finally, *she* began to take shape. A tall lithe figure, standing just a few feet away from Josiah's bedside. At first, the image was fuzzy. Distilled. As if he was looking at something through a glass of water. But the more he focused, the more defined the figure became, until he could slowly make out the short-cropped blonde hair and angular face. The pouty lips caked with blood-red lipstick. The thin, but pleasantly built physique and the unholy black eyes that stared gleefully down at his struggling grandmother.

Candace?

But that made no sense. She wasn't one of the Kindred. Maher had never mentioned any experiments with her. How could she be here? Alive? Unlike the spirits of the Kindred who'd been mindlessly walking the halls of Aion Pharmaceuticals since their deaths, Candace's shade had haunted him personally from the day he'd first found her mutilated body in a grave at the Devil's Teeth. Though he wanted to wrap his mind around the puzzle, he knew he had to put it aside for now. At the moment, it didn't matter. Whoever, or whatever, this particular creature was, it was evident that she was responsible for the carnage being done to Granny at that moment. And that was going to stop right now.

"GRANNY!" he shouted. But although he'd broken free of whatever had kept his mind in a fog, he still found himself unable to move.

Candace turned to look at him, a bright smile spreading across her pretty face. "Oh, Ezekiel. Poor sweet boy," she said with mock concern. Oddly her voice sounded very little like the Candy Staples he'd known all his life. Instead, it sounded somehow grandmotherly. Ancient and deceptively kind. It was a voice he knew all too well. "Whatever are we gonna do? Your poor Granny's almost at death's door! Why don't you run to her aid, boy? Run to her aid!"

But Crane remained perfectly still, unable to break free from whatever mystic bonds the Staples-creature had cast on him. Seeing the distress in his eyes, she giggled merrily. "Oh, how the mighty have fallen. The great Ezekiel Crane has been reduced to a mere puppet in my hands." She clapped boisterously, savoring her prey's paralysis. Her voice had suddenly changed. It was now distinctly Candace Staples. Spiteful. Biting. It was as if two beings were occupying the same body.

"So hard to imagine why so many people fear you. Why *I* feared you."

"Today is not the day to find out why they *do* fear me, witch!" Crane growled, his eyes fixed on Granny as she continued her struggle. A subtle moan slipped out from her lips as one of the coyotes tore a chunk of meat from her thigh. Crane felt his blood begin to boil at the sight, but still, he was unable to move anything below the neck. Slowly, he looked up at Candace and spoke. "You do an excellent impersonation of Ms. Staples." His voice was eerily calm. "Though why you'd attempt the pretense with me, I've no idea. You, of all…people…should be aware that I know Candace isn't in there."

She gave a contemptuous shrug. "It caught you by surprise though, didn't it?" She let out a coughing giggle.

"But you've shown your hand too soon," Crane continued. "I know what you're up to. Leave now, and I'll allow you to live."

For a moment, a look of dread spread across Candace's face. Her eyes widened in surprise before the act melted away in a fit of contemptuous laughter.

"If that's so, then you know there ain't nothin' you can do to hurt us," the voice from inside Candace's body said.

"That remains to be seen, skinwalker," he said, chiding himself for not seeing it sooner. He'd known the stories about the Willow Hag. Had grown up hearing how she'd survived through the ages by killing people and stealing their skins, as a means of disguising her true nature. But he'd never imagined in a million years they were actually true.

Another moan arose from Granny, reminding him he had little time left. But he couldn't do her any good until the binding spell was weakened enough by time and distraction…and for that, he'd need more time to work his own unique brand of magic. "What I'm really curious about is how long?" He had to delay her. The more concentration she used to talk with him, the less aggressive her coyote familiars behaved. For the moment, they had all but forgotten Granny and were now staring him down with hungry eyes. "How long did you pretend to be Delores McCrary? How long did you play upon Granny's love of the old woman to get closer to her? To learn her secrets, as well as mine?"

A look of genuine confusion crossed Candace's face.

"Oh, don't give me that. Don't deny it," he said. "It's in your voice. You spent so much time assuming Dee's identity that it's affected your speech pattern. You sound too much like her even now."

Slowly, the look of confusion melted away from her face and she shrugged. "Six years," she said. "Though to be honest, it wasn't all the time. Most days, Delores was herself, completely unaware that I was taggin' along for the ride. I'd only manifest when the need suited me...like when she grew close to that Staples boy. When I realized she wanted nothin' more than to bring his momma back to life...well, that's when things got a little more interestin'. That's when she sought me out herself. And I was only happy enough to oblige, let me tell you.

"I would've been content with just habitatin' with her for as long as I could, but her heart just weren't strong enough. She was dying, and I needed a replacement quickly. One not so subject to the laws of life or death."

"Which is why the experiments with the Kindred," Crane said. One glance around the room told him that *they* were finally gathering. Any second now, he would have amassed enough assistance to press an attack. Granny just needed to hold on a few more minutes. "You needed a body that would prolong your life even further than you somehow already have. One that would transcend the boundaries of physical ailments or human degeneration." He recalled his conversation with Dr. Maher just a few hours earlier. How, after Asherah had brought them the seven victims of One-Eyed Jack, Delores McCrary had shown up at Aion. She'd approached Jael with a proposition. She'd assist her. Use her own magic in conjunction with Jael's science and unravel the mysteries of the One-Eyed Jack spores in order to save Josiah's life. For Granny's sake. Jael had been reluctant to accept the assistance. But Delores had been insistent. Eventually, Crane's sister had relented and the two had worked in tandem together. All the while, the Hag had watched through stolen eyes. Had learned from a hijacked mind. And, unlike his sister, the Hag had deduced the truth about the teratoma tumors and the possibilities they represented. "You took what you learned about the Kindred, and created a perfect facsimile of Candace Staples to be your new vessel."

Candace shrugged. "I certainly wasn't going to use any of those so-called 'Kindred', that's for sure. They weren't nothin' but a complete failure. It's just a matter of time before they wither away to the dust they are. They's ravenous now. Cancer, after all, needs to feed. But soon, they won't have strength enough for even that. They'll just shrivel to nothin', and all them who thought they got their loved ones back...well, they'll know what you've known for a while now. The Dead don't come back." She paused. "Well, *most* of the time anyway."

A lump formed in Crane's throat. "What exactly does that mean?"

Ignoring his question, Candace looked down at her own body. Her fingers sensually traced every curve and contour of her figure with deep introspection.

"Does this body please you, Ezekiel?" the voice asked. She'd reverted back to sounding like Candace Staples again. "I remember the two of you having a little crush on one another back when y'all were in high school together...'til her rotten daddy put a stop to it, of course." She smiled seductively as she traced a finger over the curvature of her hips. "Do you still desire her? She could be yours, you know. The way I'd planned Asherah to be yours." When he failed to give her the reaction she'd hoped for, she continued. "Or maybe...hmmmm...maybe you'd prefer someone else. Someone with bright red hair, perhaps?"

Crane's eyes narrowed. His rage burned even hotter as he considered the foul implications of what she offered. "I warned you not to test me today, but you didn't listen." His voice was little more than a growl. "I'd advise you to leave. Now."

The Candace-creature cocked her head to one side, as if reflecting on his strange threat.

"And what, dear boy, do you think you can do to me?" she asked, once more sounding like an aged crone. As if sensing their mistress's confusion, the three coyotes moved away from Granny's still form and padded quietly over to Candace. Their jet black eyes never wavered from Crane's as they moved. "Who do you..."

She continued her tirade, but Crane was no longer paying any attention to her. Something from the corner of his eye had caught his attention. He glanced to the left and immediately saw her. She stood perfectly still. Her flowing white hair had turned golden blonde...just as it had been when she was a young lady, before the pressures of raising three ungrateful orphans had weighed so heavily upon her. A sad smile crept onto her face, and she nodded lovingly at him.

He blinked, hoping the apparition would be gone when his eyes cleared of unbidden tears, but she was still there when he looked again. Even younger now. Maybe mid-forties. But despite the age regression, he'd recognize her wise and beautiful face anywhere. It was that sweet smiling face, after all, that he had so often looked up at while being rocked to sleep. It were those kind, gentle hands that had doctored his knees whenever they'd been scraped or bruised after falling down. It had been those beautiful blue-gray eyes that had wept with him every time he'd nearly given up on life or love, and it was the same comforting arms that had held him time and again.

Granny?

She, of course, didn't respond. She couldn't. Shades, after all, have no true consciousness. Her own spirit had already moved on. Already gone to be with the Lord…with his parents and his siblings. Gone for good, but forever tormenting him in this maddening effigy of a ghost.

Like the rest of his family, she was gone. Stolen from him. Ripped from his life by the claws and fangs and hate of dark magic…

…And he had *had* it!

"…can assure you, Ezekiel Crane," Candace was still speaking. Still threatening him and his very existence.

He didn't care. She could do whatever she wished—or try anyway. At that moment, he felt something inside him fracture. Something fragile, shattered in a million pieces. Rage, carried into his soul on the tide of molten fury, filled his entire being, as he stared helplessly at the lifeless body of his now dead grandmother.

And he roared.

Instantly, the Willow Hag-controlled Candace went perfectly still. The coyotes cowered behind her, as Ezekiel Crane turned to glare at all four of them, fire burning in his eyes.

"You. Killed. Her."

A sudden gust of wind whipped past his head, rushing throughout the room, and barraging the chimes into a chaotic maelstrom of sound.

"What… What are you doing?" Candace asked, looking from Crane to the chimes and back again. She raised her hands in a placating gesture. "I'm not sure you know what you're doin', boy. Stop it. Stop it now!"

But Crane heard none of it.

"You killed Granny," he repeated, not taking his eyes off them. The coyotes' blood-soaked muzzles ducked down, cowed. Cautiously, they moved as close to the wall opposite Crane as they could, with their tails sweeping between their hind legs while whining piteously.

But if he noticed, he showed no sign. Instead, he closed his eyes, raised his face and arms skyward, and screamed furiously to the heavens.

Candace, fear etched across her face, was backing away from Crane, stumbling back against the window where the coyotes now huddled.

And just as swiftly as it had arrived, the wind softened to that of a mere breeze, and the chimes ceased their cacophonic madness. The silence was almost deafening.

The calm before the storm.

Slowly, Crane opened his eyes and glared at the undead woman.

"You really should have listened to me," he whispered before unleashing all the fury of Hell into a twelve-by-twelve-foot hospital room. A renewed gust of wind rushed all around them, followed immediately by a strange unearthly green haze swirling and weaving through the air that began to form familiar ghostly shapes.

The Dead, led by the flapping of the ebony-hued wings of a raven, had come to Crane's grief-stricken aid.

The coyotes, riled by the sudden burst of light, wind, and sound, howled with fear before their lips curled into vicious snarls once more. In unison, they leapt toward Crane, only to be intercepted by the intangible tendrils of the angered shades. One of the mongrels, the one that had been closest to reaching its murderous mark, was picked up and hurled through the air. With a sickening crunch, the coyote struck the far wall and fell to the floor without a sound. Its siblings whined piteously as they spiraled uncontrollably through the air toward their dark mistress. Wild-eyed with terror, the creature bearing the resem-blance of Candace Staples dashed out of the way and watched as the two remaining canines became entangled with the thick, velvet curtains and crashed through the window. No one paid any attention as they plummeted to the parking lot below. No one took notice when the broken remains of all three animals slowly dissolved from existence, leaving no trace they'd ever been there.

"Crane!" Candace shrieked. It sounded more like the Candy he remembered now. The Willow Hag's feeble attempt to appeal to his sense of chivalry, no doubt. "Call them off!"

But he ignored her screams, choosing instead to focus his attention on the bloody mass huddled on the floor next to his brother's bed. He moved over to her, oblivious to Candace's pitiful attempts to bat away the incorporeal hands that sliced through her body like knives, cutting away at her flesh with unseen talons. Indifferent to the Hag's plight, he knelt down beside the tattered remains of his grandmother. The shades that haunted his every waking moment could have their way with her. They could do whatever they liked. The only thing that mattered right now was...

"Granny?" he asked while rolling her over onto her back. For the first time, he managed to see what she'd been huddling over —an ossuary. A bone box. Presumably containing the cursed bones of Dr. Eli Smith and the power to control the will of the Witchhunter's Leechers. "I'm so sorry. I was too late."

He pulled her tight against his chest. Tears—the first to fall in over fifteen years to his knowledge—streamed down his face, as grief flooded every inch of his soul. The Dirge had warned him, yet he'd allowed himself the smallest hope. Allowed himself to believe that he could somehow change destiny...somehow wrest the bony fingers of the Reaper away from the one he loved most in the world. The one he relied on more than any other. How foolish he'd been to think he had power over something as omnipotent as that.

"Crane! Crane!" Candace screamed from somewhere in the distance.

He was only vaguely aware of a single form materializing from the ghostly green haze that filled the room. A form that twisted and stretched into a tall, lithe feminine figure with short-cropped blonde hair, an angular face, and full, pouty lips. The visage was nothing new to him. He'd been seeing her every day of his life since he'd dug up her mutilated corpse last year. But the passing glance he gave the shade of the real Candace Staples spoke volumes.

Her eyes burned with a fury few had ever seen, and the full brunt of that rage was directed entirely at the one inhabiting her revived body. He thought it odd that a shade would have any emotion at all, considering they were merely after-images of their eternal souls. Then again, Candace had been a horribly vengeful woman in life, so perhaps it made sense after all.

"Crane, call them off! Please."

He didn't so much as glance her way as he sat there, cradling his grandmother in his trembling arms. "Don't you worry none, witch," he said bitterly. "As you've already elucidated, there isn't much anyone can do you." He paused before letting out a slow, cold chuckle. "But that new pristine body of yours? Well, that just might be a different story. Would be a horrible shame to live the next few hundred years in a scarred, broken body, don't ya think?" He looked over at the shade of Candace Staples. "I have a peculiar feelin' Ms. Candace—the real Ms. Candace there—has the same opinion as me."

And as the shade horde, led by the real Candace Staples's specter, continued their ruthless assault on the Willow Hag's puppet, she turned to the window and leapt through, falling to the pavement below. Not willing to give up their prey so easily, the ghost-like army flew after her, howling into the late after-noon sky like banshees in the night. They would continue hounding her until the last vestiges of the spell he'd woven before entering the institute had all but disappeared. Then, as always, they'd return to him...all two hundred and thirty-seven of them.

No, he thought grimly. *Two hundred and thirty-eight now.* He looked over at the single remaining shade in the room and wiped away a tear with his sleeves. "Two hundred and thirty-eight."

EPILOGUE

The Crane Homestead
One week later

They were going to be late to the funeral. Alex Davenport had only one job to do: get Crane to the funeral on time. And he was going to screw that up. Not that there was anything he could have done about it. Heck, there was probably nothing anyone could have done about it—save maybe Granny.

Gotta love the irony of that, Davenport thought as he strode purposefully down the hall, before chiding himself for the crassness of the observation.

However, the point remained valid. The way he'd heard it, Crane had always been difficult to manage...even at the best of times. Throw in the untimely death of his beloved grandmother, and all bets were off. But bereavement was the least of his problems. Add sibling troubles in the mix and one might begin to understand the insurmountable odds the stalwart reporter was facing at that very moment.

Ah, the siblings, Davenport thought. *Talk about dysfunctional.*

Truth was, Crane's mood had gone from morose to just plain

foul ever since returning from Chicago to confront his sister about Josiah's medical treatments. Apparently, the meeting had not been pretty.

Since Granny's death, he had moved his brother back to the ancestral homestead. He'd kept Heather, his brother's love-stricken nurse, on payroll and had moved the entire hospital room into one of the spare bedrooms. His sister, Jael, hadn't liked it, so Crane had flown up to the Aion Pharmaceuticals home office, and they'd hashed things out. From the bits and pieces he'd picked up on in conversations he'd inadvertently eaves-dropped on, Crane had made it abundantly clear to Jael that as he was now the patriarch of the family, there was little she could say about the medical care their brother received.

To be fair, Crane was sparing no expense on the treatment. To a nosey reporter like Davenport, that, of course, begged the question as to where a hillbilly from Po-Dunk, Kentucky could acquire the considerable fortune Crane seemed to have amassed over little more than a decade. However, he decided to leave it alone for the moment...out of respect, more than anything else.

Besides, as he made his way down the hallway to the back of the house, Davenport had more pressing matters. Namely getting Ezekiel to the funeral home as soon as possible. He was just thankful the funeral wasn't at Overturf & Sons.

"Ezekiel? Buddy, you about ready to go?" he asked quietly. Whatever Crane was doing in the makeshift hospital room, he'd rather not disturb either of the two current residents.

A pang of regret struck the reporter like a bag of bricks. Kili had yet to recover from her ordeal at the Devil's Teeth and had been catatonic for the last week. There'd been only a couple of instances of semi-lucidity, but even then, she was unable to fill in any blanks as to what had happened.

Crane insisted that she had not murdered Delores on that sacrificial stone, but that everyone—including Kili herself—was supposed to believe that she had. He never explained how he knew this with such certainty, but any argument made by Sheriff Slate or his deputies were met with severe tongue-lashings, and a handful of not-so-subtle threats, by the most feared man in Boone Creek.

Still, despite it all, neither Crane nor Asherah Richardson, in all their arcane wisdom, had been able to help Kili much at all. It had been suggested that only time would heal the particular wounds she'd suffered—meaning the deep-seated emotional injuries cast upon her by the Willow Hag's curse. To Davenport, it sounded like a cop-out. But then, who was he to judge? After all, he was about to abandon the poor girl completely, in the name of ambition.

An urgent call from an editor the previous day necessitated an immediate trip to Dubai...something ridiculous about a ghostly pirate ship haunting the harbor of Port Jabel Ali. But his editor had been rather insistent. He might be freelance, but if he expected any more paychecks from *The Fortean Inquisitor*, he had to accept the assignment. His only consolation was that the story should be fairly straight forward and he would be able to return in less than a month—barring any unforeseen complications. All he knew was he'd do everything within his power to get back to Kili as quickly as he could.

"Crane?" he said again. He was a little more insistent this time. "You there?"

He nudged the bedroom door open and peeked in. The lighting was dim, designed to be as relaxing to the occupants as possible. The room was filled with state-of-the-art medical equipment that beeped and hummed in a strangely relaxing cadence. Two beds sat flush against opposite walls and contained Crane's current patients, both appearing to be resting comfortably. A large rabbit's foot, similar to the one Crane had given her during their first encounter with the Leechers, hung over Kili's bed. By contrast, some sort of bird's claw hung just above the head of Josiah Crane.

There was no sign of the nurse, but Ezekiel sat on the edge of a doctor's stool near the foot of Josiah's bed and seemed to be mumbling incoherently to himself.

"Crane?" Davenport whispered, stepping into the room.

But the mountain man ignored him as he continued speaking.

"Ethics? Really? You're lecturing me on ethics now?" he said, throwing his arms into the air with a derisive laugh. "Besides... what else am I supposed to do? I can't possibly deal with what's coming without her assistance." He paused as if listening intently for several seconds before responding. "I know it's not the *real* her. But any her is better than none at all. Besides, if I have to endure this, why not make the best of it? Why not utilize it to my advantage?"

Was Crane talking to himself? Had the strain of everything driven him over the edge?

"Crane?"

"Yes, Alex," Crane responded. Though his tone was just as soft-spoken as normal, Davenport could detect an almost imperceptible trace of tension. Frustration, perhaps. "I know. It's time to go. But I have to clear something up first." He then turned his attention back to the open space in front of him and continued his strange argument. "You know as well as I that doom approaches. We've not endured a Ghostfeast in these parts for almost two hundred years, and I'm not certain I've strength enough to deal with it on my own. Every man, woman, and child in Boone Creek is in immense danger, and Granny was the only person I know who had the knowledge to put a stop to it before it even begins. We need her now more than ever."

Davenport's ears perked up at hearing this. What was coming? A Ghostfeast? Did this have something to do with the Leechers again? Crane still hadn't told him what he'd done with the Witchhunter's bones. Presumably, he'd hidden them. Someplace better than the last time. He didn't understand why they just couldn't grind the stupid bones up and be done with it. After all, no bones meant no Leecher's right? But whatever the reason, Crane had insisted that destroying them would make things much worse. Is that what he was talking about now? If not, then what could possibly be more evil than Eli Smith or his Leechers?

And just who the heck was he talking to? The Little People, maybe? No. Kili had told him that Crane had never been able to communicate with them. That even though they seemed to respect him—seemed to help him even from time to time—he'd just never been able to communicate with them. That was something only Granny could do. Or maybe Kili as well, if she ever woke up from the madness that now gripped her.

"The Ghostfeast, Alex," Crane said. When Davenport returned to the here and now, he could see that Ezekiel Crane was now standing and looking him over with dark, red-rimmed eyes. At least he was already in his Sunday's finest. Just needed to slip his tie on and they could be on their way to the funeral home in no time. "I'm discussing the Ghostfeast. Something out of legend. Something to be gravely feared, and the signs are clear. It's coming. Soon."

Davenport could only stare, trying to comprehend what he was being told. After a few immeasurable seconds, he found his voice again.

"Um, but what exactly *is* a Ghostfeast?" he asked. Though it sounded ominous enough, he knew it must be infinitely more dangerous if Crane feared it even more than the Leechers.

Crane's jaw tightened visibly before he shook his head.

"Honestly, it's rather difficult to explain. The Ghostfeast seems to manifest differently each time it occurs, but whenever it does, it brings nothing but death and sadness." He let out a sigh, slipped on his tie, then slapped the reporter on the shoulder with a forced smile. "But now isn't the time to concerns ourselves with such matters. Now is the time to reflect on the life of a great woman. To honor her memory and bask in the light her life brought to so many people. We can worry about nightmares tomorrow."

Without another word, he walked over to the door, opened it, and gestured Davenport to proceed first.

"Um, so are you going to tell me who you were talking to in there?" the reporter asked as he walked into the hallway. "And don't tell me you were talking to yourself or make any crazy jokes. I've been around you and this nutso town long enough to know better than that."

Crane smiled and it reached his eyes when he did. For the first time in a while, it was genuine.

"Never you mind," he said, tapping the face of his watch. "No time for such tomfoolery at the moment. We're running late."

"But I…"

"Don't forget the car keys. Oh, and perhaps you might want to bring your cane," Crane said moving toward the front door and tapping his foot impatiently.

"I haven't needed it ever since Asherah did her mojo thing to my hip."

Crane's smile faltered. His eyes darkened ever so slightly.

"Be that as it may," he said, pointing to the stick hanging from the hat rack next to the door. "Indulge me. You never know when a good blade might come in handy." He ushered the reporter out of the house once he'd grabbed the requested items, and they moved toward Crane's truck. "No, a sword cane might be handy indeed," he said as he climbed into the driver's seat and held out a hand for the keys. "Especially when one is attending a funeral in *this* town."

When Davenport was in, Crane started up the truck, put it in gear, and started making his way toward the funeral home.

ON THE SUBJECT OF MIND AND MAGIC...

When I first started writing The Dark Hollows Mystery series, I had a clear-cut definitive plan. I was going to write an urban fantasy set in rural Appalachia...or rather, a rural fantasy. Imagine it. A sort of Harry Dresden, wizard P.I., out in the hills of southeastern Kentucky, going *mano-a-mano* against the likes of giants, trolls, faery-folk and the like. After all, Appalachian folklore is rife with such beings and creatures. What better way to expose the rich, rural goodness of mountain folklore than exploring it in a modern fantasy?

Of course, you realize, that's when a completely contradictory spark of inspiration struck me. Such instances are both the blessing and the curse of creativity. The things you plan rarely ever turn out the way you expect, and the first Dark Hollows book is a perfect example of this. You see, as I began plotting and designing my characters, preparing them for the extravagant phantasmal world I had planned for them, an inexplicable desire to turn the story into a classic Sherlock Holmes-like mystery began to overwhelm me. I'd never written a mystery before, and I knew that Ezekiel Crane was the perfect protagonist to delve into the depths of murder and mayhem with a clinical detachment and the keen, scientific mind so engrossing in the best of amateur sleuths.

So the question arose: how do I proceed? Do I make *The Curse of One-Eyed Jack* a cornucopia of the fantastic, filled with fae-folk, trolls, and witches, or do I turn my creative musings toward the cold, rational intrigue of murder and crime?

Honestly, the answer came easily and without any hesitation. *Why not do both?* Why not write a mystery story involving the superstitions and folklore so prevalent within the Appalachian Mountains, while at the same time, design a very special mystery in which science and magic meet, merge, and perhaps become indistinct from one another?

This is exactly what I set out to do within the context of the entire Dark Hollows series. In the first book, it was necessary to establish the strange similarities between the seeming dichotomy of magic and science. I wanted to show a world where one might need to second guess biased, initial instincts. Take a second look at the predispositions of the way the world works. Is magic real? Or is it merely science that hasn't been explained yet? Is science little more than one view of how the world works, or could there be more to it?

So, with *Curse*, I concocted a story that seemed to blend the primal forces of biology and physics with that of magic and superstition. Did Crane use some primeval spell to bring young Leroy Kingston out of his feverish coma, or did the properties of the tree bark help sate the fever through mere chemistry, which helped to wake him up? As the author, I'll be honest with you… I really don't know. It's all part of the mystery!

But as you begin to read the newest installment of The Dark Hollows Mystery series, the book you're now holding in your hands, you will quickly discover that the rules have changed. You will quickly be introduced to a world where magic seems to have the upper hand. Where superstition and faith and spiritual forces of all kinds are at battle in the world of mortal men, and there seems to be little that science can do about it.

What happened? What happened to that stalwart bastion of rationality that mankind has come to revere? To cling to so desperately, lest reality slips right through our fingers and cause us to plummet into chaos?

Have no fear, faithful reader! All will be made perfectly clear. Perhaps not in this volume, but the future holds many secrets it yearns to give up. For now, just have faith that the author does have a plan. He knows what he's doing, even though it might seem utterly chaotic and unseemly.

For in our world, neither science nor faith can ever hope to overthrow the other. The two will always lean toward balance. The reason? Because it is this author's opinion that the two are two sides of the very same coin.